The Reunion

by Jennifer Gentry

Prologue

June - Present Year

The minivan crept along the cemetery road past rows and rows of tombstones, coming to a stop in front of one underneath an ancient weeping willow tree. A young woman emerged from the vehicle and reached back inside for a bag and a box of plants sitting on the passenger seat. She shut the door with her leg and carefully made her way over to a tombstone. Next to it was a bench, and onto this she set her armful of plants. Then, she reached into the bag for her gardening tools.

She knelt in front of the tombstone, digging holes and then planting each of the various bunches of flowers in the loamy soil. Satisfied with her work, she wiped her brow with the back of her hand and settled back in the lush grass.

With a sigh, she thought again about the day's date: June 2. Had it already been a year? It didn't seem possible. This was the first time she'd been to his grave in months. She'd last visited eight weeks after the funeral. At first, she was in no shape to even leave the house, sicker than she'd ever been in her life. Then, once she'd started feeling better, their little town of Cancun, Colorado had experienced the full brunt of a brutal mountain winter. She just couldn't risk an accident on the mountainous road between her house and the cemetery--not when she was the only parent they had left. And then in recent months, she'd been busier than she'd ever thought possible. However, no matter how busy things were at home, or how much it hurt seeing his beloved name in stone with those two dates below it, she knew nothing would keep her from being here today with him. On the very worst kind of anniversary.

Andrew Emmitt Darcy
Safe in the arms of Jesus

2

She ran her fingers lovingly over the name, melancholy once again at the gruesome thought of his life cut so violently short. He'd only been thirty. So young. It still didn't make sense to her. But did losing a loved one this way ever make sense? She wasn't the first, and would unfortunately not be the last to experience this kind of horror. Cold comfort, indeed.

She listened to the wind whispering through the leaves on the trees, closing her mind to the memories of that dreadful night. Not yet. She was not ready--there were other things to think of first. Using her sleeve to wipe the tears from her eyes, she brushed her hands off and reached once more for the bag. From inside, she carefully pulled out a small box made of marble. Lifting the lid, she extracted each item one by one. A picture drawn by her four-year-old son of his interpretation of Daddy singing with the angels in Heaven. A small plastic bag containing several wispy locks of hair taken from her two-year-old son's first haircut. Another plastic bag containing several pictures. These she removed from the bag and held up, explaining each one.

"Here's Emmitt at his fourth birthday party with the toy train set our parents chipped in and bought him. And here's Will after his first haircut." She flipped through the pictures one by one, each memory more bittersweet than the last. She would always treasure these special moments with her sons--Andrew's sons. The little boys were pieces of him she would have with her forever. They both even boasted more of his features and appearance than hers. Yet, she wished once again it could've been different. That he could've been *in* the pictures, sharing these precious memories with her.

There were several pictures separated from the others when she'd first removed them from the bag. These she now took in her hands.

"When I was here last, I told you I suspected I might be pregnant. Turns out I was. Andrew, I'd like to introduce you to your little daughter, Andrea," she said, and held up a picture of a tiny infant wrapped in a pink blanket. "I named her after both of us--Andrea Joy." One by one, she held up several pictures of their daughter taken at various stages in her short four months of life. "She was conceived that morning... My very last gift from you, my love."

A daughter. When Will was born, they'd talked about trying once more for a little girl. While he loved his sons, Andrew had always wanted a daughter. One who would be "Daddy's little girl". And of course, she had dreamed of having someone to dress up and show off. Now, they finally had a daughter. A daughter her husband would never hold close to his heart. A daughter without a father to walk her down the aisle when she married.

It was still incomprehensible to her.

She returned the pictures to the bag, gently lay them in the box with the other mementos, and then placed the box behind the flowers up against the tombstone. She'd leave them here for him. Even though she knew he wasn't actually *here*, it comforted her somehow to know the box was there.

She leaned back against the tree, drew her knees up into her chest, and closed her eyes. Even with her eyes closed, the words on the tombstone were clear enough they seemed embedded in her very mind. Against her will, the memories of that day flooded back to her. Some of the memories were achingly tender, precious. But others, like those from that horrible night...

The night of the reunion---the night Andrew was killed.

Chapter 1

June - One Year Ago

Emma Darcy awoke to the smell of coffee percolating in the kitchen down the hallway from the bedroom she shared with her husband, Andrew. There wasn't anything quite like the first scent of her favorite caffeinated beverage first thing in the morning. And thanks to Andrew's Mother's Day present last month, each morning the coffee pot was timed to wake her up with a fresh brew promptly at six-thirty. She rolled onto her side and glanced at her husband, only to realize he was already awake and watching her. She knew that look--he had something in mind.

"'Mornin', babe," he purred, leaning in for what he intended to be a lingering kiss.

She grinned at him before covering her mouth with her hand. "Morning breath, Andrew. Can I please brush first? Can *you* please brush first?"

Laughing, he pulled her into his arms and began nuzzling her neck. "Doesn't bother me if it doesn't bother you." He proceeded to trail kisses along her ear and neck, then started inching lower.

Emma giggled, placing a restraining hand on his bare chest. "Andrew! I'm serious! Can't we at least have a *mint* or something?"

He reached over to the bedside table and found a roll of mints left there for such occasions. After unwrapping two of them, he popped one into his mouth and the other one into hers, wiggling his blond eyebrows at her suggestively. "There, is that better? You know the munchkins will be up soon, so we don't have a lot of time here."

"Romantic, honey. Real romantic."

He framed her face with his hands. Brushed his lips across hers in a sweet kiss. "Can I help it if I'm madly, passionately, in love with - and can't get enough of - my wife?" he asked, tenderly caressing her lips with his thumb before kissing them again. "You are so beautiful. What did I ever do to deserve you?"

She favored him with a watery smile. "Andrew," she half whispered, half sighed. "I love you."

_____

Two hours later, Emma finished drying her hair, then slipped her feet into a pair of flip-flops. Andrew was finishing up in the shower and then they'd decided to take the boys out for breakfast this morning. It was up to her to wake them up and get them both dressed.

She snuck to the room next to theirs and carefully opened the door. Amazingly, the boys were still asleep. It was practically unheard of for them to sleep so late. She was extremely thankful for the stolen time with her husband.

Emma crept to one-year-old William Andrew's crib and gently peeled back his light blanket. Will was lying on his stomach, knees pulled up and his little bottom stuck up in the air. His blond, curly hair - so much like his Daddy's - was plastered to his head and the back of his neck in tight corkscrews. Thumb stuck firmly in his mouth, with plump, cherubic baby cheeks, he was absolutely adorable. In the toddler bed across from the crib was three-year-old Emmitt Michael. The little boy was another miniature of his father, except that his hair was not curly and stuck out in large tufts from the top of his head.

She turned slightly when she heard her husband enter the room, smiling when he slipped his arms around her from behind and drew her firmly against his broad chest.

They stood there together, watching their sleeping sons for a few minutes. Then, he turned her in his arms and lowered his mouth to hers for a tender kiss. "They take my breath away---just like their mother," he whispered, caressing her cheek with the back of his hand.

Emma melted into his arms. "I love you, Andrew."

"I love you more, Em," he whispered back, kissing her nose. "Shall we wake up the little princes?"

Forty-five minutes later, the family was settled at the corner booth in their favorite restaurant, waiting for their orders to arrive. Andrew and Emma enjoyed a leisurely conversation while the boys colored on paper place mats. After breakfast, they took the boys to a park near their house that had a playground geared more toward smaller children like theirs. They took turns pushing Will in a baby swing and chasing Emmitt between the swings and the slides. The family's delightful morning together was concluded with chocolate ice cream cones from Dairy Queen before it was time to head back home. The boys were exhausted after their busy morning and needed naps.

While Andrew made sure the boys were asleep, Emma headed back to their room and pulled out the new black dress she'd purchased for that evening's reunion. It was hard to imagine that it had already been ten years since her high school graduation! Where had the time gone? She stood in front of the full-length mirror on the back of the closet door and held the dress up to her body, trying to imagine how it would look once she'd completed her hair and makeup.

Andrew stopped in the doorway of their room and leaned on the jam, his arms crossed in front of him. He caught Emma's eye in the mirror and a slow, seductive smile spread across his handsome face. "I confess I can't wait to see my hot wife in her sexy new dress."

She rolled her eyes at him and tossed the dress onto the bed. "I'd hardly call it that, Andrew."

He sidled up to her and grasped her slim waist. "Consider what I normally see you wearing, babe. T-shirts and jeans. Trust me, it *is* sexy."

Emma favored him with a sly grin and cupped the back of his head, pulling him toward her for a kiss. As often happened between them, the passion quickly intensified.

Reluctantly, he broke the kiss and distanced himself from temptation. After a quick glance at his watch, he groaned. "As much as I'd love to crawl into that bed with you and show you just how sexy I think *you* are, it's time for me to go. I'm gonna be late if I stay much longer."

Emma sat on the bed, watching him pull together materials for both of his classes. "I can't wait until you're finished with your Master's, honey."

"I know, Em, me too. You bringing my suit tonight?"

"If you like. The black one?"

Andrew nodded.

She rose and wrapped her arms around him in a tight hug. "I'll see you later tonight."

"Count on it," he whispered, resting his forehead briefly against hers before giving her a last lingering kiss. "I doubt I'll be able to concentrate in class, I'll be too busy thinking about going home with the hottest girl at the reunion."

Emma laughed and blew him a kiss.

After watching Andrew's Durango pull out of the garage, she checked on the boys one more time and then headed back to her room to rest awhile. She knew her husband would find something to do to keep them both up late tonight and she'd need every minute of rest she could get now.

Dr. Justin Bennet slid several coins into the vending machine and pressed the button for some water. Twisting the cap off, he brought the bottle to his full lips and guzzled almost half of its contents.

"Thirsty, eh, Bennet?" came a thick Southern drawl from slightly behind him.

He turned and grinned at the sweaty man who'd spoken. "You ought to know, Williams, considering I beat your sorry self at tennis just now."

The other gentleman laughed heartily. "That's a good one. Keep on tellin' yourself that if it makes you feel any better," he quipped as they made their way toward the gym's locker room. "And what does Cancun's Bachelor of the Year have planned for tonight?"

Justin rolled his eyes and groaned. Not that again. He could not understand how in the world he'd even been nominated for that title, let alone actually *winning* it. Surely there were men on the list more befitting the title than him.

"As a matter of fact, I'm going to a high school reunion."

Williams' face mirrored his displeasure. "Sure you can't get out of it? There's a great party tonight at the Chief of Staff's mountain cabin."

Those kinds of parties held about as much thrill for Justin as that blasted Bachelor of the Year title. His idea of fun was not spending an evening watching colleagues from the hospital get plastered. Drinking - socially or otherwise - held no appeal. Not anymore. What was enjoyable about becoming so inebriated you couldn't remember what you'd done the night before? Not to mention the physical after-effects of being drunk. He'd left all of that behind him years ago, thanks be to God. "Thanks, but no thanks. You know I'm not into that."

His friend punched his arm and chuckled. "And *that's* why you won the title, my friend. A respectable, successful surgeon who's a gentleman to boot. You truly are an enigma to the people of this town. Have fun at your reunion," he called as the two headed to separate parts of the locker room.

"I fully intend to," Justin whispered softly.

After all, *she* would be there.

Chapter 2

Emma eyed herself critically in the mirror, sighing as she ran her hands over a few imaginary creases in the black dress she wore. The woman before her was passably pretty, she decided, although certainly not anything spectacular. Having children had added a curve or two to her rather boyish frame--not altogether a bad thing.

The dress was quite stylish and made her feel more feminine than she'd felt in a long time. It draped her body becomingly, long enough to just kiss her knees, with the v-neck bodice giving just a hint of what lay beneath. Her shoulder-length chestnut hair was swept up in a neat french twist, revealing a long, graceful neck. Dark eyes framed with long lashes peered back at her as she continued her perusal. She'd brushed a smoky gray shadow across her eyelids and used a bit more eyeliner and mascara than she normally wore. This gave her eyes a mysterious, almost sensual quality. Yes, Andrew would definitely approve when he saw her later tonight. The thought brought a knowing smile to her lips.

"Emma, where are you?" called a voice from outside her bedroom.

She opened the door and smiled at her sister-in-law's stunned reaction. "So I guess I look okay?"

"*More* than okay. If I know my brother, he won't like sharing you with everyone else tonight," Allie replied with a laugh.

Emma gave her husband's younger sister a brief hug, then reached for the heels that went with her dress. "I'd better kiss the munchkins goodnight and then get going. Andrew's coming straight from his class in Denver and I'm supposed to bring his suit. Thanks again for watching the boys tonight. I confess I've been looking forward to this for a long time."

Allie shot her a bemused smirk. "Really? You've been looking forward to your tenth high school reunion? I thought most people dreaded those like the plague or something."

She shrugged. "Yeah, but it'll be nice having a chance to see everybody. Besides, it's been so long since Andrew and I had any time away from the boys. I can't remember the last time we got all dressed up to go anywhere besides *church*."

Allie laughed. "And it's not like you'd wear that dress to church."

"It's okay, isn't it?" Emma asked, a finger of doubt grasping her.

"Em-ma!" she exclaimed with a roll of her eyes. "For crying out loud! That's *not* what I meant. You're just normally covered from head to toe, that's all. You know, Mrs. Turtleneck and all. Goodness--what are you, 100?"

Now it was Emma's turn for the eye roll. "Okay, okay. Point taken. Anyway, as I said before, thanks for doing this. The boys have been looking forward to playing with you--Emmitt in particular. He's been asking me all day if it was time for you to come yet."

"Awww, he's so sweet. It's no big deal, really. They won't be up long and then I'll do some sketching. I want to finish the sketches of the boys for Dad and Andrew's Father's Day gifts. There are only a couple more weeks left until Father's Day, so Mrs. Hunter has promised to help me out with the paintings when I'm finished sketching."

"How sweet of her to offer, Allie! You know, Noelle and I walked through the gallery a few weeks ago and were amazed at how talented the whole family is. Mrs. Hunter is famous around here for her watercolors of course, but neither of us had any idea that her children, Devon and Lily, are also very talented artists as well."

"Devon is talented, very handsome, and very *single*," Allie replied with a grin. "I'm hoping that he'll ask me out soon."

Emma raised an eyebrow and laughed. Leave it to her sister-in-law to find yet another handsome single man-- one who was also interested in art no less. "Why don't you ask *him* out?"

"He's got women swarming around him like bees," she replied regretfully. "Besides, I want him to be interested enough to make the first move. Right now he only sees me as his sister's best friend."

Emma certainly understood that sentiment. More than Allie probably realized. Squeezing her shoulder on her way past, she quietly opened the door to the boys' bedroom and smiled at the sight that greeted her. Will was standing up in his crib, holding onto the railing, babbling to his older brother. Emmitt was pushing a toy truck in circles on the rug in front of the crib, giving his little brother a running commentary about the truck's driver.

When Will looked up and spotted his mother standing in the doorway, he grinned at her, lifted up both arms, and cried, "Up! Up!"

Emma lifted him out of his crib, nuzzling his chubby cheek. "Hello, my darling. Did you have a good nap?"

"Nap! Nap!" he parroted. Almost everything he said was loud and repeated at least once.

She sat him on the floor next to his brother and carefully knelt next to Emmitt. "Mommy's going out for awhile, but Aunt Allie is here to stay with you. Will you be a good boy for her, buddy?"

Emmitt nodded, climbing onto her lap. "Daddy not comin' home?"

"Not until after you're asleep. But we'll come kiss you goodnight when we get home, okay?"

"Pwomise?"

"Promise," Emma assured him, brushing a kiss across his forehead. "I love you both!"

"Wuv you too, Mommy."

At the doorway, she blew each of them another kiss before nodding for her sister-in-law to enter. Allie had thoughtfully waited outside the room so that she'd have a few minutes alone with her boys, knowing that once the boys saw her, they'd temporarily forget all about their Mommy. The boys' squeals of happiness echoed down the hallway as she headed toward to the front of the house.

Andrew was an excellent husband and father, but these classes he was taking to finish up his Master's Degree kept him away most nights and two Saturday afternoons a month, and the boys missed their Daddy. And frankly, she missed her husband as well. He was her best friend and had been ever since she could remember. In elementary school, only Andrew among all the boys in their neighborhood could outrun her, and despite the fact that she'd tried to outshine him, he'd doggedly remained her friend. They'd been each other's confidants for everything from crushes to dreams for the future. In high school when Justin Bennet had broken her heart, it had been Andrew who had pieced it back together.

It was during her sophomore year of college that she'd begun imagining him as something much more than a friend. It was as if she'd really seen him for the first time as the man he was. Of course, she hadn't wanted to be the first to reveal her new feelings for him, terrified of ruining the friendship forever. Misplaced feelings had ruined one such relationship in her life already. She wasn't about to let that happen with the best friend she'd ever known.

During Christmas break, Andrew had completely stunned her with the revelation that he felt something more for her as well. He'd been subconsciously comparing all of the women he met to her. None of them made him feel anything close to the way he felt about her.

They'd taken things slowly at first, emailing and talking on the telephone several times a week. That spring, he'd graduated from college and begun teaching at Cancun High School. It was during Christmas break of her senior year that he'd asked her to marry him. Only a week after her graduation, they were married. It had been the happiest six years of her life.

At the high school, Emma found a parking space next to a vintage blue Corvette, eying the convertible curiously. There was something familiar about that car, but she couldn't quite put her finger on it. Besides, no one she knew could afford a car like that. Most of their friends were teachers and drove modest vehicles. Obviously, someone in her class had done well for themselves in the ten years since high school graduation. She turned in her seat to make sure Andrew's suit was still hanging from the hook above the door behind her. When her phone beeped, alerting her that she'd received a text message, she reached across the seat for her tiny handbag and flipped open the phone. *Just leaving, be there in 30.* There was certainly no point waiting for him in the van if he was just leaving the city.

Emma tossed the phone back into her purse and locked the van. Not accustomed to wearing heels, she gingerly picked her way across the parking lot and into the gym. Just inside the door was a table with adhesive name tags and a bunch of black Sharpies. She scrawled her name on a name tag, briefly glancing at it before sticking it onto her left shoulder. *Emma Johnson Darcy.*

Seeing Andrew's last name at the end of hers still brought a smile to her face. Darcy. Just like the romantic hero of her favorite novel, *Pride & Prejudice*. She'd loved the story of Elizabeth Bennet and Fitzwilliam Darcy since she'd read it for the first time as a teenager. Amazingly, she'd never really thought about Andrew's last name until she'd fallen in love with him. The first time she'd dreamily written their names together, it had suddenly struck her. Laughing, she'd realized that her initials, "E.D.", were the same as Elizabeth Darcy's married initials.

She searched the gym for any familiar faces, smiling and nodding her head as several hellos were called her way. Finally, she spotted her friend Noelle Jenkins and made her way over to the group of tables where she was sitting.

Noelle stood and hugged Emma, grinning in delight at her friend's appearance. "You look absolutely beautiful, Em! Andrew had better get here soon if he doesn't want a bunch of men stealing his wife away to dance."

"Pu-leeze," Emma groaned. "You look beautiful, too, Noelle. Where's Joe?" she asked, referring to Andrew's best friend and Noelle's boyfriend.

"He's on duty tonight," she replied with a frown. "What's the point in having a handsome boyfriend if I can't show him off at my ten-year high school reunion?"

"That *is* a bummer, all right."

They both laughed and then took seats next to each other at the table. Emma resumed her perusal of the room. At 290, their senior class had been somewhat large for their little town, a suburb approximately 30 minutes southwest of Denver. She wondered how many people would actually show up. Then she remembered the Corvette.

"I ended up parking next to a very nice car--one that looked oddly familiar. Do you happen to know which one I'm talking about, Noelle, or why it might be familiar?"

"You mean the Corvette?" Noelle replied with a smirk.

"So you noticed it, too." Emma leaned closer to her friend and lowered her voice. "Did you happen to see whose it was?"

Another smirk, this one accompanied with a raised brow. "Are you sure you want to know?"

"Of course I do! Inquiring minds always want to know," she added with a grin.

"Let's just say that the owner did not graduate with us, but he's someone you know."

"Noelle, I've lived in this town my entire life. I know just about everyone--including the people who graduated before and after us. You're gonna have to give me more than that."

"Okay then. How about this? He's behind you dancing with Izobel Sanders."

Emma turned in her seat, scanning the crowd for the former captain of the cheer squad. Her stunningly exotic looks made her easy to spot, but for the moment, her partner's back was to Emma and she couldn't identify him. He did look vaguely familiar though. Something about the way he moved...

He turned her way. Sudden recognition froze her to the core before giving way to complete and utter shock. It couldn't be. It just *couldn't* be! If she didn't know better... *No!*

Not twenty feet from her stood Justin Bennet, the one who had shredded her heart to pieces all those years ago.

He wasn't supposed to be here! He was supposed to be in Boston. Not Cancun. And especially not at her high school reunion. Dancing with Izobel Sanders, of all people. He wasn't even in their graduating class, for crying out loud.

Although... She did have to admit that after twelve years, he still looked amazing. Better than ever, actually, if that was even possible. His ebony hair was cut in the latest style, emphasizing his boyish good looks. His tall frame was encased in a superbly tailored black suit. A burgundy tie and crisp white shirt peeked through his buttoned suit jacket. As she watched, his face lit up in a huge grin at something Izobel said.

Emma quickly turned back in her seat and closed her eyes, finally realizing why the car was familiar--it was Justin's, or rather, his father's. She'd spent enough time in it as a teenager that she really should've recognized it sooner.

Noelle watched the varying emotions playing across her friend's face and felt sorry for her. How would she feel if an ex-boyfriend unexpectedly showed up in town? And with an old nemesis no less? She reached over and placed her hand atop Emma's in sympathetic support. "They came in together. Neither of them are wearing rings, so he must've come as her date."

She shook her head, trying to clear her thoughts. "It doesn't matter. I think I'll wait for Andrew outside--it's kind of stuffy in here."

Noelle nodded. "You want me to come with you?"

"Noelle! Emma!"

They glanced up to see some friends of theirs making their way over to the table.

"No, you stay here with the girls. I'm sure Andrew will be here in a few minutes," she answered, risking a quick glance at the dancing couple. A pair of cool blue eyes locked onto hers in surprise before she quickly turned away and made her way back outside.

Justin's jaw dropped in shock.

He'd expected to see Emma tonight. Indeed, one of the reasons he'd agreed to accompany Izobel was so that he could have an excuse to see her. And he knew she'd look pretty--he'd always thought she was. But the woman who'd confidently breezed in the doorway moments ago was more breathtakingly beautiful than any other woman he'd seen before. His eyes followed her to a table where Noelle Jenkins was already sitting. Then, he watched as her eyes swept the room, looking for her husband, no doubt.

"Justin, earth to Justin," Izobel softly whispered, giving him a playful nudge in the ribs with her elbow. "You know it's rude to stare. Particularly at a woman other than your date."

Justin snapped his gaze back to the woman in front of him and grinned sheepishly. "I'm sorry, Iz. I'm being a lousy date, aren't I?"

She arched a brow. "This I've always known, my dear friend."

He bestowed a face-splitting grin upon her. "I have no doubt where you received that little bit of information."

Izobel nodded. "Now, my *Matty* on the other hand...."

He heaved a little sigh at her wistful tone, wishing for the thousandth time that his twin brother, Izobel's former fiancé, had not enlisted in the Marines following their high school graduation. It had been five years already. Five years without his other half! Even after all this time, he still felt the loss keenly.

And now Emma was lost to him as well. Against all hope, he'd somehow imagined finding her anxiously awaiting his return to Cancun. Alone. Unmarried. Still in love with him.

He'd been a fool.

Hearing her name yelled by one of her friends, his gaze was drawn to her table once more. Their eyes met and he froze, a jolt racing up and down his spine. He watched as she looked quickly away, said something to Noelle, and then practically ran out of the gym.

On her way out, he also saw the appreciative looks thrown her way from several of the other men in the room.

A hopeless desire to talk to her, dance with her, swept over him. He pressed a kiss to Izobel's cheek, led her over to some of her friends, and walked away in search of Emma.

He was *still* a fool.

Twenty minutes later, there was still no sign of Andrew and it was growing colder. Emma rubbed her arms, wishing she'd thought to bring a shawl. At this altitude, the nights could be quite cool. She took out her cell phone to check the time and frowned. Andrew was late. He was never late. He was the most punctual person she knew. Then, she noticed the mailbox sign in the corner of the phone and realized she'd somehow missed a text. She opened the message and frowned again. *@ the store, b there soon. luv u.* He'd stopped at the store, knowing he was already running late? That was really not like him at all. A nagging feeling of unease began in the pit of her stomach and she shivered, but this time not from the cold.

She gave herself a mental shake and decided to give him another ten minutes before calling. After all, this was Cancun. What could happen? Resolved, she turned to go back inside. There was no telling how long he'd be and she was freezing. Breezing back through the doorway, she nearly collided with Noelle, who was on her way outside to find Emma.

"Where's Andrew? I thought he'd be here by now."

"He texted that he had to make a quick stop at the store."

Noelle's face wrinkled with confusion. "What on Earth for?"

Emma shrugged. "I honestly have no idea--he didn't say. I'm gonna give him 10 more minutes and then if he still isn't here, I'll call."

Her friend pursed her lips primly. "Gimme your phone."

"Why?"

"Just do it."

With a shrug, Emma handed over the phone. Noelle promptly flipped it open and took a picture of her friend.

After pressing a few buttons, she grinned smugly and tossed the phone back to Emma.

"There. That ought to get his attention."

"What did you just do?"

"Duh, I sent him a picture of you. If that doesn't speed him on his way, nothing will."

With a laugh, both women stepped away from the gym door where it was warmer.

"You are never going to believe what happened after you left."

"What?"

"Mr. Corvette himself asked me to dance."

Emma was a bit shocked by this news. "He did what?"

"He asked me to dance. Wanna know what we talked about?"

"C'mon, Noelle. Just tell me already!"

"You."

A jolt raced through her at hearing this, and she grabbed both of Noelle's hands in hers. "You talked about *me*?! But why? What did he say?"

"He said--" she stopped mid-sentence, briefly squeezed Emma's hands, then let them go. "He's coming this way," she whispered with the barest of lip movements.

Emma only had a few seconds to prepare herself before witnessing Noelle's smile and feeling the light tap on her shoulder.

"Hello, Emma. It's been a long time."

She turned and slowly raised her eyes to his. "Yes, it has. Hello, Justin." He was even more good-looking close up. Instantly, Emma was sixteen years old again.

She'd been in love with Justin for almost a year. He'd asked her out on a few dates, and had even kissed her a couple of times---but had never really returned her feelings. He couldn't see her as anything but his best friend's kid sister; certainly not someone he'd have romantic feelings for.

"Would you like to dance?" he asked, emotion thickening his already deep voice.

She glanced quickly at Noelle, who graced her with the slightest of nods, before bestowing a smile upon Justin. "Sure," she agreed, sliding her arm through his.

He led her to the dance floor and took her into his arms, being careful to leave adequate space between them. "I noticed that your husband hasn't arrived yet, and I wouldn't want to give him the wrong impression when he finally does," he explained with a sly grin.

Emma laughed and shook her head. "He knows he doesn't have anything to worry about."

His laughter joined her own, their awkwardness toward each other beginning to melt away.

"How did you know I was married?"

He smiled. Then, her left hand still firmly clasped in his, he slid his finger over to tap her diamond solitaire wedding ring. "This sparkler was a dead giveaway. But I already knew."

"Checking up on me, were you?" she teased, a bit taken aback.

Yes. And I didn't like what I discovered. "Aaron and I met for lunch the other day, and he told me about you and Andrew," he explained. "I should've known, really, considering how close you two were in high school."

Aaron had seen Justin? And hadn't told her? Did her big brother not consider Justin's return to Cancun newsworthy--especially given how she'd felt about him all those years ago? "When did you get back in town? The last I'd heard, you were out in Boston."

"I was offered a good position in the surgical department and couldn't turn it down. I thought it was better, considering..."

Emma squeezed his hand. "I'm sorry about your brother, Justin. I meant to write after it happened, but....well, I just didn't know quite what to say," she admitted soberly.

The soft smile he gave her was tinged with regret. "I understand, Em. After how I treated you, I don't blame you for not writing."

"I appreciate that, but it's still no excuse. You were my friend. The least I could do was send a condolence card. He was your twin brother, after all. And then to lose your dad last year. I'm so sorry. I can't even begin to imagine what it's been like for you and your mom."

Neither said anything else for a few moments, each stuck in the regrets of the past.

"So now you've returned home. Was this because of your mom?"

What he wanted to say was, *I'd hoped against hope that you'd somehow waited for me. That there wasn't anyone in your life.* But what actually came out was, "No, not entirely. After being away for so long, I just started to miss this place and my friends as well." Dare he say it? Yes. "Believe it or not, Emma, but I even missed *you*."

She blushed and looked at her shoes. "Yeah, right."

With one finger, Justin gently raised her chin until her eyes were level with his again. "I really did. You were always fun to be around. And you were the only one who ever laughed at my jokes," he teased.

"Of course, I did. I was desperate for you to like me," Emma boldly replied.

He groaned. "Don't remind me. I was an idiot! If I'd known how beautiful you'd turn out to be, I wouldn't have walked away." This confession stuff was good for the soul.

His compliment warmed her from head to toe. "I'm sure Andrew is grateful you did."

They both laughed.

Just as the dance ended, his beeper erupted. He glanced at the numbers and pulled a cell phone out of his pocket, excused himself, and walked outside where it was quieter.

Noelle immediately rushed over to interrogate her friend. Emma was busy relaying the details of their conversation and almost didn't notice that Justin had rejoined them.

"I'm sorry I can't stay and talk--there's an emergency and I've been called into work. It was great seeing you, Emma" he added, giving her a quick side hug. "You too, Noelle."

"See you around, Justin," Noelle replied for them both.

He quickly glanced around the room, a frown lurking at the corners of his mouth. "I don't see Izobel. Can one of you please let her know that I had an emergency and had to leave? We came in separate cars, so she'll be able to get home without me."

They promised to pass on the message and then made their way back to an empty table and sat down.

"I'll bet she's in the powder room. Want me to take care of that, Em?" Noelle asked, knowing that Emma had never cared much for Izobel. Somehow, she doubted that arriving with Justin made her friend like the beauty any better, either.

Emma gratefully nodded. Alone for the moment, her thoughts kept drifting back to her dance with Justin. Well, that...and their conversation. After all these years, he thought she was beautiful? Interesting. A part of her wondered how things would've turned out if he'd felt that way twelve years ago.

Her wedding ring caught the light above her. Its sparkle shot a prickle of guilt through her, reminding her she had no business thinking of another man when she was so happily married. She resolutely shoved all thought of

Justin from her mind and chose to direct her thoughts to her husband instead. Andrew really was the love of her life. She'd never felt about anyone - including Justin - the way she felt about him. She loved him passionately. Even after six years of marriage and two children, all it took to get her fired up was a look. He loved her just as passionately, and was absolutely devoted to their sons. He would do anything for them. Would even die for them.

Where is he already? she thought, glancing at the huge clock on the gym wall across from her. It was 8:30. He should've been there at least thirty minutes ago.

She was interrupted from her reverie by Noelle's stunned, "It's Joe!" She hadn't even realized her friend had returned.

Emma took one look at his grim face and rose to her feet, her heart racing inexplicably with fear as he quickly barreled over to their table.

Joe Peterson glanced at her, not quite meeting her eyes, before greeting Noelle with a kiss. "I'm glad you're here, hon. Emma, you'd better sit back down."

Her pounding heart skipped a beat, then dropped into her stomach. When a cop tells you to sit down, it can't be good. "Did something happen at home? Is it my babies? Allie?" she cried, panic making her voice shrill.

He shook his head. "No. It's Andrew." He swore under his breath and kicked the table leg. "I hate to tell you this, Emma, I hate it more than anything," he began, pinching the bridge of his nose dejectedly. "Andrew's been shot."

"He's been *what*?!" she cried.

"Joe, how is that even *possible*? He texted her that he was stopping at the store for something and then was coming straight here. Surely there's been a mistake," Noelle quietly reasoned, taking Emma's hand in hers. "There *has* to have been a mistake, Em."

He shook his head again. "No mistake. He did stop at the store--a large bouquet of roses and a card with your name were found next to him."

Her heart dropped. Roses. He'd stopped to buy her roses. So like Andrew.

Noelle squeezed Emma's hand. "But what happened?"

"A cashier heard a gunshot and ran outside in time to see two men driving away in the Durango, then noticed Andrew on the ground."

Emma burst into tears, nearly sliding out of her seat. "Is he--is he--" She couldn't bring herself to finish the sentence.

"He's not dead. But I'm not gonna lie, Emma. He's in very bad shape. They've rushed him to the hospital. It doesn't look good."

"Joe, that just doesn't make any sense. Who in their right mind would shoot someone over a rusty old *Durango*?" Noelle asked.

"The detectives have just begun the investigation, but the jewelry store next door was robbed a few minutes before the shooting. They believe that the thieves car-jacked Andrew's car as a get-away vehicle," he replied grimly.

"Have to go, have to go," Emma mumbled, standing awkwardly to her feet, then instantly swaying.

Joe quickly scooped her up in his arms and ran for the door. After he placed her carefully in the back of his police cruiser, Noelle slid in next to her, offering what comfort she could.

Emma clung to her friend and sobbed, repeatedly crying "No!" during the entire trip to the hospital.

Chapter 3

Aaron Johnson was waiting for Emma when she raced through the doors of the hospital, Joe and Noelle on her heels.

Spying her older brother, she launched herself into his arms. She didn't stop to wonder why or how he was even there. It was just enough that he was. "Andrew's been *shot*, Aaron, shot! I just can't believe it!"

He held her tightly, rubbing her back soothingly. "I know, Em, I know. When the nurse assisting Justin called us, we were as stunned as you. Thank God for him. He knew you'd need the support. Julia's on her way over to your house even as we speak so that Allie can be here, too."

Again, without a thought to how *Justin* had even known, Emma was grateful to him for calling her brother and sister-in-law, Julia. Fresh tears ran down her cheeks when she realized she was going to have to call Andrew's parents as well. She just couldn't do it! She just couldn't say those words again. There was a part of her that didn't believe he'd been shot. *Shot*! Her precious Andrew!

Joe laid a hand on her shoulder, somehow instinctively knowing what she was thinking. "I'll call Mom and Pop, Emma. Don't worry." They were like parents to him, his own having been killed in a car accident when he was a teenager. He knew how hard this would be for them.

"Thanks, Joe," she softly replied with a watery smile, watching him exit the hospital for a better phone signal.

"Where is Andrew now, Aaron? Can she see him?" Noelle asked.

Aaron shook his head. "He's already in surgery. I got the call just after they'd started, and it'll probably be awhile. You know Justin will do everything he can for Andrew, Em."

She nodded. Of course, that's how he'd known. At least there was some comfort in that thought. Justin's surgical successes had been quite the talk around town for the last couple of years. She knew he'd move heaven and earth to save Andrew's life if there was even the remotest of chances of doing so.

"Do you want to go home and change, sis, or head up to the OR waiting room?"

Emma rubbed her arms. A chill was sweeping its way through her body and yet she wasn't physically cold. "I'm not leaving."

Her brother took off his jacket and laid it over her shoulders. "Then, we'll wait upstairs."

However, once upstairs, Emma found that she just couldn't be still. There was only one place to go for comfort, and she desperately needed to be alone to think. As much as she loved her brother and friend, their attempts to comfort her only served to remind her of her fear and worry for her husband.

"Noelle, can you go back downstairs and wait for Andrew's family to get here, then make sure they know how to get up here? And Aaron, can you please wait here for any family members or in case the doctor brings any news?"

Both agreed.

"Where are you going, Em?" Aaron asked, concerned.

"To the chapel."

They both hugged her before letting her go, knowing that there wasn't anything either one of them could possibly say or do that would take away the pain she was in. Prayer would help--they were certain of it.

Justin yanked off his surgical gown, letting it pool around his feet on the floor. Then, he peeled off his surgical gloves and threw them in the corner, stalking from the operating room in frustration and anger. How could this happen? And *why*? The man had a wife and two small boys! He leaned against the hallway wall, then slid slowly to the floor, his face in his hands. How was he ever going to tell her? He thought back to the way she'd looked tonight. She'd looked all lit up inside, almost ethereal. He'd never seen her look like that before. Being a wife and mother agreed with her. She was obviously very happy. And with a few words, he was going to completely shatter her world.

He began to pray that the Lord would give him the words to say, knowing that nothing would prepare her for what was coming. Only Jesus Himself could ease her pain and give her any semblance of peace tonight.

In the chapel, Emma prayed as she never had before. She pleaded with God to spare Andrew's life--not just for her, but for their boys as well. Wouldn't God want Andrew there to raise their sons alongside her? After all, what in the world did *she* know about raising boys?

She tried to pray for the men responsible as well, but anger and bitterness seemed to choke her. "Jesus, I can't do this. You've asked me to love these men because they are Your lost children and they need You. But I can't do it. I *hate* them for what they did to Andrew! To me and my sons. Don't ask me to love them. To forgive them. It's too much."

She sank to the floor of the chapel and pressed her face into the padded altar bench before her, overcome. After awhile, she felt a warmth and a peace deep inside of her, and knew she was not alone. The One who created her was with her in the tiny room. She found enough strength to push herself up off of the floor and sit down on one of the pews in the front of the chapel.

God was with her while she continued to pray for a miracle for her beloved.

And He was with her when she heard the door open and half rose from her seat to see Justin walking toward her. With just one glance at his face, she knew.

Andrew was gone.

"Oh, God, *no*!!" A strangled cry emitted from her lips as she sank to her knees, overcome once more.

Justin threw himself down next to her and enfolded her in his arms, rocking her back and forth. "I'm so sorry, Emma, *so* sorry! We did everything we could."

She turned and wrapped her arms around his chest, squeezing him tightly in return. "I know," she managed to choke out. "I know you did. Thank you for trying to save him."

He held her while she cried, the force of her sobs threatening to tear his heart in two. Finally, after awhile he realized that the rest of the family still hadn't been told. He released her, then reached for a tissue from the box on the floor next to the altar.

"I have to go break the news to the rest of Andrew's family. Do you want to come with me or stay here?"

She knew she should go with Justin and share in the family's grief, but she just couldn't make herself hear what he was about to tell them. Besides, one look at her face and they'd know before he even opened his mouth. Didn't they deserve a few seconds of hope before it was ripped forever from them? She slowly shook her head, further indicating her choice by returning to her pew.

He kissed the top of her head and gave her another quick hug. "I'll be back, okay?"

Once Justin was gone, it was hard for her to feel that soothing Presence, even though she knew deep in her heart that He was still there.

Andrew was dead. How could it be? She did not understand, and probably never would. She was now a twenty-seven-year-old widow, and her sons were fatherless at the ages of three and one. The thought that her babies would likely not remember their own father broke her heart and brought fresh tears to her eyes.

On top of it all, her very best friend in the world - the one who knew her better than anyone else, and always had - was gone. Whom would she cling to now?

My daughter, I am with you always. Cling to Me.

This time, she could feel the Presence with her like a gentle hand atop her head. The warmth and peace once again flooded through her and she cried with relief.

It was time to join her husband's family--her family. She needed them even more than before. After all, she was now a single mother of two small boys.

The boys. She couldn't imagine telling them that their Daddy would not be home tonight, or any night. But somehow, as difficult and as painful as this was for her, the tears didn't come.

She woodenly walked through the doors of the chapel and down the hall to the surgical waiting room. To her surprise, none of the family members were there. Instead, a lone man was sitting on one of the plastic chairs reading a newspaper.

"Excuse me," she said quietly, surprised by the raspiness of her voice. "My family was gathered in here earlier. Do you happen to know where they went?"

He glanced at her puffy, tear-stained eyes, and patted the seat next to him, setting his newspaper down on a little table nearby as she walked over.

Once Emma was seated, the kindly elderly man surprised her by taking her hand in his. "That new surgeon took them all into a private room a couple doors down. I've been around this hospital long enough to know that they only do that when there's been some unhappy news. Is there something I can pray with you about?"

She suddenly realized that he was wearing a clerical collar. "It's my husband, Andrew. He---he was shot earlier tonight and..."

The priest nodded in understanding. "Your husband was the young man shot in the grocery store parking lot, one of the English teachers from the high school."

"How did you know?"

He sighed and his face puckered, as if he'd sucked a lemon. "My dear, you need to prepare yourself for another unpleasant experience when you leave this hospital. Reporters are waiting downstairs. Hospital administration won't allow them up here for now, but they are waiting for any members of the family - you, in particular - to leave so that they can hound them with their questions."

Emma gave a hysterical little laugh. "Why can't they just leave me alone? Leave *us* alone?"

He patted her other hand. "I understand perfectly. And I agree whole-heartedly. Sometimes the media can be a little overzealous in its attempt to cover the news."

After a few moments of silence, he offered a tiny smile. "My name is Father Miller. Would you mind if I prayed for you and your family?"

She gave him a watery smile. "Emma. My name is Emma. And no, I wouldn't mind."

After Father Miller's simple prayer asking for comfort, she made her way slowly down the hall in search of Justin and the rest of her family.

Glancing in the window, she could see the various reactions on the faces of those gathered within. Her mother-in-law was sobbing in the arms of her father-in-law, whose face was drawn and pale. Joe was angrily pacing back and forth. Allie was in a chair in the corner of the room, bent over at the waist, her shoulders shaking with her quiet sobs.

She took one last fortifying breath, squared her shoulders, and opened the door. Immediately, all eyes shot to her. Out of the corner of her eye, she saw Justin take a step toward her and then freeze, uncertainty written on his face. She purposefully made her way over to Allie and placed her hand on her sister-in-law's shoulder.

Beth Darcy, Andrew's mother, stepped closer and enfolded Emma in an embrace. "I'm so sorry, honey."

Emma shrugged. Shouldn't this be a something she should be saying to *her*? Yes, Andrew was her husband. But he was the woman's son. A precious life she'd carried in her womb, nursed, and raised from infant-hood. Shouldn't that relationship be held every bit as dear?

"It's a shock, Beth. I mean, *how...?*" she let the question trail off as tears rained down her cheeks once more.

Soon the women were all gathered together, holding each other and sharing their mutual sorrow through quiet sobs.

After awhile, she absentmindedly noticed that the room was divided into two groups: one, the grieving family and Joe, her husband's best friend; and two, Aaron, Noelle, and Justin. Over the sounds of weeping, she could faintly detect traces of a conversation taking place amongst the latter group. As best as she could discern, they were talking about *her*. There was concern about how to get her out of the hospital without being mobbed by the media waiting downstairs. Apparently some of her family members had not been so fortunate in eluding them when they'd arrived a couple hours ago.

A couple hours ago. Had it been that long already? Or had she sat in the chapel longer than she'd thought before Justin's appearance there? She rubbed her upper arms, then slid them all the way through the sleeves of Aaron's jacket. But even this was not enough to ease the chill that had spread throughout her entire body.

Justin slowly crossed the room and squatted down in front of her, ignoring the curious glances directed his way by Emma's mother-in-law. He'd purposely kept his distance from her, unsure how the Darcys would perceive his help. Until now, that is. For even from across the room, he could see that she was struggling. She looked like she was desperately trying to shrink in upon herself. When it was clear the rest of her husband's family seemed to be immune to her grief, he'd made up his mind to help her any way that he could. "Can I get you anything?" he asked softly. "Some coffee, maybe?"

Without looking at him, she nodded. "Thank you, Justin."

He remembered that even as a girl of sixteen, she'd loved nothing better than a good cup of coffee. "If memory serves, you take it with cream and two sugars."

"Yes, she still does," Aaron confirmed.

"I'd like it black," she requested dully, finally raising her eyes to Justin's.

The utter hollowness he saw mirrored in their depths shocked him, and he nearly fell over. He'd never seen that look in her eyes before and it frightened him. In the next instant, every protective instinct he possessed rose to the surface. How he longed to *really* comfort her. But with a room full of watching eyes, he could do nothing. He rested his hand briefly upon her shoulder, giving it the lightest of squeezes, then vacated the room for the coffee.

Aaron and Noelle exchanged confused glances. She never took her coffee black, preferring instead to take the edge off the bitterness with cream and a little sugar.

Beth speared her daughter-in-law with a quizzical look, pasting a watery smile upon her face before speaking. "Emma, honey. I wasn't aware you knew Dr. Bennet." When there was no reply, she decided to probe with more force. "How *exactly* do you know him, dear?"

Emma released a long sigh, thoroughly exasperated. Her husband lay dead somewhere on this floor, yet his mother was interrogating her on her relationship with Justin? As if there was even anything worth reporting!

After all, she'd only seen him again for the first time in *years*, just this very evening! "Beth, he's----"

She was cut off mid-sentence when her brother's own sense of protectiveness prompted him to speak. "He's an old friend of mine, Mrs. Darcy. Emma's known him since she was a young girl. He's been out east for the last twelve years and only recently moved back to Cancun. He's like a brother to Emma."

She'd been nursing a bottle of water someone had given her, and with that comment, she gasped, accidentally choked on some of the water, and began coughing. Allie pounded her back, shooting her a look fraught with concern. "Sorry," she sputtered, "Guess it went down the wrong pipe."

'He's like a brother to Emma'? she thought, thoroughly astonished. Although she understood Aaron had only made the comment in an attempt to nip Beth's suspicious train of thought in the bud, she knew she would never be able to see him that way. He could *never* be a brother to her. There was too much history between them for that. The fact that he was even here, suddenly back within her notice, was enough to strain incredulity.

At that point, she realized she was quickly reaching her limit of what she could handle in one night. She either had to get away for a few minutes by herself or she would positively bust. Excusing herself with the explanation of needing to visit the ladies' room, she quickly slipped from the room into the relative quiet of the hallway.

She aimlessly wandered down the hall without the least regard to where she was going, thankful to be away from watching eyes. *Why are hospitals so cold?* she wondered to herself as another chill swept through her body. She clutched Aaron's jacket tighter to her frame, catching the barest whiff of his favorite cologne in the process. It was a scent that also happened to be her husband's favorite. A wave of grief raced through her and she felt herself crumbling.

Before she would've hit the floor, strong arms caught her shoulders and steadied her on her feet once more. She was then pulled tightly into a powerful embrace. Justin. Only Justin. She clung tightly to him and sobbed until she was utterly spent. Even after her tears had ceased, he continued to hold her, loath to let her go.

Finally, however, he reluctantly released her, allowing the wall to offer her the support he much preferred providing himself. He'd gotten the coffee and had almost reached her side with it when he spotted the grief pierce her anew. Quickly, he'd deposited the coffee cups on a nearby table and rushed to stop her descent to the floor. Now, they retrieved their cups from the table and made their way slowly back to the waiting room in silence.

Inside, everyone was clustered together in chairs, carrying on a quiet discussion. Emma quickly realized they were trying to figure out what should be done about the media presence downstairs. They all felt that having a family spokesperson was necessary, but none felt they were sufficiently calm enough to serve in that capacity.

Sympathetic gazes met hers. It was almost more than she could bear. She suddenly realized she wanted nothing more than to go home, crawl into her bed, and never leave it. Intuitively, she knew she needed to be strong for her children. But she hadn't the faintest idea how to do it. The thought of raising her boys alone overwhelmed her, and she swayed.

Quickly, and without thought, Justin's arm snaked out and caught her to his side, lending her his strength once more. Glimpsing Beth Darcy's narrowed gaze, he glanced down to see Emma's reaction to it and was thankful to see her eyes closed. He looked across her head and made eye contact in what he hoped was a clear signal to her brother.

Aaron nodded imperceptibly and stepped over to them, easing his own arm around his sister so that Justin could distance himself from her. There was no sense in antagonizing her in-laws further.

After several more minutes of discussion, it was decided that Aaron would act as the family spokesman. Hospital staff would announce to the press that he would be downstairs shortly to make a statement on behalf of the family. While that was happening, Justin would sneak Emma out of the building through the ground floor employees' entrance - a gated area of the parking garage that required a pass key to enter - and then take her home. Noelle and the remaining Darcys would leave the hospital via the third floor garage entrance, where Joe would await them in his police cruiser. They hoped that Joe's presence - as a tall, burly uniformed police officer - would deter any persistent media from harassing the family. They also hoped that with Aaron's announcement and with the rest of the family leaving on the third floor, Emma's presence would not be missed. While Beth was less than thrilled that Justin was escorting her daughter-in-law home, she grudgingly accepted his offer of assistance.

Within an hour, Emma had been safely delivered to her door, where Justin had offered her one final hug and promised to call her soon. The boys were still sound asleep, blissfully unaware that their lives would never again be the same. A part of her wanted to gather each of them to her and smother them in kisses. The other part, the grieving wife part of her, wasn't ready to deal with their questions. Instead, she said goodbye to her sister-in-law, Julia, and made her way to her bedroom.

Turning on the small lamp next to her bed, she was startled by the reflection that stared out at her from the mirror across the room. Mere hours ago she'd stood in this very spot, eagerly anticipating her romantic evening with Andrew. The pretty woman she'd caught a glimpse of earlier was now gone. In her place was a woman who seemed to have aged a decade in the span of a few hours. Despair once again overwhelmed her and she suddenly wanted nothing more than to feel the bliss of forgetfulness.

She climbed into her bed fully clothed and sobbed for what felt like hours before finally succumbing to a dreamless sleep.

Chapter 4

Emma awoke the next morning to the comforting aroma of percolating coffee. She reached over to Andrew's side of the bed and was surprised to find it empty. As church didn't start until later in the morning, he usually took advantage of the opportunity to sleep in. One of the boys must've awoken him. Like as not, she'd find him in their room, reading or playing quietly in an attempt to give her a few more minutes' sleep. It was a little odd, however, that he'd been the one to hear them and not her. Andrew could sleep like the dead. With that thought, something pinged on the fringes of her memory. When no further recall came, she shrugged. It was just too early for her brain. Coffee. She required coffee. And judging by this strange fog she was in, lots of it.

She brushed back the covers and frowned, confusion crinkling her forehead. Why was she wearing the dress she'd purchased for the reunion instead of her silky nightgown? Had she really been so tired the night before that she hadn't even bothered removing her dress? Apparently so. She caught her tangled hair up in a loose pony tail, stuffed her feet into her fluffy slippers, and shuffled down the hall to the boys' room. Peeking in, she was surprised to find them both still sound asleep. There was no sign of Andrew. Perhaps he'd settled them back down and then headed to the kitchen for some coffee.

Except that he wasn't there, either. Maybe he was in the bathroom. After all, she hadn't looked to see if their en suite bathroom door was open or not. She retraced her steps to the bedroom, unease knotting her stomach when she still couldn't find him. A memory continued to lurk just at the edges of her consciousness, but managed to elude her once more.

Back in the kitchen, she picked up her favorite coffee cup from the mug rack and poured a steaming cup of coffee. She held the cup in both hands and lifted it to her face, inhaling the soothing aroma. The smell of freshly brewed coffee really was one of her favorite scents. She pulled open the refrigerator and frowned. No creamer. She'd have to take her coffee black after all. Yuck.

Realization dawned, and she smacked her forehead with her palm. "Of course! He's gone to get some creamer," she replied aloud. That was Andrew, all right. Her knight in shining armor.

Cup in hand, she shuffled to the garage door and peeked out the window--to a garage empty of not only Andrew's Durango, but her minivan as well. Confusion reigned for only a moment before the previous evening's events came flooding back to her in one frightening, agonizing rush. The mug slipped from her fingers and crashed to the floor.

Tears streaming down her cheeks, she sank to the floor in a heap, sobs forcefully tearing through her body. She wasn't sure how long she lay there before feeling warm breath at her neck and tiny fingers wiping her tears away.

"Don't cry, Mama. Don't cry."

Emma raised her head to see Emmitt's green eyes peering intently down upon her. She wordlessly swept her son into her arms, burying her face into his small neck, and rocked him back and forth. He may not have understood what it was that had caused his mother's despair, but he responded to it nevertheless. He wrapped his small arms tightly around her neck, raining kisses over her cheeks.

"Jesus is gonna make it better, Mama," he whispered, framing her face tenderly in his hands as he'd often seen his Daddy do. "I know He will."

A fresh round of sobs overtook her. Wasn't she supposed to be the one who was strong for them? Not the other way around. Besides, she hadn't even had a chance to break the horrible news to them yet. How did one explain such a thing to small children? If *she* couldn't even understand it, how in the world would they?

A voice from the now-open door into the garage behind her startled her. "That's right, Emmitt. Jesus *will* make it all better." It was her mother.

"Nana!" Emmitt exclaimed, jumping up and racing into her open arms. "Something's wrong with Mama, Nana." It was evident just how concerned the little boy was for his mother.

Grace Johnson knelt before her grandson, gently sweeping the hair back from his face. "Yes, sweetheart. I know. She'll tell you about it later. But right now we just need to let her be sad. Do you understand?"

He nodded soberly. "Like when I get a boo-boo an' it hurts for awhile?"

"Yes, darling. Just like that."

The three-year-old glanced around the kitchen with a frown. "Where Papa?"

"He's in your room getting Will up. How would you like to go fishing at the lake?"

Emmitt's eyes widened in surprise. "On *Sunday*? Won't Jesus be mad we missed church?"

"No, sport," came the deep-throated voice of Emma's father. He stood in the kitchen doorway holding a sleepy-eyed Will. The strain of the morning more than evident on his care-warn face. "I know Jesus understands."

Taking his grandfather's words to heart, the little boy jumped up and hugged his knees tightly. "I can't wait to go fishing, Papa! It's been a long time since we went."

Emma watched her parents exchange rueful glances. The "long time" in Emmitt's mind had, in reality, only been a few short weeks. She mustered her best effort at a smile, grateful for her dad's thoughtful offer to take the boys out for a few hours. His somber eyes pierced her heart with the knowledge that they grieved with her. While technically only a son by marriage, their relationship with

41

Andrew had been closer to that of their relationship with Aaron. That of a blood son.

"Is he gonna be all right with them...alone?" she asked, painfully aware that Andrew was always the one whose job it was to corral their rambunctious boys on these excursions. Fishing with two small children always required more than once person.

"Don't worry, dear. Your brother's meeting them out there."

Emma could hear the boys chattering excitedly down the hall as her father helped them dress. "They'll be thrilled to have Uncle Aaron join them."

When she moved to clean up the spilled coffee and broken mug, her mother stayed her arm, gently pushing her over to the breakfast bar, where she'd placed a fresh mug. "I'll take care of that, honey."

She doubted her numb fingers would be able to support the mug without dropping it. Instead, she wrapped her fingers around it, praying the warmth would ease the chill that had spread through her body. She carefully raised the cup to her lips for a sip, then gently pushed it away with a grimace. She'd forgotten--no cream.

Grace dumped the last of the broken pieces into the trash, then swept her gaze in Emma's direction. "Would you like me to make you some tea instead? It won't take but a minute."

She nodded.

Her mother set the water on to boil, then got down the pretty porcelain tea pot and two tea cups that had been part of a set Emma had received as a wedding present. She set out the sugar dish, poured a little milk into the creamer, then placed it on the table with the other pieces. Once the tea was ready, each woman doctored hers according to taste preferences.

Before Emma was half-way through her first cup, her father reappeared in the kitchen with the two boys.

"Well, my dear. We're off. Do you have those lunches ready?"

Grace pointed to a soft-sided cooler on the counter. "There's peanut-butter-and-jelly for the boys and ham and cheese for the two of you. Plus some chips, baby carrots, juice boxes, bottles of water, and cookies as well. And I've filled your thermos with coffee. How does that sound?"

"Yummy!" Emmitt exclaimed, thoroughly excited about the thought of fishing *and* a picnic at the lake.

"All right then. Bring me back a big one and we'll fix it for supper."

Once the boys were gone with her dad, Emma speared her mother with a look. "When did you do all this?"

"Neither of us got much sleep last night. And we realized that this morning would be pretty difficult for you--especially with the boys not knowing. So we decided to give them a few more hours of normalcy before the news was sprung on them. After dropping your dad off at the high school, where your van was still parked, I stopped at the store and picked up the ingredients for a good picnic lunch. If I'd realized you were out of creamer, I would've picked some of that up, too. If you'll remember, you gave us a set of spare keys when we stayed with the boys while you and Andrew spent your anniversary weekend in Denver. Keys to the van were also on that same key ring. We knew we'd need the car seats this morning, and there was no sense in just letting it sit in the high school parking lot."

Emma waved her hand in dismissal. She had no plans to leave the house anytime soon, so what did it matter where the van sat? She was, however, a little shocked that it hadn't occurred to her the boys would need their car seats. Thankfully, her parents hadn't lost *their* mental faculties and had planned accordingly. In this current state, she wasn't even sure she should be left alone with two young children. Perhaps it was really for the best that the boys were gone for the day.

"How is it that I didn't see either of you - or the cars - when I got up?"

Her mother squirmed uncomfortably. "That's because we were busy outside," she answered, nodding toward the window.

Emma pulled the curtains back slightly and peeked through the window. A hoard of reporters strolled back and forth on her front lawn. It was clear that some were on camera, giving reports. Others were merely waiting for that all important signal from their news desks. She let the curtains slide through her fingers with a groan. This was a nightmare.

"We have no idea how long they've been here, but they were here when your dad arrived in the van. Not quite so many as there are now. But enough. We saw the reports from last night, Em, and determined they were not going to get to the boys. Especially since they still don't know about Andrew. When I got here, your father was out there talking to several of the reporters. He got them to agree to temporarily move away from the house and into the street, explaining that the boys are far too young to understand what was happening and that seeing so many new faces would only scare them. Anyway, knowing he was going to be leaving shortly anyway, John left the van in the driveway. And as overcome as you were, I'm not surprised you didn't hear me drive in."

As relieved as she was that the reporters had apparently agreed to leave her sons alone, a deep sinking dread began to spread through her heart. "They're not going to go away, are they? They're camped out there just waiting to ambush me! I'm stuck in this house, aren't I?" she cried shrilly, panic overwhelming her as she paced. "Oh, God, *why*?! Why me? Why *Andrew*?! What possible good could come from this?" The questions continued to pour out of her, hysteria threatening to completely take over.

Grace rubbed her daughter's back, frowning. When Emma finally succumbed to the sobs, curled in a heap in the corner of the kitchen, she quietly left the room to make a call. She couldn't think of any one else to call besides him, thankful he'd had the foresight to give them his phone number last night. She only hoped he'd be able to come.

"It's Grace. Are you working today?"

"Not until tomorrow. How is she?"

"Not good. She's hysterical and I can't get her to calm down. I'm worried she's going to make herself ill if she continues like this. Can you come?"

Without hesitation, he agreed. "Give me fifteen minutes."

"Hurry, please. Have you seen the news?"

"Yes," he replied angrily.

"Then you know the situation over here."

"Is she aware of it?"

"It's what sparked the hysteria."

"I really have no desire to talk to any of them. If they try to corner me, I'm afraid I'll do or say something out of anger that I shouldn't."

"I understand that sentiment perfectly. Text me when you're a couple houses away and I'll open the garage door for you."

She disconnected the call, placing the phone in her pocket. Then, she took a fresh washcloth from the linen closet and soaked it in warm water. Thoroughly wringing the excess water out helped take an edge off the anger. But only an edge.

She squatted before Emma in the kitchen, placing the warm cloth in her hand. "Here, honey. Press this to your eyes."

Emma took the proffered cloth gratefully. Her head ached terribly from weeping, but she just couldn't seem to stop. Every time she thought she'd emptied the pot of grief, it would fill again. Deeper than before. She wasn't sure how much more of this she could take.

Turn to Me, My child. I am here with you.

The Presence was back, bringing comfort to her wounded heart.

But then, just as some of the panic was dissipating...

You just know one of those reporters is going to say something in front of the boys before you have a chance to tell them. They're never going to leave you alone until they've seen you at your worst.

This other voice had a point. She knew it. And feared it. One again, the panic and hysteria ratcheted back up to full volume. She didn't even notice when her mother's phone beeped. Nor did she notice when her mother rose and opened the garage door. She didn't hear the car drive into the garage, or the cacophony of the reporters outside before it was silenced by the closing of the garage door. She didn't hear, see, or notice anything until strong arms drew her into an embrace. Confused, she raised her tear-filled eyes in an attempt to see who was holding her.

Justin. How had he gotten there?

While speaking in hushed tones to her mother, he tightened his embrace briefly as if trying to draw all of her grief into himself. Then, he picked her up and carried her into the living room, settling her gently onto the couch. Once she was seated, he sat down next to her, placing one arm around her shoulders, and squeezing her left hand with the other. "Emma, I have something that I'd like you to take. It will help you relax a little bit."

When she started to protest, he dropped her hand and placed his fingers against her lips to silence her. "I know you don't want to take this, but as a doctor - and your friend - I really think you need some rest."

She glanced first at Justin's earnest face and then at her mother's worried one before nodding. She accepted the pills from her mother and washed them down with a few gulps of water.

"Do you like having the reporters here, Em?"

She vigorously shook her head, glaring at the window. What kind of question was that? Of course she didn't! "I'm so afraid one of them is going to say something to the boys. They don't know yet, Justin. I haven't...been able to bring myself to...." she admitted, tearing up again.

He pulled her back into his arms, torn between the desire to comfort this special woman and the desire to personally escort each and every reporter off the property. Violently, if necessary. "I have an idea of how to get you away from here. If you'll promise to get some rest, I'll explain it all to your mother and take care of the arrangements. Can you trust me to do this?"

She lifted her head enough to meet his gaze. "Of course, Justin. You're my friend. I know you'd do anything in your power to help us."

He caressed her cheek tenderly. "Yes, I would. Now, close those eyes and get some sleep. I'm not going anywhere."

She braved a slight smile. "I'm glad you're here."

There's nowhere else I'd rather be, he thought, allowing her to cuddle more snugly against his chest. He kept his lips clamped shut until he felt sure she'd finally fallen asleep, content to simply enjoy the delightful sensation holding her in his arms produced.

"Thanks for the coffee, Grace," he replied, pausing for a sip from the cup she'd placed on the little table at his elbow. "While she's sleeping, I'm gonna need you to pack some clothes for Emma and the boys. Just enough to last a couple days. They can always run laundry if they need to."

Emma's mother settled into a recliner placed at an angle to the couch and peered at him over the rim of her own cup. "Oh? Where might they be going, Justin? If you're thinking of having them stay with us, I'm not sure that's such a good idea. If she's with us, she's sure to be found eventually."

"No, you're right. They can't stay with you, or with the Darcys, either. And they certainly can't stay with me. How would that look?" he asked with a rakish grin.

Grace reached over and slapped his knee. "Be serious. So where *do* you intend for them to stay?"

"At my dad's old fishing cabin in the foothills. When he died last year, my mom wanted to sell it. But I convinced her to let me have it. An ex-Marine buddy of my brother's is now a contractor, and he's been helping me with it. As luck would have it, he finished the repairs just a few weeks ago. There are three bedrooms and a big, comfortable couch in the living room, so there should be plenty of room for Emma and the boys--and anyone else who wanted to stay with them. The closest neighbors are about a half-mile away and only use their house as a vacation getaway. It would be peaceful and quiet."

She sighed wistfully. "Oh, that sounds wonderful. I'd say that's just what they need right now. Thank you, Justin."

"It's the least I can do. I may not be able to bring Emma's husband back. But I can at least offer her a bit of privacy in her time of grief. A veritable port in the storm, as it were."

"So how are we going to manage this?"

"I've been thinking about that. Once you've gotten some bags together with things you think they'll need or the boys will want to have, we'll put them in the back of the car. Just in case my plan was accepted, I went ahead and borrowed my mom's car for the day, leaving her the Corvette."

"Good thing you did. Besides the fact we would not have been able to fit everything *and* two extra passengers in that car, it *does* stand out just a bit."

"Just a bit," he agreed with a low chuckle before continuing with his plan.

"Once everything is packed, we'll have Emma lay down in the back seat so that she's not spotted. My mom's car has heavily tinted windows, so they won't be able to look in and see her. We can raise the garage door and you can stand at the kitchen door and yell back into the house that we're going for groceries or something, but will be back soon, and then shut and lock the door, like we're leaving for a few minutes and she's remaining at the house."

Grace nodded slowly. "That could work. Do I need to pack any food?"

He shook his head. "No. When I first thought of this last night, I called Aaron and explained my idea to him, just to make sure it wasn't overly presumptuous or anything. He thought it was an excellent idea. Then, when I woke up this morning, there was a voice mail from him informing me of the plans to take the boys fishing. Once they are finished at the lake, Aaron will bring them over to the cabin. He's been there a couple times and knows the way. At some point, he and I will run out for some groceries.

"Grace, I don't like the idea of Emma being alone-- especially in a strange place. And especially since she's had that sedative. To be brutally honest, I don't think she should be alone for awhile, period. But maybe that's just me."

She bestowed a warm, motherly smile on her son's oldest friend. She'd always liked Justin, despite the way he'd sometimes treated Emma when they were younger. But then, Emma *had* worn her feelings for him for all the world to see. She really couldn't blame him for running away--few young men were mature enough to handle that kind of emotion at that age. Now, while she had some suspicions about his motives for helping Emma, she decided to keep them to herself and just wait and see. That he cared for her daughter was quite clear. According to Aaron, it had been almost painfully obvious--especially to Beth Darcy. But beyond that? It was a little too early to tell. For now, it was enough that they were friends again. "I guess you've thought of everything, Justin. I appreciate all that you've done, and all that you're doing for my little girl. All of us are in shock, but I'm afraid the next several weeks are going to be pretty rough on her in particular. She has a funeral to plan. And she's got to learn how to be a single mother."

"Unfortunately, the only way to learn that is just by doing it. As for the funeral, I'm sure between you and Andrew's family, there will be enough people to help her make arrangements."

"Steve and I were planning on staying with Emma and the boys for awhile--at least until the funeral. Our suitcases are already in the guest bedroom. So if you don't mind, we'll just stay out at your cabin with them instead." She waited for his nod of consent before adding, "And for the record: I agree with your assessment that she shouldn't be left alone. As her mother, I don't intend to. Now, if there's nothing else we need to discuss, I'll get some things packed for Em and the boys."

Justin watched as she left the room to begin packing, relieved to be alone with Emma for awhile. He glanced down at her sleeping form, a fierce tenderness building inside him. Against his will, memories of the night before ran through his mind.

He'd arrived at the hospital amid pandemonium. Cops had filled the hospital lobby. He'd briefly wondered at their presence, but soon forgot about them. Upstairs, he'd been given the patient's medical status while he hastily donned his surgical scrubs and scrubbed in.

By the time he'd finished, the patient was being wheeled into the room on a gurney. Justin took one look at the young man's face and paled as full recognition hit. It couldn't be! God, *no*! This couldn't be happening.

But it was. The man lying on the gurney with a life-threatening gunshot wound was Emma's husband, Andrew Darcy.

He didn't think the man was awake until he heard his name spoken in a raspy whisper. "Yes, it's me, Andrew," he acknowledged, leaning closer to the injured man in order to hear him better.

"Tell her I love her. The boys. And tell her...she looked beautiful tonight."

Justin's brow furrowed in confusion. How did he know how she'd looked if he'd never made it to the reunion? He'd started to ask, but Andrew's next statement completely knocked the question from his mind.

Andrew gave a slight smile that was tinged with great sadness. "So glad it's you. Take care of her. Please. I don't want her to be alone."

"Me?" Justin repeated, incredulous. "You're asking *me* to take care of her? Are you sure?" he added softly.

He nodded almost imperceptibly, unconsciousness clasping its frigid tentacles around him. "God...told...me. It's...okay."

Those were the last words he'd uttered.

Hours later, once news of Justin's friendship with the deceased's family was more widely known around the hospital, an orderly had brought him Andrew's phone. It had fallen out of his shirt pocket when the ER doctors had hastily removed it from him. Justin had decided to check the phone, just to make sure it was really Andrew's before returning it to Emma. An image had popped up immediately and he'd sucked in his breath. It was the picture Noelle had taken of Emma outside of the gymnasium. Instantly, the conversation from earlier came to mind.

Andrew was right--she'd looked absolutely gorgeous. Not that he'd ever had the chance to see her in person that evening.

Somehow, Noelle had managed to capture a playful, almost sultry expression on Emma's face. A most definite come-hither pose, meant to immediately entice her overdue husband to her side.

Circumstances were such that he'd never arrived at the reunion. Never danced with his wife, nor had the chance to express to her how beautiful she'd looked.

Everything Justin had been able to do.

The reminder had cost him many hours of sleep as he tossed and turned in bed, guilt steadily creeping into his heart.

Now, holding the dead man's wife in his arms, despite the pang of guilt and the feeling of unworthiness, he recognized that a heavy responsibility had been laid on his shoulders.

But it was not an unwelcome one.

Far from it.

Still. He'd promised to look after her, and he was determined to keep that promise.

Regardless of what the future held for them.

Chapter 5

The ploy worked perfectly. After Justin loaded all of the luggage into the trunk of the car, he helped Emma stretch out on the back seat, a pillow under her head, and a blanket pulled to her chin. Once in the car, he opened the garage door and awaited Grace's performance.

"Okay, dear, we're leaving now. We'll be back soon. Call me if you need anything---and don't open the door for anyone," she called into the house from the door, making sure her voice carried enough for the reporters closest to the garage to overhear. Then she locked the door and quickly raced to secure herself in the car, both of them making sure the car doors were locked and the windows closed.

Justin backed out of the garage and closed the door, easing carefully down the driveway even as reporters attempted to get either of them to comment on camera.

The ride up to the cabin only took fifteen minutes. He stopped the car and glanced back at Emma. Her hollow expression haunted him. "We're here," he replied with a slight smile.

The smile was returned without conscious thought on her part. She slowly raised herself into a sitting position, then opened the car door. Instinctively, she braced for the flash of the cameras. Instead, only a chorus of birdsong and the trickling of rushing water met her ears. She leaned against the car and closed her eyes, drawing in a deep breath of the fresh, pine-scented air.

The crunch of gravel alerted her to Justin's presence moments before he clasped her hand in his. "Ready to go inside?" His excitement to show off his home was palpable.

She surveyed the property appreciatively, taking in the beauty all around her. The cabin had been built in the foothills surrounding Cancun. Off in the distance, she caught a glimpse of the rugged peaks of the Rocky

Mountains. The cabin itself was perched on the side of a slope, one side nestled against the hill and the other ending in a wide deck. It was toward the deck that Justin now lead her.

Plush chairs were grouped to allow intimate conversations while taking advantage of the best views. To her great surprise and delight, the deck wrapped around the back of the house. A large table and chairs were placed just steps away from French doors which she assumed led to the kitchen. It was a place she could certainly envision herself spending a considerable amount of time.

From the main deck area were stairs which led down to a rushing stream. At the edge of the stream was a free-standing bench swing, more plush chairs, and a fire pit. Just downstream from the seating area, the land leveled enough for the water to pool, creating a natural pond before cascading over more rocks on its way to the base of the mountains.

Grace stood next to Emma at the deck railing, whistling at the spectacular view before her. "My goodness, Justin. I can certainly see why you didn't want your mother to sell this place."

He laughed. "This has always been one of my favorite places to come. The inside of the cabin doesn't quite compare with this, but that's okay. I spend most of my time out here, anyway. Do you see that patch of blue down there?" he asked the women, pointing to a spot downhill from the cabin.

"Yes. What is it?" Emma asked.

"That's Smithton Lake. Just down the road is a trail that leads directly to it. We mostly spent our time fishing down there. But every once in awhile, when dad felt more like staying close to home, we'd fish from a little pond around the bend from the cabin."

It seemed strange to think that her father, brother, and sons were down there even now, fishing in the lake. "Can you see the house from there?"

He shrugged. "I suppose if you had binoculars and knew what to look for you could. I honestly can't say I've ever tried. Would you like to go inside and look around?"

She nodded with a smile. His excitement was contagious.

"If you don't mind, I think I'd like to sit out here awhile longer," Grace called, claiming one of chairs that was in the shade.

"Suit yourself. Come on in when you're ready."

Justin placed a hand to the small of Emma's back and directed her through the main door. Before moving to Cancun and reestablishing his abandoned friendship with Aaron a few months ago, he'd dreamt of this moment. Everything he'd done in the way of improvements to the cabin had been with Emma in mind. He'd long envisioned bringing her here to live---as his wife. That dream had been shattered during his first lunch meeting with Aaron.

They'd met over Justin's lunch hour at a popular deli around the corner from the hospital. He'd worried that seeing each other after so many years would be awkward. Especially since neither had remained in contact with the other. But it hadn't been. It was as if no time at all had passed as the two caught up and reminisced over days gone by. When his curiosity could wait no longer, he'd casually inquired after the one woman who'd managed to capture his heart.

"She's doing great," Aaron replied, sipping from his soda, then taking another bite of his sandwich. "It's still hard for me to imagine my baby sister a mother though," he added with a chuckle.

Justin's heart ached. So she was married. Lost to him forever. Because he knew that she'd never have children without marrying first. She'd always been adamant about that, even as a teenager. Why had he pushed her away then? What a fool he'd been! If he hadn't... Heartsick, he couldn't even finish that thought. "Yeah, that *is* hard to imagine," he agreed, trying not to let his friend see how crushed he was. "Who did she marry? Anyone I know?"

"Sure you know him. Remember Andrew Darcy?"

He frowned. "Wasn't he that shy kid who used to hang around her a lot back in high school?"

"Yeah, that's him. Only he's not shy anymore. Being married to my sister has really brought him out of his shell. He's a completely different guy now. He teaches English at the high school. Actually, he's just been voted Cancun County's Teacher of the Year--the youngest teacher to ever receive the award. Pretty impressive if you ask me." Aaron was clearly proud of his brother-in-law.

"Definitely," Justin reluctantly agreed.

They'd discussed other topics after that, but his heart hadn't been in the conversation. It was on the woman he wanted more than any other---the one woman he couldn't have.

Emma's soft gasp jolted him from his thoughts.

"Justin, this is beautiful!"

Warmth flooded his heart. "Thanks, Em."

Just inside the door, the room opened into the main living areas of the cabin. There was a largish kitchen on the left. Emma noticed that the French doors she'd seen on the deck did indeed lead into this room. To the right was a comfortable family room, a large rectangular dining table separating the two spaces.

The kitchen had been updated to include all the latest amenities. Granite countertops. Stainless steel appliances. Cherry walnut cabinets. The window over the old-fashioned farmhouse sink overlooked the deck and the hills beyond.

In the family room, a comfy-looking sectional and several chairs were grouped facing a large wood-burning fireplace, twin bay windows flanking either side of it.

The floors throughout the entire space were gorgeous hard-wood floors that had been recently sanded and refinished. Colorful rugs covered the floor underneath the dining table and seating area. The colors throughout were understated, consisting of varying shades of brown and red. Earthy tones.

"It fits you," she murmured softly.

He didn't bother contradicting her. The decor of the cabin prior to the renovations had been much more masculine. It had always reminded him of a rustic hunting lodge. Most of the furniture was made of oversized leather. And his father certainly hadn't been concerned about rugs to soften the look of all the wood, nor had he bothered with the latest conveniences in the kitchen. It was a man's retreat. And he'd loved it. He'd somehow known, however, that Emma would never feel at home in such an overtly masculine space. She'd be completely overpowered. So he'd asked Ryan to help him create a more female-friendly living space. When the cabin was completed, he'd been stunned to realize he felt as much at home in it as he ever had. The rustic hunting lodge was one side of him. But this was another.

Perched on the edge of a chair, he enjoyed watching her take it all in. The pleasure on her face gave him goose bumps. After all, he'd done it all for her. Only for her. For her to receive some measure of comfort from this place made all of his planning and preparation worthwhile.

After several minutes, she finally stopped and raised over-bright eyes to his. "Thank you for this, Justin. I feel like I can breathe here."

As tears slipped unbidden down her cheeks, he rose and took her in his arms. She in turn wrapped hers around his waist. Face buried in his chest, she gave free reign to the tears. He wished there was something he could say to comfort her, but knew no mere words would ease the pain. So he did the next best thing he could think of. He tightened his arms around her and held her while she cried.

When her tears were finally spent, she sank onto a corner of the sectional. He slipped down the hall to the bathroom, returning with an unopened box of tissues and a warm washcloth. "Why don't you stretch out and get some more rest? You look a bit like a limp noodle."

She didn't even put up a fight this time. "Will you wake me when the boys get here?" she pleaded.

"Of course. And when you feel up to it, I'll show you the rest of the house. There's not much more to see, anyway."

"Okay," she mumbled.

Once she was asleep, he stepped outside and quietly brought the luggage into the house. With some help from Grace, the things belonging to Emma and the boys were put away in the master bedroom, with her parents established in the second bedroom.

Not long after they'd finished unpacking, Aaron arrived with his father and the boys. Their noisy arrival awoke Emma. Justin watched her paste a smile on her face for her sons' sake as she listened to Emmitt recount their adventures at the lake. While his brother chattered excitedly, little Will shyly climbed upon his mother's lap, thumb planted firmly in his mouth, and gazed curiously at Justin.

It was the first time he'd seen her with the boys. The first time he'd seen the *boys*, for that matter. They both clearly favored their father. His heart instantly melted for these two who, in the blink of an eye, had lost their wonderful, loving father. Something he could relate to. His father's heart attack last year had been sudden and severe. He'd been dead even before medical help could arrive. The difference was that he'd had thirty years with his father.

The boys? Three, at the most. Little Will, barely even a year old, would likely never remember Andrew. That thought broke his heart. The reality of Emma's situation became crystal clear, perhaps for the first time.

He looked up at her, watching her with her sons. Their presence was a stark reminder that she was now a mother. A *single* mother! Gone was the carefree girl he remembered. The sole responsibility for these two precious lives had been thrust squarely upon her slender shoulders. She met his gaze briefly. In her eyes he glimpsed just how heavily that burden sat. Not for the first time, he wondered why Andrew had entrusted their care to him. If he'd been in the man's shoes, the very last person he'd want looking out for his wife and sons was the one other man she'd cared most about. He determined anew that no matter what it took, no matter what must be done, he would not allow her to fall under the weight she now carried.

"It sounds like you had a great time, darling. Did you bring back a fish like Nana asked?"

Will bounced up and down on Emma's lap excitedly. "Fiss! Fiss!"

"*Three* fish," Emmitt clarified proudly. "And they're pretty big fish, too, Mama. Papa and Uncle Aaron are outside cleanin' them for Nana."

"That's my boys. Good job, guys."

Emmitt leaned closer to her. Glanced at Justin and back at his mother. "Mama, who's that? Why are we here? And where's Daddy? I don't see him."

Justin saw a look of panic momentarily cross her face. That was his cue. He knelt in front of the boys and gave them his brightest smile. "My name is Justin. This is my cabin. I'm a friend of your Uncle Aaron's...and your Mama's," he added softly, raising his eyes to hers.

She nodded, a tiny smile forming at her lips.

He wasn't quite sure what else to say. Particularly since the boys had yet to hear the news of their father's death. How exactly did you explain such a thing to small children?

She seemed to accept that the moment had arrived. "Boys, there's something Mama needs to talk to you about." She stopped to gather her thoughts, trying to decide how best to break the news.

He excused himself and slipped outside where Grace was chatting with the men while they cleaned the fish. He stepped up to her and gently pulled her to the side. "She's telling them now," he informed her quietly.

She turned anxious eyes on him, then looked down at the stream. "Oh, Jesus, help my girl," she prayed aloud. "Thank you, Justin. I'll go in. Do you pray?"

"Most certainly."

"Good. Please pray for her now."

"I have been," he assured her.

Emma's eyes were drawn to the open door. Seeing her mother enter the room instantly settled her nerves, and her eyes briefly slid shut, grateful once again for Justin's thoughtfulness. Her mother knelt on the floor in front of them, a hand on each of the boys, her eyes closed.

Emma knew she was praying. For her. For the boys as they received the worst news they could ever receive. She cuddled Will closer to her chest and wrapped her other arm tighter around Emmitt, seated next to her. "Something happened last night. To Daddy."

Lord, how much do I tell them? I don't want to terrify them, or make them think someone is going to hurt me or them. But I need to help them understand Andrew isn't coming back.

"There was an accident and Daddy was hurt very badly."

"Is he okay? Is he at the hopital?" Emmitt asked hesitantly, fear filling his eyes.

"Yes, he had to go to the hospital. And no, he's not okay." She paused for another moment, desperate. *Lord, help!* "Do you remember when we talked about Heaven? How people that know Jesus go and live there when they die?"

"Like Gramma Mary after she got really sick?"

"Yes, like Great-Gramma Mary."

Emmitt was quiet several minutes. When he finally spoke, he spoke so softly that Emma had to strain to hear him. "Mama...did Daddy go to live in Heaven? Is that why we haven't seen him today?"

"Yes, baby, he did," she whispered, her heart breaking at her son's grief-stricken expression.

"That's why you were crying?"

She merely nodded, unable to speak.

He wrinkled his nose in thought, then said, "Daddy's just gone for a visit, though, right? Is he coming back soon, Mama?"

At his innocent, hope-filled question, Emma could bear no more. Tears rained down her cheeks in torrents. "No, Emmitt, he's not. When you go to Heaven, you stay there forever."

The little boy buried his face in his mother's shoulder and sobbed. "I'm---gonna---miss---him---so---much," he brokenly cried.

At the sight of both his mother and brother crying, Will immediately burst into tears as well. Soon, all four of them were sobbing.

The muffled sounds of weeping filtered through the front door to where the men stood on the deck. Aaron and Steve Johnson exchanged wordless glances, pain lancing through each of them. Their gazes shifted over to Justin.

He set his jaw and narrowed his eyes, unspeakable anger filling him. Anger at the men responsible for this family's pain. Anger at God for allowing it. He wanted to hit something. Pound something. No. *Annihilate* something. Anything to ease the pain and anger inside.

Steve used the outside spigot to clean his hands, then yanked off the apron he'd worn to cover his clothes while cleaning the fish. He cast one more mournful glance at his son before heading inside.

Aaron quickly cleaned himself up as well. He recognized that his friend was ready to explode, although he couldn't quite understand why. Sure, anyone with a heart would be upset for the family. But this? Justin was literally seething! Maybe a few root beers would loosen his tongue and get him to explain what was going on. "Let's get outta here."

A few hours later, the men returned with enough groceries to last several days. Aaron stayed long enough to ensure that everything was carried inside and put away before driving home, promising to check on them later.

Justin watched as Grace continued the dinner preparations. Despite the fact that she was working in an unfamiliar kitchen, this woman was clearly in her element. The delicious aroma of baked trout filled the kitchen. His mouth watered just thinking about how good it would taste. How long had it been since he'd enjoyed a home-cooked meal? Even though his mother lived nearby, their work schedules didn't allow them to share many meals together like this. Most of his dinners were hastily prepared, then consumed standing at his kitchen sink. Not exactly the best dietary habits for a doctor. But he wasn't the type to go to a lot of fuss just for himself. For friends, on the other hand, or for his mom, then, he went all out on the planning and preparation.

Steve emerged from the back bedroom, leaving the door slightly ajar. "The little guys are still asleep. Between our fun at the lake and the upsetting news, they were completely exhausted. I wouldn't be surprised if they sleep straight through." After the boys had sobbed themselves to sleep, Emma and her father had carried them back to the master bedroom and put them to bed. Thankfully, the bed was big enough for all three of them. Even if it hadn't been, she just couldn't stand the thought of the boys having to sleep in a strange room by themselves. She wanted them with *her*. Within arm's reach.

"Emma with the boys?" he inquired curiously.

"She's on the swing," Grace replied without looking up from the potato she was peeling.

"I think I'll go check on her."

She cut her eyes at her husband, who'd begun preparing a salad at the counter next to her.

"You do that, son," he replied, winking at her.

"This will be ready shortly, so don't stay out there too long," she called over her shoulder.

The sun had already descended over the mountains, taking its warmth with it. Justin grabbed a blanket off the back of the couch along with a high-powered flashlight before leaving the cabin. Without street lamps, it got dark very quickly up here once dusk set in. He didn't want either of them to fall, nor did he particularly care to stumble across any wild animals in the dark.

Emma's father had laid a fire in the fire pit for her. Its luminescent glow silhouetted her body on the swing. Completely lost in thought, she didn't notice him until the swing dipped as he settled onto the seat next to her. The eyes she turned to him were red-rimmed from weeping. The hollowness from earlier had remained, along with a crushing melancholy.

One arm thrown across the back of the swing, he turned his gaze to the fire, unsure of what to say to the grieving woman beside him. When she scooted closer to him and leaned her upper body against his, curling her legs beneath her, a jolt of electricity shot up and down his spine. His heart leapt within his chest. She was actually turning to him for comfort, like she'd done as a young girl. He settled the blanket over them, holding her just a bit tighter to his side. All thoughts of the meal Grace was preparing abandoned him. How could he think of food when *she* was near? Next to him. Snuggled in his arms.

Emma burrowed a little closer to Justin's warm chest. She'd been so cold before he'd arrived. And not just from the cool night air. This chill had seeped into her very being, creeping in while listening to her sons' sobs of grief. After putting the boys to bed, she'd escaped out here for some time alone. To process everything that had happened. And to try to imagine a future without Andrew in it.

They remained on the swing for awhile longer, silently rocking, listening to the gurgling stream and crackling fire. He left her alone with her thoughts, content to offer his support the best way he knew how. By just being there.

He suddenly remembered Grace's warning about dinner and sighed regretfully, knowing that their time alone had come to an end. "Your mom's probably got supper all ready. Shall we go up?"

She sat up, swinging her legs to the ground. "I suppose. I guess I am kinda hungry."

He tucked the blanket around her shoulders, allowing the flashlight to illuminate the ground as they walked back up to the house in the semi-darkness. Then, he held her elbow as they ascended the porch steps to ensure she didn't trip over the blanket's edge. Someone had switched on the back light, bathing the area in an warm glow.

She placed her hand on the doorknob, but didn't open it. Instead, she just stood there.

He touched her shoulder, concerned. "Emma? What is it?"

She turned and looked up at him, eyes bright with unshed tears. "Justin," she whispered. "I know you've probably got to work, and I know that you probably ought to go home. But please...please stay. *Don't* go."

His heart pounded at the raw need in her voice. He wrapped her in a bear hug, then swiftly released her, acutely aware that they were fully visible to her parents inside the cabin. "Are you sure? I mean, your parents will be here, and I hate to intrude."

She continued to gaze at him, eyes pleading.

"What about the boys? Will they be uncomfortable with me here?"

She set her jaw. He wasn't going to agree. "Let me worry about them, okay? *I* need you here. I need a friend who isn't emotionally involved in this. Someone who won't feel sorry for me or my boys. Someone who won't keep reminding me that my husband's dead."

Justin's own jaw dropped in shock. Desperate to hide his feelings, he tore his gaze from hers. How could she think he wasn't emotionally involved? Just because he wasn't a friend of Andrew's didn't mean he didn't have an emotional stake in this. *She* was hurting. That was enough.

"Please, Justin."

How could he refuse her? "All right. If you really want me to stay, I'll stay."

Her shoulders sagged with relief. Tears brimming, she leaned into his embrace. "Thank you. I couldn't ask for a better friend."

He let out a long sigh and followed her into the house for dinner.

Friend. How he'd give anything to change that.

Chapter 6

Emma awoke early the next morning, despite the fact that she'd slept little during the night. She lay motionless, watching her sons' peaceful slumber. Before she'd retired the previous evening, her dad had helped her push the bed against the wall, careful not to wake the boys. She'd slept on the open side of the bed, shielding them from rolling off, as neither were accustomed to sleeping in such a big bed. Emmitt had smacked into the wall a couple times while he slept, reaffirming her decision.

She gazed tenderly into their little faces, struck anew by just how much they looked like *him*. Knowing they would be a walking, talking reminder of him every day for the rest of her life was both thrilling and painful. Especially since it meant she would not for one minute be able to forget him. And that's exactly what she longed to do. To forget. To numb her aching heart with the busyness of everyday life.

Emma smoothed Will's hair out of his face and lightly kissed each of their foreheads. She eased out of bed, wrapping her robe tightly around her body, and stepped down the hall to make some coffee. Once it was ready, she filled a mug and curled up on one of the twin window seats. She stared, unseeing, at the mountains in the distance. Drawing her legs up, knees folded against her chest, she wrapped her arms around them tightly, desperately trying to keep the thoughts already assaulting her at bay.

In the smallest of the three bedrooms, the pervading scent of coffee beckoned Justin from a fitful slumber. Having slept in only a pair of flannel pajama bottoms, he pulled on a worn t-shirt he'd rescued from the dresser in the master bedroom the night before. Seeking his own cup of liquid energy, he headed into the kitchen, wondering briefly who was awake. Deep down, however, he knew it was Emma. Had she even slept at all? He sincerely hoped so. If not, he fully intended to make sure she got the rest she needed later today. Even if she didn't like it.

Cup in hand, he perched on the edge of the window seat, nudging her leg with his knee. "Hi."

Empty eyes met his. "Hmm?" He could tell the moment she emerged out of her daze and recognized him. "Oh. Hi, Justin."

"Did you sleep?" he inquired, peering at her intently over the rim of his cup.

She leaned her head back against the cool window pane. "Define *sleep*. If by sleep you mean 'laid in bed and stared at the ceiling', then yes. I slept."

"Do you need me to prescribe something?"

"Yes... No... Maybe... Oh, I don't know."

He frowned, covering her hands with one of his. "Just think about it, okay? I'm not gonna force you to take anything. Yet," he added with a straight face, then allowed a tiny smile to peek through.

"I will."

"How about some breakfast? I'm an expert waffle chef."

She wrinkled her nose in distaste.

"Don't tell me you don't like waffles. Everyone likes waffles, Emma. How can you not like *waffles*?!"

"I just don't, okay? What about pancakes? Mmmm, with chocolate chips in them. Do you have the ingredients?"

He gripped her shoulders and gently shook them. "Wait a minute. You like pancakes, but you don't like waffles? Which, by the way, are the very same thing as pancakes but with indentions in them."

She raised her chin defiantly, crossing her arms in front of her chest. "They are *not* the same as pancakes."

Justin laughed. "You take the cake, woman."

"Mmmm, cake. I could really go for some cake right about now. With lots of frosting," she added dreamily.

"I'll speak to the hotel manager for you. Perhaps something can be arranged."

She shoved his arm. "Ha, ha."

"So pancakes. You sure that's what you want?"

"With lots of chocolate chips. Don't forget about the chocolate chips."

"I can't promise the chocolate chips. Does that affect your decision?"

"It might. What're pancakes without chocolate chips?"

"A whole lot healthier for you, that's what."

Emma rolled her eyes. "Doctors," she muttered under her breath.

He grinned. This was the Emma he remembered. Playful. Teasing. Fun. It was nice to know she was still there after all. "Okay. Since we don't have chocolate chips, and since you won't eat pancakes without them, what would you say to a western omelet?"

She scrunched her eyebrows, seemingly deep in thought. "All right. But only if you promise to pick up some chocolate chips at the store on your way back here from work later. And *no* mushrooms."

"No mushrooms," he agreed with a shudder.

"When do you have to go in?"

"I won't be going to work today. Or for the rest of the week for that matter." Last night he'd called in a favor, securing the week off. He'd readily agreed, however, to remain on call in case of emergency. "Someone else will have to pick up those chocolate chips."

"Really? You've got some time off?"

"Uh-huh. You asked me to stay here with you. So how could I not?"

She eyed him for a split second before her lids slid shut over tears that threatened to overflow. "Thank you," she softly replied, taking in a shuddering breath.

"It's the least I can do, Emma. Really."

As she seemed to crave a little time to herself, he pressed a kiss to the top of her head and moved into the kitchen to prepare breakfast.

I'd do anything to bring even a tiny bit of happiness back into your life, my sweet friend, he thought.

Anything.

A few hours later, while the boys helped their Nana bake peanut butter cookies, their favorite, Emma took advantage of the distraction and garnered some time to herself. It was an absolutely beautiful June day. Breezy, but not too windy. Warm, but not hot. She sat in the lounger on the deck, allowing the sun's rays to soak into her skin, and enjoying the trickling sounds of the stream.

Her father and Justin had driven over to her house to pick up a few extra items and to bring back the copy of Andrew's will they'd kept in a small safe in their bedroom closet. And to pick up a bag of chocolate chips, she thought with a small smile, already anticipating what she knew would be on tomorrow's breakfast menu.

She'd almost fallen asleep when she heard the rumble of an engine and assumed they'd returned. However, she was surprised to see two cars pull up in front of the house. Her brother's, and Joe's.

"Hey, sis. You look like you're doing a bit better today," Aaron commented, planting a kiss on her forehead, then stretching out his tall frame on the lounger next to hers.

"A bit," she answered, uncertain. What was Joe doing here?

"Hello, Emma. You're a hard woman to catch up with," her husband's best friend remarked, hands on hips. "Perturbed" was written all over his expressive face.

"Hi, Joe. I wasn't expecting to see you. Please have a seat."

He grudgingly sat.

"Em, he has some news about the shooting he thought you'd want to hear. When he couldn't find you, he called me."

"I went by the house, but obviously you weren't there. Mom and Pop are worried sick."

Emma palmed her forehead. "Ugh! I'm so sorry. With all the excitement of moving out here---temporarily," she added, noticing his frown, "I forgot to call them and let them know where we'd be. I'll call after awhile. I promise."

"I think that would be a good idea, Emma. Mom's got it in her head that the men who shot Andrew somehow found out where you live and decided to come after you and the boys."

"What?" she gasped. "How in the world would they even know who I am?"

Aaron grimaced. "Because you're all over the news, Em. Pictures of you have been included in most of the broadcasts."

She'd somehow forgotten that little detail. Tears formed and flowed down her cheeks. "Why can't they just leave me alone? Leave *us* alone? Why are they doing this?"

Her brother reached across and clasped her hand in his. "It's quite a sensational story, Emma. Once you hear the details from Joe, you'll understand. Even if it weren't, he was a most beloved teacher at the high school and a well-liked member of this community to boot."

It did make sense. But that didn't mean she had to like it. "What new information, Joe?"

He cleared his throat. Looked down at his shoes briefly, then out at the view before allowing his gaze to finally rest on hers. "We don't know much, Emma. All we do know is from video taken from a surveillance camera. And the cars were just too far away to get a good look at the men responsible."

She stifled a horrified sob. "So the men who did this will get away with it?"

"I didn't say that. There was a witness."

"You already told me that yesterday. You told me that the clerk saw the men driving off in his car. He couldn't have seen their faces, though. So how does that help us?"

Joe shook his head. "Not the clerk. There was an actual witness to the whole thing. From what we've managed to piece together, the two men who robbed the jewelry store sought a getaway car in the grocery store parking lot. They attempted to steal a young woman's car that was parked next to the Durango.

"This is going to be hard to hear, Emma. Are you sure you want to know what happened?"

She wrapped her arms around herself. Nodded slowly. "As much as it pains me to hear it, I need to know, Joe."

"Very well. Andrew walked out of the store, saw the woman in distress, and tried to intervene. He got into a scuffle with one of the assailants, giving the woman enough time to get to her car and drive away. They ran. What he didn't know, however, was that they'd snuck back around to the Durango. They forced him out of the car while he appeared to be distracted with something, and in the scuffle, he was shot. We don't know how much the woman saw, but she could certainly identify the attackers. There might also be video surveillance in the jewelry store of the men's faces. If they were not wearing masks."

Aaron squeezed her hand supportively. "I'm so sorry, Emma."

She remained quiet for several minutes before turning back to Joe. "What does all that mean exactly? I mean, for getting some justice for my husband?"

"We're going to discreetly ask this woman to come forward. Perhaps she's seen the news reports of you and your family. If so, we're hoping she'll be willing to help you get the justice you deserve."

Emma stood and leaned on the railing overlooking the creek, allowing the wooden frame to partially support her weight. This was a lot to take in. Her husband had died trying to save someone. Through the tears and pain, a half smile formed on her lips. Andrew had died the hero she'd always known him to be. While this wasn't what she wanted, she and the boys would always be proud of the way he'd lived his last moments. She thought back to all the ways he'd saved her over the years. Maybe not quite the same way he'd saved this woman. But he'd saved her nonetheless.

The time that stood out to her the most right now was when Justin broke her heart. Perhaps that memory was uppermost in her mind because of her renewed friendship with the man himself. Or perhaps it was because she was a guest in his home. Whatever the case, Andrew had been the one to help her pick up the broken pieces of her heart and move on. Without Justin. He'd truly been her knight in shining armor. Her confidant. Her best friend.

The night before Justin was supposed to leave for college in Boston, they'd had a date planned. She'd spent the day in emotional hysterics, depressed that he was leaving and she wouldn't be able to see him every day. But she'd believed herself so head over heels in love with him that she couldn't be depressed for long. Thoughts of him would send her into rapturous smiles.

When he'd arrived for their date, he'd been far more reserved than normal. Instead of greeting her with his customary flirtatious grin and kiss on the lips, he'd barely mumbled hi. There had been no physical contact.

And she'd been too blinded by her deep infatuation for him to notice.

All throughout dinner, he'd been quiet and wouldn't quite look her in the eye. She attributed it to the same emotions she was feeling--he was dreading their time apart and didn't want to say goodbye.

If only.

After dinner, they were supposed to have gone to the lake for a walk around the trails there. But he'd surprised her by driving her straight home.

Although confused, she'd blithely ignored the warning in her heart.

"What time does your plane get in tomorrow?" she'd asked.

"Just before 6."

"Oh. Well, I'm sure you'll be too busy getting unpacked tomorrow, but you can call me on Saturday to let me know you've made it okay."

When he'd glanced at her, there was something in his expression she couldn't quite define.

"Emma..." he'd begun softly.

"We'll see each other when you come home for Thanksgiving and Christmas, and of course we can talk on the phone every weekend when the rates are lower. My dad would kill me if I tried to call more often than that," she added with a forced laugh.

"Emma," he stated again, this time a bit more forcefully.

She didn't like what she heard in his voice. Her heart pounded and she wanted nothing more than to cover her ears against whatever it was he was about to say.

"You know I think you're great, right? You're a sweet girl. Really. But..."

Tears filled her eyes. "'*But*'? Justin, I love you. Don't you love me?" He'd never actually said it, but she'd always assumed he did.

Something flickered across his expression and he looked away for the longest time. When his eyes returned to hers, his face was cold and hard. Distant. "No, Emma."

She'd swallowed her tears, fighting for control. Not for anything would she let him see her cry.

And then as if that hadn't been bad enough...

"You'll always just be Aaron's kid sister to me, Emma. That little girl who used to follow us around everywhere we went."

She'd jerked as if he'd struck her. A little kid? *That's* how he saw her? "How could you?"

"I'm sorry."

But he hadn't *sounded* the least bit sorry.

She'd nodded once, biting her lip in her continued fight for control. "I am too. I thought you were someone who cared about me. I guess I was wrong." With that, she'd gotten out of the car and slammed the door. She'd barely made it halfway to the house before he sped away from the curb.

In her grief, she'd failed to notice the figure sitting on the porch steps. Waiting for her. She stood in the middle of the yard, giving free reign to the bitter tears of a broken heart, when arms spread around her and pulled her into a warm chest. Soft words of comfort were whispered into her ear.

Andrew.

Not knowing about Emma's date, he'd shown up on her porch, wanting to hang out with his best friend. He'd been waiting about ten minutes when he'd seen Mr. Bennet's Corvette pull up at the curb. Had seen the hurt expression on Emma's face, and had wanted nothing more than to yank the jerk out of the car and give him a piece of his mind for hurting her.

Emma had long believed that was the night things had slowly, subtly, started to change within their relationship.

The sounds of another car heading up the road pulled her back to the present. This time it was Justin and her dad. Both men exited the vehicle and joined the three on the deck.

Joe took in the man who'd once captured Emma's heart with eyes narrowed suspiciously. What was he doing here? Was the man trying to ingratiate himself with her once again?

Emma's father extended his hand to Joe, forcing his gaze away from Justin. "Good afternoon, Officer Peterson. It's good to see you. What brings you out this way?"

"Please, call me Joe, Mr. Johnson," he requested, shaking the man's outstretched hand.

"All right then. But only if you'll call me Steve."

"He has some news about the shooting, Dad," Aaron explained.

"Have the men who did this been found?"

Joe crossed his arms in front of his chest and shook his head. "Not yet, but we're confident that they will be. There was a witness to the shooting that can give testimony of the whole thing--including identify the shooters. That's *if* we can somehow get her to come forward," he added.

"It's a step in the right direction at least. Was there anything else?" Steve asked.

The police officer glanced hesitantly at Emma.

Soon, all eyes were on her. "Go ahead and tell them, Joe," she whispered, turning back to face the yard once more.

As he relayed the same information he'd given Emma, Joe was frustrated to see Justin stand beside her at the railing, his back to the yard and his right arm mere inches from hers. But when the doctor reached out and gently stroked her arm with a finger, his blood boiled. He would not idly stand by and watch this man put the moves on his best friend's widow--and mere days after Andrew's death, no less! His scowl deepened.

Aaron shot Justin a look of warning and was relieved to see him distance himself from Emma. He knew that his friend's motives were pure, but Joe didn't. Clearly the man was suspicious, his feelings hostile toward the man. He wondered if those feelings were also shared by the rest of the Darcy family as well. Knowing what he knew, he sincerely hoped they were not. Otherwise, things could get ugly. He needed to get Justin away from his sister for awhile. "Justin, can you go inside and see if mom needs anything?"

"Sure. I'll just take this stuff on in. Steve, where should I put those bags? Your room or mine?"

"We can put them in our room for the time being," he said, reaching for one of the bags. "I'm on my way in as well. I want to see if any of the cookies are ready. Joe, thank you for personally bringing us the news. Be sure to get some of my wife's homemade cookies before you go."

"Will do," he replied with a forced smile.

As soon as the two were inside, Joe rounded on Aaron and Emma. "What is Justin Bennet doing here?" he angrily demanded, lips clenched tightly.

Emma sighed, then turned to face her husband's best friend. "This is his cabin, Joe."

"Look," he began, forcing himself to calm down. "I understand why he invited you here. I do. And if I had a place like this, I would've made the same offer. But that doesn't mean he should *stay* out here with you, Emma."

"It's not like they're alone. Besides the boys, mom and dad have been here with them," Aaron pointed out.

Why were they even having this conversation? As if anything remotely inappropriate was likely to happen. She'd only been a widow for less than 48 hours, for crying out loud! "I just lost my husband! As if I'd even be thinking of anything else! Justin is my *friend*. He's the only one who does not have an emotional stake in this. The only one who isn't also grieving. Maybe it was selfish of me, but I needed that."

"Wait a minute---are you telling me that you *asked* him to stay? Em-ma! What were you thinking?"

She glared at him. "I'm a grown woman and don't need you to approve the decisions I make, Joe Peterson! I've got a lot of things to think about and plan for in the next few days, and I really don't need anyone causing me extra grief about what I do or don't do."

Joe raised his hands in surrender, wisely backing up a few steps. He opened his mouth to apologize, but she wasn't finished.

"Just so that there's no more confusion, or no more dirty looks directed at Justin, I want to get one thing perfectly straight with you--and anyone else for that matter. If you think for one second that I'll be ready to even *look* at another man for a very long time to come, you are one step away from the loony bin!" That said, she spun on her heel, burst into the house and slammed the door.

Joe stood staring after her, dumfounded. "I guess she told me."

Aaron valiantly tried to wipe the satisfied smirk off his face. Go, *Emma*! "Maybe you'd better go. She'll cool down after awhile."

He nodded. "You're probably right. Give her a hug from me, please? And make sure she calls the Darcys. They've been worried sick about her."

"Sure. By the way, we really do appreciate you coming all the way out here with the latest news from the investigation."

"Not a problem. But if I hear anything else, I think I'll just call instead."

Aaron laughed. "Wise choice."

Inside, Justin and the older Johnsons were stunned when Emma burst into the house, slamming the door behind her, then stormed down the hallway to the master bedroom, slamming that door behind her as well.

As both Steve and Grace were up to their elbows in cookie dough, Justin took it upon himself to check on her. He tapped gently on the door and waited for her muffled response before opening it.

She was sprawled face-down on the bed, sobbing into a pillow.

They'd all overheard her diatribe against Joe, so the last thing he wanted to do was to create more suspicion. Therefore, he purposely left the door halfway open and refrained from sitting on the bed. Instead, he pulled a chair over to the edge of the bed and sat on that.

Justin sat with her quietly, letting her get it all out. Sometimes the physical release of grief was just what was needed. Soon, her sobs lessened. She turned her head and looked at him for a minute before her heavy lids closed. He realized with satisfaction that she'd actually managed to wear herself out enough to sleep. He covered her with a light blanket and silently left the room, closing the door behind him.

He thought back to what he'd overheard, and his heart swelled with pride. He was proud of her for standing up for herself, and for him in the process. Proud, yet still frustrated at the same time. As Aaron had reminded him, it could be a long time before she ever saw him as anything other than a friend--if she ever did. He could certainly be patient. He'd waited several years, what were a few more?

But what if she *never* saw him as anything else?

He'd have to keep reminding himself that she'd just lost her husband and trust that if God meant for them to have any kind of a future together, He would bring it about in His time.

God's time. Not Justin's.

Chapter 7

The delicious aromas of freshly baked lasagna and garlic bread permeated the house, drawing Emma out of a deep sleep. She opened her eyes and looked around, momentarily disoriented, before recognizing her surroundings. She was back in her own bedroom at home. *Home*. After a week at Justin's cabin, it felt strange to be back in the home she'd shared with Andrew.

Tears slid down her cheeks as her thoughts drifted back to the funeral held earlier that afternoon. Over 150 of Cancun's residents had come to pay their final respects to her husband. She'd been stunned at the turnout.

The funeral had been at their church, a pretty large non-denominational congregation of about 200, near the high school. There was music, scripture readings, and a short sermon on the importance of trusting Jesus for salvation. All planned by Andrew weeks before. Why he'd suddenly felt compelled to plan his own funeral, she wasn't sure. She hadn't even realized he'd done it until they'd read his will.

Following the sermon, the pastor gave everyone an opportunity to stand up and share their stories of Andrew. Friends from college, church members, Andrew's fellow teachers - even many of the students - had stood up one by one, sharing just how much he'd meant to them.

Story after story was shared of his selflessness. His generosity. His love of teaching, his family, and his Savior. The latter had surprised Emma a little. Of course they went to church most Sundays. They tithed regularly. Contributed a few hard-earned dollars whenever missionaries came and spoke in church. Andrew had even taught a youth Sunday school class for the last several years. Short of praying over their meals, however, religion was not something they ever talked about at home. Sure, they'd had discussions about Heaven with Emmitt after her grandmother died six months earlier. But it was *certainly* not something they talked about in public. Well, outside of church, anyway. This afternoon, hearing stories of how he'd quietly shared his faith with his colleagues had shown Emma a side of her husband she'd never witnessed before. She'd found herself oddly jealous of those who'd known her husband that way. Why hadn't they ever talked about it at home? Why had he never told her about any of it?

As surprised as she'd been to hear some of those stories about her husband, there was one that had unsettled her more than anything else, from the very last person she'd ever thought to see.

A soft knock on the door interrupted her train of thought.

A second later, her mom opened the door a crack and peeked her head in. "Oh, good. You're awake. I was just coming to tell you that dinner's ready."

"Be there in a second, okay?"

Grace nodded, closing the door behind her.

Emma stepped into the bathroom and dashed cold water into her face. Next, she quickly ran a brush through her hair, then pulled it back from her face with a scrunchie.

Her parents were already seated in the tiny dining room off the kitchen, heaping platters of lasagna, garlic bread, and tossed salad clustered on the table.

She glanced at Emmitt's empty booster seat and Will's empty high chair questioningly. "Where are the boys? I thought Justin would've had them back by now."

"He called just before you woke up. After spending the morning and afternoon at the state park, he took them to McDonald's for supper," Steve explained, loading a large portion of his wife's homemade lasagna onto his plate. "They should be here soon."

"Those boys are bound to be positively worn out from all that time playing outside in the fresh air," Grace remarked. She regarded the scant amount of food on

Emma's plate with a worried frown. She had hardly eaten while at the cabin, prompting the concerned mother to make her daughter's favorite dinner, hoping it might tempt her to eat a bit more.

She opened her mouth to make a comment when Steve gently placed a hand on her knee. Her eyes flew to his. Spotting the almost imperceptible shake of his head, she sighed. She'd let it go for now. But if this continued much longer...

They were half-way through their meal when the back door opened and Justin walked in carrying the boys, tiny heads perched on each shoulder. Steve and Grace both shoved back from the table and took the boys from him, carrying them back to their room to prepare them for bed.

Justin leaned against the wall, eying Emma intently.

She set down her fork before meeting his gaze. A tiny smile peeked out at him. "Hi."

He grinned. "Hi."

"Have you eaten?"

He nodded. "Although if I'd known Grace was making lasagna, I would've waited. It smells amazing."

"There's plenty leftover if you'd like to take some home."

"I might just do that. It's not every day I get to enjoy a home cooked meal. But hey, don't let me keep you from your dinner."

She pushed her half-eaten meal away, then placed her napkin on the table. "I'm finished, anyway. Do you have to get back home right away, or can you stay and talk for awhile?"

"I can stay awhile."

She walked over to him and slid her arms around his waist in an embrace.

"What's that for?" he asked, returning the hug.

"For taking the boys today," she answered against his chest. "I didn't want them at the funeral. I'm just not

81

sure they'd understand. And with Andrew's parents insisting on an open-casket... Anyway, someone filmed the funeral, so the boys will be able to see it when they're older. If they *want* to see it, that is."

"I'm sorry, Em. I know that's not what you wanted."

She led him into the living room, chuckling bitterly. "No. I really caused a scene, too."

"I doubt that."

"I wish it weren't, but it's true. For thirty straight minutes, I kept hearing person after person saying, 'Doesn't he look so natural?' Honestly, why do people *say* that? I can only assume they're trying to make it seem like the deceased is merely sleeping. But seriously! I've never seen sleeping people *look* like that! I watched Andrew while he slept often enough to know *he* certainly didn't. So to hear this ridiculous phrase over and over again this afternoon... I just lost it."

"Uh-oh. That doesn't sound good. What did you do?"

"I yelled - actually *yelled* - at poor Mrs. Goodson. She repeated that same comment to Beth, who was also standing there with me. And I just went off. I screamed back at her, '*No*, he doesn't! You think this waxy look is *natural*?! There's nothing *natural* about it!'"

Justin valiantly tried not to laugh, but he wasn't very successful. "I'm sorry Emma, I know it's not funny."

She shrugged. "I'm sure one of these days I'll be able to laugh about it. But right now I'm just mortified. The look on that poor woman's face... She was absolutely horrified. She mumbled an apology and made a beeline for her seat. As far away from me as she could get, I might add."

"What did Beth say?"

"I think she was sorry they'd pushed so hard for the open casket. But she let it go. Not long afterward, the funeral director closed the casket."

They sat in silence for a few minutes--Emma staring at the wall, Justin quietly watching her. She'd buried her husband today. *What must that be like?* he wondered. How must it feel to say goodbye to your best friend and life companion? He'd lost his twin brother and his father in just a matter of years. Both were painful losses, yes. But to lose one's *spouse*? And at such a young age in such a horrific manner? He couldn't imagine it.

"How many people came?" he asked, wanting to keep her from brooding longer.

"The church was pretty packed. I had no idea he'd touched so many lives. It was surreal."

"Sounds like a good portion of the town were there."

"Just about. Except I wasn't expecting to see---"

She halted mid-sentence when her parents walked into the room.

"We got the boys in their jammies and tucked in bed," her father reported. "Your mom and I just want to clean up these dishes for you before we go."

"Did you eat dinner yet, dear?" Grace asked Justin.

"Yes, ma'am, I did. I guess I should've called you *before* I ate with the boys."

"There's plenty here. Why don't I just fix you a plate to take home? You can heat it up for a meal tomorrow."

"That sounds perfect Grace, thanks," he answered, glancing briefly at Emma. She was back to staring at the wall again, a distracted look on her face. "Say, do you mind if I take Emma for a quick drive? Maybe stop for some ice cream?"

"Not at all, Justin. Not at all. But don't rush back. It's probably good for her to get out of the house for awhile," Steve reasoned.

"Well, Emma? Want to get some ice cream?" he asked.

She continued to stare at the wall until he touched her arm. "I'm sorry. Did you say something to me?"

"I asked if you'd like to get some ice cream with me."

"What? Oh. Yeah, that sounds nice. Mom, Dad, we won't be long."

"Take your time, dear."

He led her to the curb where his car was parked, then opened the door for her. Once they were both comfortably seated, he reached into his pocket and handed her a set of keys. "Before I forget, here are the keys to your van. I've got to say I felt a bit like a soccer mom driving the boys around in it today."

Emma laughed. "As much as they would've enjoyed riding in your car, there's no way two car seats would've fit in here."

"Not a chance, no. So. Shall I leave the top up, or put it down?"

She eyed what she could see of the starry night sky through the window, suddenly longing to be able to see it better. To feel the wind in her hair again. "Down."

He grinned. "Down it is."

They got chocolate ice cream cones from Dairy Queen and took them to a nearby park--the very park she and Andrew had taken the boys to just a week before. Had it really only been a week? It felt, somehow, that it had been at least a month or more.

She sat on one of the swings, making designs in the sand with her toe. "I love swings. No matter what's going on, I just have to sit in one and I'm instantly a little girl again," she replied, finished the last of her cone, then brushed her hands on her jeans.

"Really? I can't remember the last time I did any swinging."

She gaped at him. "Now, that's just plain sad. Do you even remember how it's done?"

He gently shoved off with his toe. "Oh, I think I can manage."

"I'll bet you can't swing as high as I can," she challenged.

"Is that so?"

"Yeah."

For the next ten minutes, they laughed and taunted the other to go faster, higher. In the end, Justin won, mainly due to his longer legs.

"You have the unfair advantage of being taller than me," Emma complained.

He laughed. "Nothing I can do about that, is there?"

She smacked him lightly in the arm. "No, I guess not."

Justin slid his swing to a stop, then reached over and did the same to hers, bumping her knee with his in the process. The brief contact was a lightning bolt to his senses. He swallowed, then cleared his throat. "You were telling me something about the funeral back at the house when your parents came in. What was it?"

She instantly sobered. For a few brief minutes, she had forgotten she'd buried her husband today. The largest part of her felt guilty about it. But there was a small part of her that felt only relief. Relief that, for those fleeting moments, she'd experienced a glimpse of what it felt like not to mourn. To ache inside. She wished that blessed relief could last longer.

Suddenly chilled, she rubbed her arms, wishing she'd thought to bring a sweater. "Justin, can we please sit in the car and talk? It's getting cold."

The thought of sitting close together in an enclosed space both thrilled and unnerved him. But being the gentleman that he was raised to be, how could he refuse her request? "Sure."

Once again, he opened the car door for her. Inside, he raised the convertible top and even turned on the heater for her. "Better?"

She nodded, favoring him with a grateful smile. "Thank you."

He turned sideways in his seat, leaned against the door, and waited for her to speak.

"I saw someone I didn't expect to see, and I'm not quite sure what to make of it."

"A friend? Someone from church?"

She shook her head to both. "Someone I've never seen before."

A twinge of uneasiness began to take root in the pit of his stomach, but he didn't quite understand why. He knew it wasn't anyone from the media. After she'd seemingly disappeared for almost a week, they'd collectively lost interest in trying to find her. Other stories had broken. She'd become old news. Thankfully.

"Justin, it was the woman Andrew saved the night he was shot."

Not in a million years would he have guessed that. "Did you just see her, or did she speak to you?"

"She spoke to me."

"Wow, Emma. Man. What in the world did she say?"

Justin was clearly as shocked as she'd been, which was somehow comforting to her. She allowed her mind to drift back to the end of the funeral, trying to remember exactly how it happened.

The line of people waiting to offer their condolences was slowly dwindling, much to Emma's relief. Most of these people she only barely knew, some she'd never even met before today. Yet, each of them had some connection to her husband, had been touched by his life in some way. Many of the stories she'd heard had swelled her heart with pride for the wonderful man she'd married. How had she been so blessed as to be chosen by such a man?

Her father had already gone to pull their car around. Justin had used her van to take the boys for the day, something she was immensely grateful for. There's no way they would've understood what was taking place today. And watching their Mama grieve was getting harder and harder for them to see.

She accepted hugs from the last of the well-wishers and turned to collect her things. They'd chosen to make the funeral a public event, but the burial a private one. Only family - and close friends like Joe and Noelle - were invited. At the time it had almost seemed cruel to limit those at the gravesite service to family. But after she'd seen how many people packed into the church to pay their final respects, she believed they'd made the right choice. Just getting all those people to the cemetery would've been a logistical nightmare.

"Mrs. Darcy?" queried a soft feminine voice.

She turned and saw a beautiful young woman standing in the aisle next to the pew. "Yes?"

The young woman wrung her hands nervously. "You don't know me, but I just had to come here today."

Emma's brow wrinkled in confusion. Who was this girl?

"My name is Anna," she said, darting her gaze around, as if looking for someone.

"Nice to meet you, Anna," Emma replied, holding her hand out. "How did you know my husband?"

The young woman placed her cold hand in Emma's. "I didn't. Not really." She resumed her nervous hand-wringing.

Now her curiosity was piqued. This girl couldn't be more than twenty. Too young to be in any of Andrew's Master's level classes at the university. And she thought she'd remembered all of the students he'd taught in the last couple years. So how in the world did she know, or not know, him?

Anna squeezed her dress absently, looked down briefly, then raised her eyes to Emma's. "I'm the one your husband saved that night."

Emma's heart dropped and her face went ashen. She immediately sat before she collapsed. She squeezed her eyes shut and desperately tried not to picture it.

The girl quickly sat next to Emma and took one of her hands in hers. "Please don't be upset! Oh, I probably shouldn't have come. But I just had to be here - to tell you - that I owe your husband my life. I don't want to think about what those men would've done to me if he hadn't come to my rescue. You're not mad that I'm here, are you?"

Emma shook her head violently. Mad? How could she be mad that this girl was alive and her husband was not? Fat tears rolled down her cheeks. This girl was the very last person she expected to see today. Yet here she was. Right next to her. Holding her hand.

Okay, maybe she was a *little* mad.

"I'm just so grateful for what he did, Mrs. Darcy. You see, I've got a little sister I'm taking care of. And I'm the only family she's got. If something happened to me..."

Emma's heart filled with compassion for this girl, squeezing out all traces of anger. "Then I'm glad."

Anna gave her a watery smile. "Thank you. I wish it hadn't ended like it did. Lucy still has her sister. But you don't have a husband. Your boys don't have their Daddy. I feel so guilty."

"Please don't, Anna. We've got wonderful friends and family members who are helping us get through this. Don't you feel one bit guilty about being alive. I know Andrew wouldn't want you to."

They each wiped their eyes and stood to leave.

"If there's ever anything I can do for you.."

"Actually, Anna, there *is* something you can do for me."

"Oh, please name it! I'll do anything!"

"You have to go to the police and tell them about that night. Give them descriptions of the men. They need you as a witness so they can convict them."

Fear whitened her face and she took a step back, holding her hands in front of her as if to ward off a blow. "Oh, no, I couldn't do that! What if they find out who I am and come after me?"

Emma pulled a piece of paper out of her purse and wrote Joe's name and phone number in her flowing script. "Just think about it, okay? Please? For my sake. If you change your mind, call this man. He's a police officer and a very dear friend of mine. In fact, he was my husband's best friend. He'll do what he can to help you."

Anna hesitantly took the paper. "Okay... I'll think about it. I'm not promising anything. But I'll think about it."

At that moment, Steven Johnson appeared at the back of the church. "Emma!" he called, "You ready to go?"

The young woman glanced at Emma's dad fearfully before racing out a side door without another word to her.

"Wow," Justin whispered once Emma had finished speaking. "I can't believe she actually came to the funeral to talk to you. Did she give you her last name? Maybe you should mention it to Joe. I'm sure they have ways of finding people."

"No, no last name. Just a first name. And while I assume she's from Cancun, I really don't know that for certain. She could be from one of the surrounding towns or even Denver as far as we know."

"True," he agreed. "Well, I should probably get you home. I'm sure your parents are ready to call it a day."

At the house, he leaned over and hugged her as best as he could with the console between them. "I'll be praying that Anna realizes how important her testimony is and decides to come forward."

"Thanks, Justin. I appreciate that. Until then, can we keep this between ourselves, please?"

"Sure. But don't you think the rest of the family would like to know?"

"Probably. But then it might get back to Joe. And I don't need him bugging me about this. It's not like they've even caught the guys yet or anything."

"Emma," Justin warned, "I wouldn't wait too long on this. Joe needs to know."

She frowned. "All right, all right. I'll tell him. But in a few days. Is that soon enough for you?"

He nodded, enveloping her in another hug, then pressing a light kiss to her forehead. "If you need anything, please call me. Okay? Day or night."

"Thanks, Justin. I will. And thanks again for today. The boys were so excited to get to see you this afternoon."

He grinned. "We're buddies, your boys and me. Hey, do you mind if I hang out with them later in the week?"

She eyed him skeptically. "You want to hang out with my boys?"

"Sure do. They're a lot of fun."

"All right then."

"I'll give you a call."

"Goodnight, Justin."

"'Night, Em."

Inside, she hugged her parents goodbye, made sure the house was locked, then decided to peek in on the boys before heading for bed.

They were each sound asleep, blissfully unaware of the tumultuous day their mother had experienced. She brushed gentle kisses across tiny foreheads, then stood in the doorway for a moment, just watching them sleep.

Just a week ago, she'd done this very thing after a wonderfully passionate morning with her very-much-alive husband. And in a moment, for the first night in a week, she'd climb into their queen-sized bed alone. Without the warmth of his body next to hers. The sound of his breathing as he slept.

Tears slid down her cheeks. How her heart ached. When would it be better? When would she be able to take a breath without her chest compressing in agony? She slid to the floor and wept silently, begging God to take away the pain.

Chapter 8

August

Emma stared at the double magenta line. Shock reverberated throughout her entire body. Pregnant. A wave of nausea swept over her and she held herself as rigidly as possible, praying for it to ease. After the fourth morning in a row of rolling nausea, she'd guessed. After the seventh, she'd strongly suspected. But after the fourteenth, she'd *known*. And now this positive test confirmed it. *Pregnant*! How could it be? As if taking care of two small children on her own wasn't hard enough, now she'd have a third young life to nurture. And nurturing others was really the last thing her shattered heart wanted to do. How on earth could she raise three children without Andrew?

"It's not fair!" she cried aloud, for the umpteenth time in the last two-and-a-half months.

That's right--it's not fair. Why should this happen to you when you've been nothing but good? Now, you have nothing. Now, you have no one.

No, My daughter, I am with you. You have Me. Turn to Me.

As always, the voices warred within her heart, one tinny yet strangely melodic, the other soothing and gentle. Which one to listen to? Sometimes they each had such great points. Although, if she were really honest with herself, the melodic voice usually left her feeling even more angry and bitter than she'd been to begin with.

A knock at the back door enabled her to drown out both voices. She could make out Justin's form through the lacy curtains over the door. Quickly, she swept the pregnancy test into the trash so that he wouldn't see it. She was definitely not ready to reveal her news.

"Hey, Emma," he said in greeting as she opened the door, his hands jammed into the pockets of his jeans. Then, with one look at her ashen face, he stepped into the house and pulled her into a tight embrace. "What is it? Has something happened?"

She shook her head against his warm chest, the soft cotton of his t-shirt mashed against her cheek. Most other people stayed away from her, unsure of what to say. Even visits from family members had tapered off in the last several weeks. But not Justin's. He'd developed the habit of stopping by the house every day, either before or after his shift at the hospital, just to check on them. Never staying overly long, he'd play with the boys a bit, rolling around on the floor and rough-housing with them the way she couldn't. And at some point of each visit, he'd spend several minutes just holding her, allowing her to cry on his very broad shoulders.

During their years apart, she'd somehow forgotten how tall he was. She and Andrew had been very nearly the same height, something she'd loved. There was just something soothing about that. But despite her taller than average height, Justin still towered over her. In his embrace, her head rested at the level of his heart. She had to admit there was something soothing about that as well. It often reminded her of Will's teddy bear that made heartbeat sounds.

Emma was quickly coming to depend upon him more and more each day. He was her rock. The strength she desperately needed. Yet despite their new closeness, she just couldn't bring herself to tell him about the baby. Not yet, anyway.

"I lost my husband, Justin. My children lost their Daddy. Isn't that enough?"

"Of course, Em. It's just that you looked like someone'd kicked you in the gut when you opened that door. I just assumed something horrible had happened."

Of course something horrible happened! My husband was killed, leaving me alone with two small boys and another baby on the way!

Grasping her arms, he gently set her away from him and then leaned down slightly to peer into her face. "C'mon, Emma. This is *me* you're talking to here. Remember? The guy who's known you since you were six years old?" He took two steps away from her and leaned against the kitchen counter, crossing his arms in front of his chest. "Spill it."

She glared at him in exasperation and frustration. Like that was gonna happen. "Maybe I don't wanna talk about it yet, okay?"

He briefly glanced down before allowing his azure eyes to meet hers. "Fair enough. But I really think you'd feel better if you spoke with *somebody*. Your pastor, a counselor--Noelle, even. Just don't let it stew and fester."

"Leave it to a doctor to tell me not to let it fester."

"You get my point, though, Em. If you can't - won't - talk to me, at least promise me that you'll talk to *someone*."

Why did he sound so sad when he said that part, "won't"? She gave him a sidelong glance, trying to see if the answer was written on his face. It wasn't. He wore an expressionless mask that told her absolutely nothing. Something he was irritatingly good at.

With a long sigh, she rested the palm of her hand briefly against his chest, then quickly let it drop to her side. "I didn't mean to be nasty, Justin. I'm just not ready to talk about it all yet. I appreciate you worrying about me, though," she added, allowing a small smile to peek out.

His heart skipped a beat at both her proximity and vulnerability, certain that the imprint of her palm would be forever seared into the skin on his chest. Would he ever be able to tell her? How much time needed to pass before she'd be ready to hear how much he loved her? Had *always* loved her. If only he'd realized it sooner--back when she'd still looked up at him in complete adoration. But of course, he hadn't realized the depth of his feelings for her until it was too late.

Then, to his shock and delight, she stood on tiptoe and kissed his cheek, nearly bringing his heart to a stop. He sucked in a deep breath and tried to act as nonchalant as possible, all while a hurricane of emotion was swirling around inside. He wanted so badly to engulf her in his arms and kiss her until she was breathless. Until all thoughts of pain and suffering were erased from her mind. He wanted to let her know how special, how strong, and how oh-so-desirable she was. But it was too soon---*far* too soon. *Lord, help me to forget about my feelings and be the caring friend she needs me to be.*

"Of course, Emma. Anything for you, you know that," he added with a grin. "Now. Where are the boys? I've been looking forward to this all day."

She resumed her perch at the breakfast bar. "Hate to disappoint you, Justin, but my parents came and took them for the night, claiming their grandparental right to spoil."

"So you've got the night to yourself, huh?" *If only things were different...* Realizing the gist of his thoughts, he gave himself a firm mental shake. *Get a grip, man! If things were different, she'd be spending a romantic night alone with her husband.*

"I guess," she stated flatly, picking at a loose fingernail.

"You don't sound all that excited about it."

She shrugged. "Should I be?"

He sat on the stool across the bar from her and took her hands in his. "I don't know about 'excited', Em, but you do need some time to yourself. You've been going at full steam since the funeral."

Another shrug.

"Are you sleeping?" he asked, his fingers gently stroking the backs of her hands.

She gave a little snort. "Is that your way of telling me I look tired? That I don't look very good?"

*Yes....and most emphatically, **no**. You are beautiful. Always.* "What I'm telling you is that you need to take a break so that you can continue to be a good mommy to the boys. You can't keep going on like this indefinitely, Em."

Emma sighed once more. "I know. Thanks for the medical advice, Dr. Bennet," she added with a humorless laugh.

"Yes, I am saying this as a doctor. But I'm also your friend." *And someone who loves you deeply.*

"You're right. I am kinda tired. Maybe I'll soak in a bubble bath or something."

"Just don't fall asleep in the tub," he warned with a chuckle.

At the door, he drew her into another bear hug, attempting to draw all of the hurt and pain out of her and into him. Oh, if only he could.

After several minutes, he tried to pull away, but she clung even tighter to his waist. "Emma?" he questioned, suddenly feeling her tears soaking through the thin material of his t-shirt.

"Please don't leave me. I - I can't - can't be alone," she whispered before racking sobs shuddered through her body.

Justin inwardly groaned. Unable to control himself any longer, yet unwilling to do anything to jeopardize their friendship, he settled for tenderly pressing a kiss to the top of her head. "I know it doesn't feel like it right now, sweetheart, but I believe that one day it *will* get easier."

"Promise?"

"Promise."

God, he prayed, *please make it easier.*

"Do you want some popcorn to go with your water?" Emma called from the kitchen. While she still felt rather embarrassed for being so needy, she was also relieved that Justin had agreed to stay and watch a movie with her. The thought of being alone in the house with all the silence was...horrifying. The memories only invaded once she was still. If she could just keep moving, keep *doing*, she could keep them at bay.

Almost.

"If you're making some, then yes. Otherwise, don't worry about it," he called from the tiny family room.

He glanced through Emma's stack of movies with a frown. Selecting one that didn't remind her of Andrew was like strolling through a mine field. Okay, so that pretty much ruled out anything in the romantic comedy genre. And *definitely* not her favorite movie, *Pride and Prejudice*. What a disaster that would be! But what *wouldn't* remind her of her dead husband? Action! Nothing romantic about blood and guts. Er---on the other hand, it was probably better not to remind her of the shooting that took her beloved's life. Hmm. Okay, so there went another entire movie genre. That left....one of the boys' movies. Pulling one from the shelf, he chuckled. He was 31 years old and Cancun's Most Eligible Bachelor (regardless of the fact that, in his mind at least, he was *very* taken). Yet here he was, spending his Friday night with a grieving widow, watching a children's movie.

Emma breezed into the room with a tray that contained a large bowl of popcorn, a can of cherry soda, and a glass of water. "So, what did you pick?"

Sheepishly, he held up his selection.

"*Monster's, Inc.*?" she smirked, one eyebrow raised.

He shrugged. "We watched part of it the other day and I've been curious to find out how it ends. Do you mind?"

She flashed him a grateful smile, impulsively hugging his neck. "You're not fooling me, Justin Bennet! But thank you."

They settled down on the couch with the popcorn between them and watched in companionable silence until he noticed that her head kept dipping onto her shoulders. He placed the nearly-empty bowl on the table next to him and lifted his arm, inviting her to snuggle in.

Emma wasted no time in burrowing into his warm chest, sighing in contentment when he lowered his arm and settled her just a bit tighter to his body. It wasn't very long before she fell asleep, but Justin was in no hurry to leave. He finished watching the movie, enjoying the sensation of holding her snugly pressed to his side.

At the conclusion of the movie, he reluctantly tried waking her. While he could just ease away from her and let her sleep where she was, he knew that she'd sleep more restfully in her own bed. As it was, it appeared that she wasn't getting much sleep at all. After several failed attempts to wake her, he resolutely swept her up into his arms and carried her to the back of the house where he knew her bedroom was located, trying to ignore the thrill holding her produced. Her room was the one room in the whole house he'd never once stepped foot into.

Until tonight.

There was enough light spilling in from the hallway, so he didn't bother turning on the lamp at her bedside. Ever so gently, he laid her down in the middle of the bed. Then, he covered her limp body with a colorful quilt that had been draped over a bench at the foot of the bed.

Justin stood and gazed down at the woman he loved. He slid a lock of hair off her forehead, then tenderly brushed his knuckles across her cheek. He bent, kissed her forehead softly, and then quickly left the room before he did something he'd regret.

Wandering down the hallway, he paused to observe the photographs neatly hung on the wall. Major milestones of the boys' short lives were displayed in chronological order, from when they were hours old until now. Although both of the boys very strongly resembled their father, he could see glimpses of Emma in them as well. Emmitt's straight hair and slightly upturned nose. Will's mesmerizing brown eyes. In another picture, it was evident that both of the boys had inherited their mother's dazzling smile.

At the very last picture, Justin froze and sucked in a breath, his heart flopping in his chest. Staring back at him was Emma - *his* Emma - resplendent in a gorgeous satin and lace wedding dress, gazing up at her brand new husband with a look of utter adoration and wistfulness. The way she used to look at him. No matter how beautiful he found her now, it did not compare with the woman in that picture, and he couldn't quite figure out why. What was the difference? With a jolt, he realized that in the wedding photograph, she was blissfully happy, facing a lifetime (or so she believed) spent with the man she was passionately in love with. Despite the fact that the woman she was today absolutely took his breath away, he knew that spark of joy, that utter happiness that infused her from the inside out, was missing. When he looked into her eyes, it was gone. Instead, pain, sorrow, and bitterness remained. How he longed to see that joy in her eyes again.

To have those eyes, filled with love and adoration, gazing into his.

Could a heart broken so completely mend and learn to love again? Dare he hope? Or was he just hurting himself in the long run - waiting, praying - hoping that one day she would love him in return?

Please, God, let it be so.

With a long sigh, he turned away from the portrait and walked back into the living room, determined to straighten up a bit for her. He placed her unopened soda back into the fridge, then bent to empty the popcorn into the trash bin...and halted, the blood leaving his face in a rush.

Peeking out from a tissue was something that closely resembled a pregnancy test. A *positive* pregnancy test.

The metal bowl slipped from his grasp, but he managed to grab it again before it fell to the floor with a clatter that might alert Emma to his presence.

She was pregnant. And hadn't told him.

Why?

His fist slammed the counter in frustration. This was the very last thing she needed right now. So why?

"Lousy timing, Lord."

My ways are not your ways, My son.

He hung his head briefly. "You're right. I don't understand this. The timing..."

Another long sigh escaped.

He quickly finished cleaning up the tiny kitchen and silently left the house, making sure the door was locked behind him.

Pregnant! This changed everything.

Didn't it?

And why did it hurt so much that she hadn't been able to trust him enough to tell him herself?

Chapter 9

The next two months drug by for Emma, each day's drudgery broken only by her severe bouts of nausea. She'd never been this sick with a pregnancy before. With the boys, morning sickness was really only an occasional thing, or struck if she allowed herself to get too hungry. But with this baby, she was sick constantly. Regardless of how much or how little she ate. Or how much or little she moved. She still hadn't told a soul about the baby. Although by now, at roughly four and a half months, she was beginning to show. Luckily, September had brought cooler temperatures, enabling her to wear bulky sweaters or sweatshirts to hide her growing baby belly.

Not only was she physically and emotionally miserable, she feared there would never be a break in her husband's case. About a week after the funeral, the young woman had met with Joe, but even with her testimony and the artists' renderings they've been able to put together from her descriptions and what little they'd been able to see from the security recording, they had still been unable to locate and arrest the two men. Each day was a constant, continuous struggle just to survive. Her will to live slowly drained away with each passing hour.

It was now the middle of October, and she dreaded the thought of the coming holidays. Only another couple weeks until Halloween. Normally, she counted down the days until the holiday was over, as she and Andrew had long ago decided not to celebrate it as a family. But this year... She struggled with the knowledge that once the dark holiday was over, she would soon be bombarded with Christmas commercials. Christmas specials. Even Christmas music. And the most joyous time of the year was the very last thing she wanted to think about. Not when joy was suddenly so foreign to her.

Today - like every day - after working so hard to get the boys down for their afternoon naps, she sprawled on the couch in the living room, mindlessly flipping through the television channels. Not that there was anything good on. Hardly. But a quiet house and a moment of stillness opened the door to thoughts she'd worked so hard to bury. In spite of the raging morning sickness, she managed to keep busy enough to keep those thoughts of her husband and his horrific death at bay. Most of the time, anyway.

At a quiet knock at the door, she eased off of the couch and shuffled over to see who it was. 3:30 in the afternoon was a bit early for Justin's nightly visit. But he might've gotten off work early. Although, considering how strangely he'd been acting lately, she wasn't entirely sure she wanted to see him without the boys.

However, it wasn't Justin. It was her mother.

When Emma opened the door, Grace's face registered her shock. A beautifully full face was now drawn and almost gaunt in its thinness. Emma's normally thick, shiny hair was dull and lackluster, hanging limply down her shoulders. It appeared as if she hadn't washed it in days. What was going on?

Emma leaned into her mother's arms, careful to keep her abdomen from touching her mother's. She'd know about the pregnancy for sure if she felt the baby bump.

Grace hugged her daughter's upper body tightly, further shocked to feel how thin her shoulders had become.

"When did you guys get home?" Emma asked, closing the door and motioning for her mother to sit. "Would you like some tea?"

The elder Johnsons had scheduled a three-week cruise months before to celebrate their 35th wedding anniversary. A non-refundable cruise. Emma had insisted that her parents go as scheduled, assuring them she and the boys would be fine.

"No, not now, dear. We got in last night. I came by to pick up the mail and check to see how you were doing."

Emma eased herself back onto the couch, angled so that she was facing Grace, then clutched a pillow to her chest. She didn't want to run the risk that she'd be able to see the telltale bump around her middle. "Aaron's got your mail, actually, Mom. It's been a little crazy over here, so he offered to pick it up for me."

"Oh. Okay, I'll make a point of stopping there next. So you said it's been busy. Is everything okay?"

She picked at a button on the pillow absent-mindedly. "As okay as it can be. The boys have just been especially clingy the last couple weeks."

"I don't mean to pry, Emma, but have you been sick? You just don't look like yourself."

"A little. You know the flu has been going around. Several families in the church have come down with it." While technically true, she felt a little guilty deliberately misleading her mother. For some reason, she did not feel like acknowledging the baby. As if not talking about it with anyone made the baby less real somehow.

"Have you been to the doctor?"

"No. There's really no need, Mom. I already know what they're going to say." Boy, that was certainly the truth. "Besides, I'm fine."

"Well, what about the boys? Have they gotten sick?"

"No, just me, thankfully."

Grace eyed her daughter thoughtfully. There was something wrong here, but she just couldn't quite put her finger on it. Maybe she was just tired. It had been a couple months since they'd taken the boys overnight. Perhaps she just needed to have some time to herself. "Listen, sweetheart. Why don't I take the boys home with me for the night?"

Emma's eyes widened in panic. "No, I couldn't let you do that, Mom. You and Dad just got home. Don't you want to rest up from your vacation first?"

"What's to rest up from? We spent three weeks doing absolutely nothing aboard ship. That's enough relaxation for anybody. Besides, we've really missed the boys. It would be nice to have them to ourselves for the night."

There wasn't much more to be said. If she put up too much of a fight, she knew her mother might get suspicious. Still, the idea of another night by herself both thrilled and terrified her. If she wasn't chasing the boys around, maybe she could actually get her stomach to settle. Then again, without the busyness of taking care of the boys, those thoughts would take over.

"Let me just get their stuff," she acceded, rising from the couch swiftly. The room spun, and she hastily sat back down.

Grace sat beside Emma and rested her palm against her forehead. "You are *not* fine, Emma Joy Darcy. I definitely think you need to go to the doctor."

Uh-oh. The full name, she thought with a smirk. She shook her head gently, closing her eyes in an attempt to keep the room from spinning. "No, it's okay. I just got up too quickly, that's all. I'm all right. Maybe it *is* a good idea for the boys to stay with you tonight. Then I can climb back in bed and get some sleep."

"Well, as long as you promise to do just that, I think that would best. You look like you haven't been sleeping much."

Why did people seem to delight in telling her that lately? Emma wondered. First Justin and now her mother. "I'll be fine," she repeated. "Do you mind getting their things? I think there are clean clothes in the dryer. There should be pajamas and something for each of them to wear tomorrow."

"Sure, honey. Not a problem. You just stay there. Maybe you should put your feet up and stretch out a little."

In practically no time at all, Grace had an overnight bag packed for the boys and had muscled their car seats into the back of her car.

"We really ought to get our own car seats. It would be nice if we didn't have to go through this every time we take the boys anywhere," she remarked.

Emma snorted indelicately. "Yeah, right, Mom. That's just what you and Dad need."

"No, I'm serious. Wouldn't it be so much easier?"

"Maybe, but it's just a big waste of money. Once the boys outgrow them, when are you ever going to need them again?"

"Oh, I don't know. I have a feeling there will be more grandchildren someday."

Emma's heart stopped, realizing what she'd said. Did she know? Had she guessed? "Mom, I..."

"I know Aaron and Julia would like to have children soon," she stated, kissing the top of Emma's head. "Besides, honey. While you may not be ready to think about this yet, it wouldn't surprise me if you found someone else to love. One day, anyway. And who knows? Maybe you'll decide you'd like to have more children."

She pressed her lips together lest she inadvertently let something slip.

"I'll just go wake the boys from their naps and we'll be out of your hair."

While her mother was in the other room getting the boys, Emma took several deep breaths, attempting to calm her pounding heart. Just as she'd managed it, her boys raced excitedly around the corner and launched themselves into her arms for a brief hug, nearly knocking her off balance.

"Do we really get to stay with Nana and Papa, Mama?" Emmitt gushed.

"Yes, darling, if you'd like to."

"Oh yes, oh yes, oh yes!" he exclaimed, jumping up and down.

They each pressed slobbery kisses to her cheek, gave her one more hug, and then practically sprinted out the door to her mother's car. "Bye, Mama!" Will called back.

"Bye, love. Have a good time with Nana and Papa. Be good!" she shouted, doubtful they'd actually heard her.

Grace planted a kiss on Emma's forehead, pressing her gently, but firmly, back into the sofa cushion. "Get some rest, honey. Or else I'll call the doctor myself."

"Yes, ma'am."

"Don't get up, I'll make sure the door's locked. Now, don't worry about a thing. You just take care of yourself and let your father and me look after these little ones for awhile. I'll check on you later, okay?"

"Okay, mom."

As if she had a choice.

Emma's ringing cell phone woke her several hours later. Just as she came fully awake, it ceased ringing. Of course. Battling a wave of dizziness, she forced herself to lay as still as possible. Once it faded, she slowly rose to a sitting position and reached for the phone. Whomever called had left a message. She flipped open the phone and gazed at the time, feeling disoriented and slightly light-headed. 8:00 already? Justin usually arrived just after dinner. Where was he? With one glance at the caller ID, she guessed the answer. Clearly he was late getting off work. The message he'd left her confirmed her guess. What now?

A wave of nausea propelled her to the bathroom just in time. Back in the kitchen, she opened the fridge in search of the ginger ale. Nothing. She'd already finished the last of it earlier this afternoon after the boys went down for their naps. This was actually the perfect time to get more, she realized, especially since she wouldn't have the boys with her. Shopping by herself, particularly for just one or two things, was always easier than shopping with the boys.

After cleaning herself up a bit, Emma drove to a drug store that was mere blocks from her house. Wave after wave of dizziness swept over her as she stepped out of the car, so she leaned against it briefly, praying for the world to stop moving.

But it didn't.

A man getting in the car next to her cast a concerned glance in her direction. "Ma'am, are you okay?"

She was most definitely *not* okay, she suddenly realized, grabbing for something to cling to as blackness descended.

Justin finished the last of his patient notes and glanced at his watch. It was almost 8. Too late to see Emma's boys before she put them to bed, he realized with a frown. He'd grown accustomed to spending a few minutes with them each night after he got off work, something he'd been doing pretty regularly the last few months. Well, there was nothing he could do about it tonight. A surgical career was not exactly nine-to-five, nor was he able to keep predictable hours. He could be ready to walk out the door after work and get called back in to assist in an emergency procedure. When she didn't answer the phone, he left a brief message, assuming she was in the middle of the boys' nightly bedtime routine.

While filing the reports and taking the time to speak to one of the shift nurses about a couple of his patients, he debated whether to spend an hour at the gym or go straight home. Although he knew he really ought to put in the time working out, tonight, he was loathe to do it. All he wanted was a nice, quiet supper. Perhaps an intriguing mystery novel to take his mind off Emma, as well. And how she *still* hadn't told him about the baby.

He hung his lab coat inside his locker, not bothering to change out of the scrubs he wore, then walked briskly past the elevator to the stairwell. Taking the stairs would have to serve as his workout tonight.

At the door to the private parking garage, his beeper erupted. *What now?* It was Harry Williams. His tennis partner was an attending doctor in the ER. He jogged around the building to the emergency room in search of his friend.

"Harry, was there something you needed?"

The doctor's face peering at him was grave. "There's someone here asking for you."

Justin's brows wrinkled in confusion. "Another doctor? Do they need a consult?"

Harry folded his arms in front of his chest. "No, a patient. Do you know a woman named Emma Darcy?"

His heart plummeted within his chest and his knees nearly buckled beneath him. "Y-yes," he stammered. "What about her?"

"She collapsed in the Walgreen's parking lot and was just brought in."

Without waiting to hear the rest, Justin brushed past his friend in search of the woman he loved.

"She's in exam four!" Harry called.

He swept into the tiny examining room just as a nurse emerged wheeling a cart bearing an ultrasound machine. At the sight of Emma lying prone on the gurney, he stopped short. Her cheeks were sunken, dark circles beneath her eyes. An I.V. attached to her left arm replenished life-giving fluids to her obviously dehydrated body. A wide strap across her exposed abdomen logged a rapid heartbeat. The baby's heartbeat. A deep sense of relief overcame him. The baby was okay! He picked up her right hand and pressed it to his lips.

Slowly, her eyelids fluttered open. "Justin," she rasped. "You came."

"Of course I did, Emma. Did you think I wouldn't? Where did they take the boys?" he asked with concern.

"They're at mom's."

Silence filled the room. Finally, hollow eyes met his before lowering to her growing belly. She closed them briefly before meeting his gaze once more. "I'm pregnant."

He favored her with a slight smile. Brushing the hair back from her face, he kissed her forehead. "I know."

Her eyes closed again. "When?"

"The night the boys were gone. I was cleaning up the kitchen and saw the pregnancy test in the trash. Why, Emma? Why didn't you tell me?" he whispered, a barely traceable catch in his voice.

Tears slid down her cheeks. She'd never intended to hurt him. Never even considered he'd known or that he would feel this way. "Because I was so ashamed."

He pressed the back of her hand to his lips again. "Your husband gave you a precious gift before he died. That's certainly not something to be ashamed of, sweetheart."

"But I don't *want* it!" she wailed, pulling her hand from his and covering her face with it.

Shock momentarily pierced his heart before understanding dawned. She was afraid. If raising two small boys alone was frightening, another pregnancy would only increase that fear.

Gently, he pulled her hand away from her face and held it firmly in his. When she refused to look at him, he turned her chin toward him. "Look at me, Emma."

She shook her head vehemently, more tears streaming down her cheeks.

"You're afraid. I totally get that. But you know you've got family here to help you. You're not alone."

"It's not the same," she mumbled.

"No. You're right. It's not. I know you'd rather have Andrew here with you. And it's not fair that he isn't."

She clenched her jaw, fighting the conflicting emotions raging inside. Emotions that threatened to tear her apart.

"I can't promise you that it won't be difficult. But, Emma. Don't you think it's worth it? A *baby*. A precious little life. Another little one in this world created out of the love you and Andrew shared. Isn't that worth fighting for? Isn't that worth *protecting*?"

Choking sobs seized her. He lowered himself into a chair beside the gurney and eased his arms around her, pulling her head into his shoulder.

"I know you're scared, Em. I know how you feel."

"Yeah, right. How can you possibly know how I feel? You've never been married. You don't have children. Your spouse wasn't gunned down by thieves."

With a sigh, he sat back against the chair. Then, he massaged his forehead with his fingertips before crossing his arms in front of his chest. "I've never been married, no. And I've never had to live with the knowledge that my spouse was gunned down by thieves. But that doesn't change the fact that I *do* know how you feel."

Emma reared back and eyed him in confusion. "How is that possible, Justin?"

"Because I lost a baby once. A baby I didn't think I wanted."

Her eyes widened and her face drained of what little color it held. "No. That's not possible."

Justin---a *father*?!

He nodded. "I try not to think about it. Not very many people even know about it, in fact. But it's true."

"How? When?" She scarcely knew what to ask. And if she even wanted to know. She'd always had a certain picture of him in her mind's eye. Of a gentleman--a knight in shining armor, almost. Someone who would wait for marriage, like she had. That's what they'd always talked about, wasn't it? Now, with one word, that picture was forever shattered. The knight's armor was chinked.

"I met Lisa during my second year of college. She was pre-med as well, in some of the same classes as me. We were together as a couple for almost a year before actually making love for the first time. I was her first, too. Not long afterward, we got an apartment together. But setting up housekeeping just wasn't as much fun as we thought it would be. After awhile, we began fighting pretty regularly.

"About three months after we moved in together, she told me she was pregnant. It was completely unplanned and definitely a shock to each of us. She was worried her parents would stop supporting her and was convinced the baby would only ruin both of our careers. At first I agreed with her. But then, Emma, I started thinking about the baby and what he or she might look like. And I realized that I wanted to be a father after all."

He closed his eyes, tears slipping past closed lids. Compassion overcame her shock and she laid a hand on his arm. He grasped her fingers in his and squeezed.

"She had an abortion, didn't she?"

He nodded. "I didn't have a say. Didn't get to tell her that I'd changed my mind about being a father. I didn't even get to hold my baby, Emma. She *took* that from me!"

Sobs ripped through him. He rested his forehead on the gurney and gave into them.

Now it was Emma's turn to offer comfort. Whether or not he'd had a chance to work through any of this, even after all this time it was clear he still grieved his lost child.

111

Tears spent, Justin dried his eyes and looked at her sheepishly. "I'm sorry, Em. I guess I'm still not over it."

She graced him with a watery smile. "So what happened after that?"

"It destroyed the relationship. Any trust and love we had for each other was aborted along with our baby. Bitterness fed upon each of us until I moved out. She got a new roommate, and I moved back into the dorm."

He swept the hair out of her face once more, stroking her cheek tenderly. "I know you would never intentionally do anything to hurt this baby. But by not taking care of yourself, that's exactly what you're doing, sweetheart. And I couldn't stand it if something happened to you or any of your children."

Before she could speak, Dr. Williams reappeared in the room. "Well, Mrs. Darcy. How are you feeling? Any better?"

"Some."

"Are you experiencing any more dizziness? Nausea?"

She shook her head.

He patted her lower leg. "You sure gave us quite a scare, young lady. But you'll be glad to know that your baby seems to be doing just fine. She's quite a fighter."

Emma's body went rigid. A girl? Had she heard that correctly?

"Harry, did you say she's expecting a daughter?" Justin asked.

He glanced at Emma's widened eyes and frowned, chagrined. "That was supposed to be a surprise, wasn't it? I'm so sorry."

She swallowed. "N-no, that's okay."

He patted her leg again. "I finally managed to get a hold of someone from your family clinic, Mrs. Darcy. Your regular doctor is visiting his wife's family in California and won't be back for another few days. But the doctor on call agreed with my plan to keep you overnight. Just as a precaution, mind. We need to make sure you're properly hydrated before you return home. So, someone from the OB floor will be down shortly to transfer you upstairs. Is there someone I can call for you?"

"I'll take care of that, Harry. Thanks."

Justin shook hands with his friend before the man left the room, then resumed his perch beside Emma. "A daughter! Emma, you're going to have a little girl!"

The shock still hadn't worn off. Andrew had given her a girl. A *girl*!

Gradually, she became aware of movement in her belly. She'd been feeling these little flutters and bumps for several weeks now, but had managed to completely ignore them. Suddenly, with a jolt, she realized what was happening.

The baby was moving. Her little daughter. Quickly, she pressed her hand to her abdomen and was rewarded with a tiny thump against her fingers. Unspeakable joy surged throughout her body. A fierce protectiveness arose within her, and she realized she'd rather die than let anything happen to this precious little one growing inside of her.

Relief and peace overwhelmed her and she wept with the joy of it.

A daughter.

Her own little miracle.

Quickly, she grabbed Justin's hand and placed it over the spot she'd last felt the tiny kick. "She's moving!"

He felt a little awkward sitting there, touching her bare belly. But just as he was about to lift his hand, he felt it. Emma's daughter moving within her. He gasped and raised awe-filled eyes to her luminescent ones. Love for the woman before him filled him anew. And for the precious life she carried in her womb. His heart filled to bursting with the potent emotion. Fearing she'd see it mirrored in his eyes, he lowered them once more to her stomach.

"I probably should call everyone with the news," she replied with a long sigh.

"Why don't you let me handle that for you?"

"You could call mom, but I should probably be the one to call Andrew's family." She wasn't sure they would take too kindly to hearing the news from *Justin* of all people.

"Does your mom have the Darcys' phone number?" Emma nodded.

"Well, then how about a compromise? I'll call her and ask her to spread the word for you."

She sighed again, this time with relief. "That would work. Thanks, Justin."

"No problem. Just so you know, I fully intend to tell them that you can't have visitors tonight. I may not be your doctor, but as *a* doctor, I know that the best thing for you tonight is rest. And that's not gonna happen with a bunch of relatives crowding your room."

"Like it's gonna happen anyway. You and I both know it's hard to get any rest with nurses coming in every hour or two to take vitals."

He grinned. "Be that as it may. You're not going anywhere tonight. So you might as well take what little rest you can get. I'm gonna go take care of one or two things and then I'll be back."

"What if they come to take me upstairs while you're gone?" she asked. For some reason, she felt a new closeness to him tonight that she hadn't felt before. It was probably due to the revelation he'd shared with her. After all, she now knew something about him that few - if any - knew. She wanted him to remain with her awhile longer.

She actually wanted him to stay. His heart soared within him, even while he tried to be cautious and not read too much into it. "Don't worry, I'll find you. I have my ways," he added with a roguish wink.

Emma laughed.

Not long after he left, the orderlies arrived to ferry her upstairs to the obstetrics wing. In no time at all, she was comfortably relocated in one of the rooms the hospital had set aside for pregnant women not delivering. The fetal monitor had been reattached to her abdomen, and the fluids continued to hydrate her body intravenously.

If her little daughter's increased activity was any indication, her rough-and-tumble sons would have a sister fully capable of keeping up with them. She relished feeling the flutters in her womb and listening to the whoosh-whoosh of the baby's heartbeat. Was there a more precious sound in this world?

About thirty minutes later, Justin reappeared, producing a single pink rose from behind his back.

"How lovely!" she exclaimed, burying her face in it's soft petals. "Mmm. Is there anything quite like the smell of roses?"

He sat on the foot of her bed. "It's for the baby."

"Thank you, Justin," she softly replied.

If they could've read each other's minds, they would've realized that their thoughts were the same. Buying his first daughter a single pink rose was something Andrew would've done if he'd lived to share this moment with his wife.

"I know you've only just discovered this baby's gender, Emma, but have you thought of any names yet?"

She gently rubbed her abdomen, reveling in another furtive kick from her daughter. "Before Will was born, Andrew and I talked about possible names for girls. He really liked the name Brenna, but I thought it was too similar to my name."

"It is pretty, though. Just like you."

She blushed. "I'll have to give it some thought, I guess."

"Well, you do have awhile."

"Yeah. The baby's not due until February. Right smack dab in the middle of a Colorado winter. Oh, joy."

He patted her leg atop the blanket. "Don't worry, Em. You'll be fine."

"So did you get a hold of my mom?"

"Uh-huh. She was initially stunned, but was relieved in a way. She said that she just knew something was wrong but couldn't quite figure out what."

"That's mom."

He snickered in agreement.

"So, is she going to call Andrew's family for me?"

"Yup. Tomorrow."

Emma saw the wisdom in that, especially given how late it was. "So what you're saying is that I shouldn't be looking for any visitors tonight?"

"Not a one. Told you I'd get my way."

She laughed. "Don't get too used to it, Justin Bennet. You're entirely too spoiled as it is."

He instantly sobered. If only she knew.

Completely unaware of his change of mood, she carefully leaned back and placed the rose on the little table next to the bed. Then, she slid lower in the bed, scooting around until she found a more comfortable position.

When long moments stretched without conversation, she eyed him warily. He was frowning pensively. Was there somewhere else he needed to be tonight? If so, she was being pretty selfish to detain him. The thought that maybe he'd had other plans - a date, perhaps - did not sit well with her, but she refused to examine her feelings closer. There was, however, something she needed to do before she let him go for the night.

"Justin, before you go, I want to say that I'm sorry I didn't tell you about the baby. I hurt you and I didn't mean to. Can you forgive me?"

He glanced at her tenderly, a smile erasing the scowl he'd previously worn. "Of course, Emma. I think I could forgive you anything," he admitted. "And I certainly understand why you didn't tell me. Please don't think anything more about it." *She's not going to let me stay*, he thought with a pang of disappointment.

He rose.

He's not going to stay, she thought with a sudden disappointed twinge of her own. "Well, I know you have to get home, so I guess I won't keep you. I'm sure you had something better to do tonight than sit here with me."

Before he could think twice, he replied, "What on earth could be more important than being here with you?"

"You mean you didn't have an important date or anything?"

He laughed. She really had no clue. "Didn't you receive my voicemail that I was working late? Or notice, perhaps, that I'm wearing hospital scrubs?"

She palmed her forehead, frustrated with herself for her density. "Duh. I'm sorry." Then another thought occurred to her. "I didn't pull you away from anything important at work, did I?"

"Nope. I was just leaving when I got the page from Dr. Williams."

"So I *have* kept you from something!"

His brow wrinkled in confusion. "I promise you haven't, Em."

"I've kept you from your dinner."

He grinned. "You sure have. And I'm simply wasting away because of it."

Suddenly ravenous, she decided to do a little fishing. It had certainly worked with her husband, so why not Justin as well? "Let me guess. You were planning on stopping for some french fries, right?"

He guessed her game in a minute, his eyes twinkling with merriment. "Of course not," he scoffed. "Surgeons do *not* eat french fries."

Her face fell. "They don't? Really? That's kinda sad, Justin. What's life without the occasional french fry?"

"You didn't let me finish. Surgeons don't eat french fries, *except* when consumed with a chocolate shake. The dairy in the shake negates the grease in the fries."

"Re-ally."

"Yup. It's a common medical fact."

"Are you sure it's not *strawberry* shakes that negate the grease?"

"Y'know, you're right. My mistake. It's *strawberry* shakes."

They both laughed.

"I assume that you're telling me you'd like some french fries with a strawberry shake?"

She nodded. "Not too obvious, was it?"

"Of course not," he replied, glancing at his watch. "I believe the McDonald's downstairs will be open for another 20 minutes, so you're in luck. I'll be right back with our snack."

At the door, he stopped and looked back at her. "And just for the record, Emma. There isn't anywhere - or anyone - I'd rather be with than right here with you."

The piercing, earnest look in his eyes made her mouth go dry.

Oh, my.

But he couldn't possibly mean it the way it sounded. Because, of course he didn't see her that way. He'd made that abundantly clear all those years ago.

However, there was a tiny piece of her heart that dared ask the question.

What if he *did* mean it that way?

Or, more startlingly: what if he *did* see her that way?

It was a question that was never far from Emma's mind as they shared a large order of fries with their shakes- -hers a strawberry, his a chocolate. And it was a question never far from her mind even long after he'd gone home for the night, promising to return bright and early in order to check on her.

She was far from ready for anyone to take Andrew's place in her heart. At the moment, she didn't feel as if she'd ever be able to move on with someone else. And if he had romantic feelings for her that weren't returned, what would happen to their friendship?

More importantly, what would she do without his friendship?

A feeling of disquiet began to form in her heart at what the future might hold.

Chapter Ten

Mid-January

A very pregnant Emma ungracefully flopped onto her couch, settling one throw pillow behind her aching back and propping her swollen legs upon another. She was exhausted and it was barely 4:00 in the afternoon.

The boys had not been awake from their nap for long. She'd managed to distract them with a coloring book and some crayons for awhile, but now they were literally running around her in circles. She thought of the long hours still to go before Justin joined them for dinner and groaned. How was she ever to manage these boys for another couple hours?

After a few more minutes spent watching the boys race around the couch, she was starting to get dizzy. "Enough, boys!"

At her firm - and louder than normal - tone, they both froze in their tracks. They were growing accustomed to hearing their Mama yell, but it still frightened them nonetheless. Their normally gentle mother was disappearing more and more each day.

Seeing their stricken faces, guilt swept over Emma and she sighed. Who was this person that was taking over? She'd never yelled at the boys so much as she had in the last month. Chagrined, she sought to find a quieter activity for them to enjoy. Glancing around the messy room, her eyes landed on the shelf of DVDs and she smiled with relief. A VeggieTale. Just the quiet activity she needed. Only for Bob and Larry would her wild sons remain still. And she'd be guaranteed thirty minutes of peace. Never mind the fact that she'd been resorting to this more and more lately. If the boys were content, what did it matter?

Their favorite was "Madam Blueberry", so regardless of the fact that they'd watched it at least ten times in the last two weeks, she selected it for the boys. As always, they sat down closer to the television than was necessary, enraptured with the animated vegetables on the screen.

With the boys settled, she waddled to the bathroom and back, once more reclining on the couch. Gone was the morning sickness of a few months ago, thankfully. Instead, the baby had recently taken up residence on her bladder. She used to pride herself on having a strong bladder. Not anymore. It felt like she lived in the bathroom. One more month and she'd finally be comfortable again.

A slow smile spread across her face at the thought of meeting her little daughter in just four more weeks. Gently, she rubbed her ever-expanding stomach and was rewarded with several thumps against her palm. "Hello to you too, sweet pea," she whispered.

With the holidays officially over, and the baby's arrival not far off, she knew she needed to start thinking about possible names. While it was one she knew Andrew had favored, Brenna was officially off the table. She just couldn't imagine having a daughter with a name so similar to hers. How weird would that be? She'd never liked the custom of naming the first son after his father. He, on the other hand, had really liked the idea of giving the boys family names. As a compromise, they'd decided to make Andrew's middle name Emmitt's first name, and gave his first name to Will as a middle name: William Andrew.

At Christmas when some of the extended family members had visited, some had tried to pressure her into selecting various names. On top of everything else she'd been dealing with, it was almost too much to bear.

For the first time in her life, Emma had not enjoyed Christmas. Her every waking thought was to do whatever necessary to just get through the festive holiday. She'd finally reached a point in her pregnancy where she felt fairly decent. And knowing how much her young sons missed their father, and how it was exacerbated by the first holiday season without him, she'd thrown herself into making sure they had the best Christmas possible. As a result, she'd slept little, worked long hours, cooked all their favorite foods, and went overboard on the decorations.

To make matters worse, her mother-in-law went out of her way to make sure the fact that Andrew wasn't with them never left anyone's mind. Emma had never seen the woman cry so much in her entire life---and she'd been around the Darcys since she was a young girl. Beth had personally hand-crafted a different memento for each member of the family, each item including a picture of Andrew with that person. They were lovely, thoughtful gifts. Of course. She felt guilty for allowing even the most infinitesimal part of herself to think anything otherwise. But it was just too much. Especially when she wanted nothing more than to forget how wonderful her husband was, what a great father he was, how blessed their marriage was....and how incredibly bleak her life seemed without him - especially during this first Christmas she and the boys were alone. All she wanted was to focus on making the best Christmas possible for the boys. Whatever it took.

And to forget - if only for awhile - that she was utterly alone.

But it seemed that Beth would not let her forget.

A soft knock at the door jarred her from her thoughts. Glancing at the clock, she frowned. It was only 4:30. A little early for Justin. With a deep sigh, she shoved her legs over the side of the couch, gingerly easing herself into a standing position. Her pregnancy was making it harder and harder to find a comfortable position. And once she did, it was making it harder and harder for her to get back up again. "Coming!" she called when another knock, harder this time, sounded through the house.

She peeled back a corner of the curtains over the door and was stunned to see Justin standing on her front stoop. He clutched two big paper bags, with one plastic grocery bag suspended from his beefy arm. Quickly, she unlocked and opened the door for him. "What are you doing here so early?"

"Hello to you, too, Emma," he replied with a smirk, brushing past her to set the bags down on the kitchen counter.

"I'm sorry. That was rude."

"Especially since I've come bearing presents," he chided, shrugging out of his warm winter gear. The coat was hung on the front door knob, the rest ended up in a pile on the floor. Then, he tugged off his boots and placed them in the little tray she'd placed beside the door.

By the time he stepped back into the kitchen, she was already busy unpacking the bags of groceries. Last night when he'd started to make dinner, he'd been shocked to see how bare her cupboards, tiny pantry, and refrigerator were.

She in turn was stunned to see just how much food he'd managed to cram into a few bags. Milk. Cheese. Bread. Peanut butter. Frozen vegetables. Cereal. Eggs. Fresh oranges. A package of chicken and a package of ground turkey. Frozen orange juice. A couple boxes of macaroni and cheese. Fixings for spaghetti. Butter. So much bounty spread on her kitchen counter!

Without a word, she slid her arms around his waist and leaned against his body in an embrace. As hugely pregnant as she was, a full-body hug was impossible. "Thank you, Justin. You're so good to us."

He wrapped his arms around her and pressed a kiss to the top of her head. "It's no big deal, Em. I'm not the one who's eight months pregnant with two small children to schlepp around." What he couldn't tell her was why he had to do this. Instinctively, he knew she wouldn't want pity and would only see his assistance as such. Especially if she knew what Andrew's last request had been. Regardless, he'd do a lot more than buy groceries if she'd let him. Every night, he dreamed of walking with her down the aisle in church, all of their friends and family gathered around, to permanently change her last name.

"So what is the chef preparing tonight?" she asked, pulling away just enough to grin playfully at him.

"How does spaghetti sound?"

"Sounds perfect to me, and I'm sure the boys will agree. They would practically live on it if I'd let them."

He glanced at the clock above the stove. "Speaking of the boys, I've got a little time to do some major rough and tumbling before I need to start dinner. Would you mind?"

"Be my guest. They've been particularly hyper this afternoon. I'm not quite sure why."

He easily read more into that statement than what was spoken. "Why don't you stretch out on the chaise lounge in your room for awhile? Maybe turn on some soft music to drown out any sounds of, er, energetic playing? I've got this."

She smiled gratefully. "You're a prince among men, Justin Bennet."

In between tickle fights and listening to the chatter of little voices, Justin tried to think of what else he could possibly do to ease Emma's burden. Every time he saw her, she looked more and more exhausted. Part of that was due to this stage of pregnancy, part to having two young sons. But what worried him more than anything was that she wasn't allowing herself to travel through the stages of grief. It was as if she had formed a wall of steel around her heart, attempting to keep Andrew's memory away. Instead of embracing each stage of grief, surrendering it to God, and allowing Him to help her work through it, she was trying to do it all on her own.

And she was failing miserably.

He'd known how difficult Christmas was for her. Of course. Even after all these years, he could still remember that first Christmas without Matt. That first Christmas without Dad. As painful as it had been to lose his Dad, the loss of his twin brother still haunted him to this day. He'd worked through his grief, thanks be to God. But that didn't mean he didn't miss his better half, as Matt had always been. More than once, he wondered why God had chosen to let *him* live instead of Matt. If it had to have been one of them...

He shook his head. It was better not to go there. Who could understand the mysterious workings of God? Certainly not a former wreck of a man who was now a successful doctor. But only by the grace of God.

Out of the corner of his eye, he spied the picture frame Beth had given Emma for Christmas. The picture she'd chosen depicted Andrew gazing into his wife's eyes adoringly, their arms wrapped snugly around each other. His gut still twisted every time he saw it. A reminder of what he'd lost when he'd walked away from her all those years ago. That could've been him in the picture with her. If only.

A scowl spread across his handsome face as he thought of Beth's continued interference in his friendship with Emma. Once she'd discovered how much time he was spending with them each evening, she'd practically moved into Emma's house the week before Christmas, ostensibly just to "help out". But he knew better. As long as *she* was there, he would not step foot inside the house. And that's precisely what she'd been counting on.

He hadn't been able to see them again until last week . His heart still ached when he saw how worn down she was. She and the boys were living off of cold cereal and milk twice a day with peanut butter sandwiches for supper. After expending all that energy trying to make this the best Christmas possible for the boys, she was physically and emotionally drained. It was then that he'd stepped in and took over. Whether or not Beth Darcy approved, he'd made up his mind to step in and do something to help Emma. To that end, he'd started coming over even earlier each day to cook dinner for all of them. It was something he enjoyed, and if it happened to bless her in the process, then so much the better.

Just let Beth Darcy try and stop him.

With a determined grin, he established the boys at the table with some puzzles and headed into the kitchen to start dinner.

Emma lounged on the small chaise lounge in the corner of her room, her favorite CD playing softly on the stereo. It was heaven to lie peacefully for a few minutes, knowing her young sons were being so superbly cared for. And soon, she'd join them for a delicious spaghetti dinner cooked - and cleaned up afterward - by Justin.

What would she do without such a good friend like him? He was the refuge in the raging storm that was her life. The boys adored him and eagerly anticipated his arrival each night. If for some reason he had to work late and wasn't able to come over before they went to bed, they were sorely disappointed. As was she, truth be told. She really depended upon the help he provided around the house, the way he played with her sons as only another man can do, and their nightly talks once the boys were in bed.

And, although she'd never admit it to herself, there was one other thing she was coming to depend upon more and more.

His warm embrace. She practically craved the feeling of his strong arms around her.

Of course, this new craving was not something she allowed herself to think about. If she thought about it at all, it was to try and rationalize these strange new twinges of feeling. She was a hugger, after all, and only missed the warmth of Andrew's hugs. That's all it was. Period. End of story.

Thankfully, the ringing phone allowed her to mentally switch gears from Justin and his amazing hugs.

"Emma? Are you able to talk?"

It was Joe.

"Sure."

"Are the boys okay for the moment?"

Not for any amount of money would she divulge the fact that Justin was taking care of her boys in the other room. Whatever Joe knew, Beth knew. And that was a war she did *not* care to wage. She already bore enough battle scars from Beth's stay during Christmas.

"They're fine. Is everything okay?"

"Yes, actually. Emma, I have some news."

As he relayed his news to her, Emma's face drained of color and her heart raced. She leaned her head back against the cushion and closed her eyes.

Once the call was over, she turned her cell phone to vibrate and set it near her bed. There would be no more phone calls answered tonight.

She needed some time to process the bomb that had just been dropped on her world.

Justin was surprised to see Emma waddle into the kitchen so soon. He'd hoped she'd fall asleep for awhile before supper. One glance at her stricken expression and ghostly pallor and he was instantly concerned.

"Are you okay?" he asked, stepping around the breakfast bar and placing two fingers against her wrist. She looked like she was about to faint.

"Joe called," she began before her knees gave out.

He steadied her, lending her his strength. "You'd better sit down, Emma."

After helping her onto one of the bar stools, he turned on the stereo for the boys. "How about your favorite VeggieTales CD? Would you boys like that?"

His suggestion met with delighted squeals.

Once he was satisfied that they were content for the moment, he stepped back into the kitchen and filled a small glass with water from the faucet. This he then pressed into Emma's hands.

She frowned at the lukewarm temperature, but drank it anyway. "Yuck."

He brushed her hair to the side and peered intently into her face. Finally, some color was returning to her cheeks. "Thank God. You really scared me for a moment, Em."

"Sorry. Didn't mean to," she added, finishing the water with a grimace. "Would it have killed you to add some ice?"

He laughed. She was definitely fine. "You were saying something about a phone call?"

She nodded, an expression of utter amazement on her face. "It's over."

"What's over?"

"The men who killed my husband are in police custody."

He sat down on a barstool heavily. "They actually caught the men who shot Andrew? After all this time?"

She nodded again, unable to speak past a sudden lump in her throat. Tears pooled in her eyes and rained down her face. Her hands covered her mouth and her shoulders shook with forceful sobs.

He hopped off the stool and wrapped his arms tightly around her, cradling her against his chest while she cried. He rubbed her hair and back soothingly, pressing an occasional kiss onto the top of her head.

After all this time. Finally. Now, maybe she could get some closure and begin to heal.

His heart kept whispering something else, as well. He tried not to listen. He really did. But it was such a breathtaking thought, he couldn't help the small spark of hope that ignited inside.

Once she'd found closure and took some time to truly grieve her husband, he'd be free to declare this feelings. A slow grin spread across his face.

The next three weeks were a mixed bag of emotions for Emma. On the one hand, both men were prepared to plead guilty to the charges. There had been such convicting evidence against them, they really had little choice. To encourage them to plead guilty, however, the district attorney had agreed not to add capital murder charges to the bevy of crimes each were being charged with.

And she was angry.

Prior to Andrew's death, she'd been staunchly against the death penalty. Now, however... With one selfish, greedy act, her husband's life was over. Her children's father was gone forever. Shouldn't at least one of the men be forced to pay the ultimate price for robbing *four* people of the person closest to them?

Instead, there would be no trial. Today, in a little over an hour, the judge would pronounce a sentence that was, in all reality, just a formality. The man who hadn't been the shooter would get a shorter sentence for turning in his accomplice, with the possibility of parole in 25 years. 25 years! The other man, however, had received life in prison. Without the possibility of parole. That was the one silver lining for Emma.

She smoothed the black pants and sweater she wore, then wrapped a red silk scarf around her neck. The scarf was a peace offering from Justin after the big argument they'd had a few days ago.

The first since he'd ended their relationship all those years ago.

After ranting and railing against the entire legal system, the men responsible for her husband's death - even God for allowing it - for several days running, he'd finally had enough.

"Enough, Em! You need to let this go," he snapped in exasperation.

"How can you say that to me? You have no idea what I've been through, Justin!" she seethed, eyes narrowed.

He sighed. "No, I don't. You're right. But then I've had my own share of tragedies, too. Trust me: it doesn't help to play the blame game. The only way you're ever going to begin to have closure in this is if you can forgive them."

"I'll. *Never*. Forgive. Them." Teeth clenched, she practically spat each word.

Justin sighed again and reached out to hug her, but she pulled abruptly away. "Emma. Come on," he pleaded, arm dropping back to his side.

"If you are really my friend, Justin, you won't ever mention that to me again. *Ever*."

"Fine," he agreed with resignation. "I'm sorry if I upset you. Really. I'm just worried about you. I care about you and don't like to see you hurting."

Emma finally allowed him to embrace her as bitter, angry tears flowed down her face.

The next night, when he'd arrived to make dinner, he'd given her the scarf. Although she'd prefer to have him by her side at today's sentencing hearing, both of them knew it was impossible. Not with Joe, Beth, and the rest of the Darcy family in attendance as well. So, since he couldn't be there in person, the scarf was a pretty reminder of his support.

It was just as well that he wouldn't be there, anyway. Yesterday, she'd asked the lawyer if she could have a few minutes to speak for the family this morning during the sentencing. Those two men were going to know just what kind of husband they'd robbed her of. What kind of father they'd robbed her children of. And what kind of teacher they'd robbed the students of this town of. Justin wanted her to face the men, look them in the eyes, and forgive them. Well, she couldn't do it. *Wouldn't* do it. Never mind his pretty speech; if he were in her shoes, she *knew* he wouldn't be so forgiving, either. She also knew that - since he hadn't gone through what she had - he'd be thoroughly disappointed in what she had to say to the men today. Better he stay here with her boys. Ignorant of the morning's particulars. Because even though she had no intention of ever caving into his request, the thought of disappointing him was utterly unbearable. Justin's was the one opinion that mattered most. The only person she turned to of late.

A shooting pain knifed through her lower back, instantly pinching her features into a grimace. She rubbed the spot, trying to ease the pain. This had been happening more and more over the last few hours. This pregnancy had been harder on her than either of the others, and she longed for it to be over. In a matter of a couple weeks, her little daughter would be here. That thought was the one bright spot of her day. Earlier this morning, when the achiness had begun, she'd briefly toyed with the idea of just staying home and avoiding the sentencing today. But nothing was going to take this opportunity away from her. Not even a little pain.

She took a fortifying breath that seemed to ease the pain a little. Determination in every line of her squared jaw, she pasted a small smile on her face for her boys. They were oblivious to what this day meant, and she planned to keep it that way.

Although Justin was coming later to stay with the boys during the sentencing, her mother had arrived an hour ago to watch them while she got ready. Once dressed, however, Emma was pleasantly surprised to find Justin already lounging on the couch reading a book to the boys.

He glanced up at her with an unknown look in his eyes. Without understanding why, her heart suddenly started to pound. She tore her gaze from his and leveled it on her sons instead. Instantly, she was pierced by their cheerful smiles and obvious enjoyment of time spent with their buddy. When was the last time she'd been so blissfully happy? Their joy seemed strangely out of place today.

A few tears slipped unbidden down her cheeks and she hastily turned away before anyone could spot them.

But Justin *had* spotted them, and his heart wrenched for her. Oh, how he hated watching her suffer. He wished she could learn from her boys and just...choose joy.

Grace glanced at her watch with a frown. "Emma, we'd better get going. It's started to snow and the roads might be slick."

She nodded at her mother, then leaned down and kissed the boys' cheeks. "I love you, guys. Be good for Justin." On impulse, she pressed a kiss to his cheek as well. "Thanks for being here."

A spark of intensity briefly flickered in the deep pools of his eyes and then disappeared again. "It's no problem, Em. We have fun together, don't we guys?"

Both little heads bobbed their assents. "We're gonna have hot choc'late, Mama!" Emmitt gleefully announced.

Her brows rose in surprise. "You are?"

"That was supposed to be our little secret, remember, buddy?" Justin gently reminded him in a stage whisper.

Belatedly realizing what he'd let slip, the little boy covered his mouth with both hands, his eyes wide.

Emma grinned. "That's okay. Mama doesn't know a thing about it, right?" she whispered with a wink.

Emmitt blinked both of his eyes back at her in his own version of a wink.

At the door, she glanced back one more time at the sweet picture her sons made, cuddled with Justin on the couch.

I'm doing this for you. For all *of you.*

Fresh determination filled her. She would go to the courtroom today. And she would speak for those who couldn't.

Andrew's children.

Chapter Eleven

The sentencing had drug on and on for reasons unknown to Emma. For what little had to take place this morning, everything seemed to be moving in slow motion.

Growing increasingly uncomfortable by the second, she shifted once more in the hard wooden chair. Out of the corner of her eye, she spotted her mother shooting her yet another concerned glance. Very imperceptibly, she shook her head to indicate that nothing was wrong.

But something was very wrong.

All morning, the pains had been increasing in intensity, spreading all the way from her lower back to her abdomen. She gritted her teeth against another intense wave. With a sigh of resignation, she slumped backwards against the seat.

She could deny the truth no longer.

She was in labor.

Not now! she groaned inwardly. Not until she'd had the chance to say what she'd come here to say.

"Before I read the sentences, Mrs. Darcy has asked to speak for the family," the judge boomed from his bench.

Finally! And not a moment too soon.

Emma gathered all of the inner strength she possessed. She rose slowly from her chair and made her way to the witness stand. Once seated, she turned to look at the murders (for that's how she saw them), leveling a glare at first one man and then the other.

The accomplice, the one the law said was not criminally responsible for her husband's death, regardless of the truth of the matter, would not make eye contact. His eyes remained leveled on the table before him. The other, however, met her glare with one of his own. Then, the corners of his lips turned up into almost a snarl.

Ice flowed through her veins and her glare deepened. Just as she opened her mouth to lambaste him, she felt trickles of water running down her legs. Simultaneously, the contractions she'd been experiencing intensified to such a degree that she doubled over in pain.

"Emma!" her mother gasped.

She angrily pounded the witness stand with one fist. "No! Not now!"

"Mrs. Darcy, are you all right?" the judge asked beside her.

"No, she's not, your honor. I think she's in labor!" her mother replied, her voice panicked and strained.

Glancing up, she saw her mother shove her way past the bailiff and race over to the witness stand. "You're in labor, aren't you?"

She nodded, tears of frustration, rage, and pain coursing down her cheeks.

As the judge called for a recess, the bailiff and her mother helped Emma from the stand and out to the courtroom. Taking one look at her pinched expression, Joe lifted her in his arms as if she were weightless and carried her to the curb, where her father awaited them in the car.

Emma gave free reign to the tears, releasing some of the pent up anger and frustration. "Why couldn't she have waited just ten more minutes?" she rasped. "I had so much I wanted to say to those men."

Her mother smoothed the hair from her forehead soothingly. "I know, sweetheart." *Maybe this is better. Maybe God stopped you from speaking.* But she wouldn't utter those words aloud. Not yet. Not until she felt sure her daughter was ready to hear them. All morning she'd been praying for God to intervene. To prevent Emma from addressing the men. She understood her daughter's pain. Certainly. But it she didn't like this angry person Emma had become. And she'd prayed without ceasing for God to touch her heart anew. To bring her healing.

By early afternoon, Justin and the boys had enjoyed their hot chocolate. He'd fixed them some lunch. Then, they'd put away the toys and straightened the living room. After that, he'd tried to do some paperwork at the table, but he just couldn't sit still a moment longer. So, while Will and Emmitt slept, he kept himself busy by washing the dirty mugs and lunch dishes.

However, none of it helped take his mind off of the fact that Emma was in the hospital across town, straining to bring her little daughter into the world.

And he was missing it.

When Grace had called earlier with the news, he'd wanted nothing more than to grab the boys and bolt out the door. But she'd suggested gently that it would be better if they remained at the house, at least until it was time for his shift at the hospital later this afternoon. If she hadn't had the baby by then, he was to bring the boys with him and leave them in the waiting room with the Grandmas.

He understood. Really. They needed their naps, and there really wasn't anything they could do there anyway. Yet it ate him up inside to know that she was in pain and there was nothing he could do for her. Realistically speaking, there wasn't anything he could do for her even if he'd *been* there. And of course he knew that. It wasn't called labor for nothing. But that didn't make the waiting any easier.

With her husband - the baby's father - gone, Emma had asked Noelle to be her breathing coach. In no uncertain terms did she want Beth Darcy in the room with her. But to ask her mother and not Beth would cause undue friction. So she'd tried to play the peacemaker by asking her best friend to fill this role and having both mothers wait in the waiting room with the rest of the family.

She'd confided to him just last week, however, that she wished he could be in the room with her. That had spoken volumes to him. Of all the people she could've had with her, she'd wanted him there most of all. They both knew that it was impossible. Besides the obvious problems it would cause with Andrew's family, neither were entirely comfortable with the implication it created. He'd at least hoped, however, to be in the waiting room with everyone else.

But of course, Grace was probably right. He certainly didn't need to be antagonizing Emma's in-laws. Especially now.

Over the last few weeks, he'd sensed a slight change in her behavior toward him. He'd caught her staring at him when she didn't think he was looking. And more than once, he'd seen a certain look of disquiet on her face. He didn't know what it meant, exactly, but something inside him kept whispering that the impossible was happening. Ever so slowly - so slowly he doubted she was even aware of it happening - Emma's feelings for him were changing into something more. Something deeper.

It was enough to make his heart pound with excitement.

He didn't want to rush her, though, or make any sudden moves she wouldn't be ready for. No, indeed. The last thing he wanted was to scare her away before she realized the depth of her feelings for him. So, as hard as it was to be patient, as hard as it was to go slowly, he was determined to let her lead the way. He would do nothing to give away his feelings until he was certain of hers.

Even if it took a lifetime.

He was just sitting back down at the table, a fresh cup of coffee in hand, when there was a knock on the door. Opening it, he was surprised to see Emma's mother standing on the porch, a huge grin spread across her lovely face.

Without a word, she enveloped him in a tight hug. Then, she stepped inside, removed her coat and gloves, and stepped out of her sling-back pumps. "Of all the days for me not to wear boots..." she muttered, plopping onto the sofa. She then yanked the afghan from the back of the couch and tucked it around her frozen feet.

"Grace, why aren't you at the hospital with the rest of the family?"

"Emma didn't get a chance to pack for the hospital stay, so I came to get some things for her."

"A bag? That's it?"

Her cheshire-cat grin spread impossibly larger. "That...and to take the boys to meet their new little sister."

He let out his pent-up breath in a relieved whoosh. "The baby's here already? That went quickly."

Grace shrugged. "It was her third delivery, after all."

"Emma's okay, then? The baby?"

"More than okay. She's perfect. And Emma did beautifully, as always."

Both of them were quiet for several minutes. Grace knew full well what he wanted more information, but was feeling a bit playful. She was curious to see how long it would take before he arrived at the end of his patience and asked.

Not long, as it turned out.

A moment later, he let out a frustrated sigh. "Are you going to tell me the baby's name, or do I have to drag it out of you?"

She grinned, wagging her finger at him playfully. "Uh-uhn. I promised Emma I wouldn't tell. I think she wants to give you the details herself."

He groaned. "But, Grace! I have to work this afternoon! In fact, since you're already here, I might as well head home so that I can pick up a few things there before my shift begins. I have no idea how late I'll be. Can't you just tell me now and let me act surprised later?"

"Now, that wouldn't be honest, would it? She knows you might be late, Justin. I think she would like it very much if you stopped by to see her and the baby on your way home tonight. No matter how late you are. And consider it this way--certain people will be long gone by the time you are off work and able to pop in."

That comment completely caught him off guard. *She knows.*

Grace laughed at his panicked expression. "Hon, I've known for a long time now. I have eyes, haven't I?"

"But if that's true, then certainly Beth..."

She nodded. "Why do you think she tries to keep you away from Emma? I believe you scare her."

"But why? Surely she can see that Em doesn't feel the same way about me." Okay, so he was blatantly fishing for confirmation of Emma's feelings, and he knew it. Nevertheless, he wasn't too proud to do it. He could frankly use a little reassurance from her mother. Particularly one so keenly observant.

She eyed him with a little smirk. "We both know that's not true."

"Maybe," he conceded. She'd seen right through him. Of course. He should've known better. "That doesn't mean she realizes it, though."

"Of course she doesn't. I'm quite sure she'd run the opposite way if she did. She's clearly not ready for another relationship, Justin, and I greatly appreciate the fact that you've been letting her actions guide yours."

He may as well admit it. It's not like she didn't already know. "I love her, Grace. Very much."

"I know you do. And I'll let you in on a little secret. I have a hunch we'll be celebrating a wedding sooner than you think," she confided, giving him a quick peck on the cheek. "I'm sure I'll see you soon. I'm going to get that suitcase packed and then wake the boys up."

"Okay," he replied, lost in thought.

Dare he allow himself to hope it might be true?

A wedding in his near future.

Emma settled her newborn daughter on her lap and gazed lovingly at the tiny features. Ten perfectly formed little fingers, ten perfectly formed little toes. A shock of dark, curly hair framing a delicate little face--she had her Daddy's curls and her Mama's dark hair. Dimples peaked out of two chubby cheeks. She gently opened one of the small fists and touched the tiny palm, smiling when her daughter's fingers immediately curled around hers. She was perfect.

Only one thing marred the bliss of the moment.
Andrew wasn't here.

She gently scooped the baby into her arms and held her close to her heart. This precious angel would never know her father's voice. Would never snuggle with him on the couch with a favorite book. Would never dance a Father/daughter dance with him at her wedding. She held her baby cuddled closer to her chest and wept bitter tears.

Moments later, at a soft rap on the door, she hastily dried her tears before calling for the visitor to come in.

Justin entered the room, still in his scrubs, a gorgeous vase of blush-hued roses in his hands. "Is this a good time?" he asked concerned at the telltale tear streaks on her cheeks and puffy, red-rimmed eyes.

"Just a bittersweet day," she admitted, forcing a small smile for his benefit.

He set the roses down on a little table and perched carefully on the edge of the bed, gazing with awe at the tiny bundle in her arms. He'd never before seen so much hair on an infant!

She turned the baby to allow him a better look. "I'd like you to meet Andrea Joy Darcy. Andrea for her Daddy and---"

"Joy for you," he finished, raising his eyes to hers. *Please, Lord. Let this little one live up to her name and return some joy to Emma's heart and life.*

"Would you like to hold her?"

"Very much. I've been looking forward to this all day," he added as she transferred Andrea into his waiting arms.

She watched as he touched the tiny cheek, her heart melting when he ducked his head and lightly kissed the baby's smooth forehead.

"She's absolutely beautiful, Em," he whispered huskily. "She looks just like you." Truly. While the boys both strongly favored their father, her little daughter's appearance was so strikingly like hers, it was as if he was looking at one of Emma's baby pictures.

Her heart swelled with pride, and another emotion she couldn't identify. "Thank you."

Justin stared at the precious angel in his arms, completely enraptured. Suddenly, the baby opened her eyes and gazed back at him with the biggest, bluest eyes he'd ever seen. A rush of love, deeper than he could've possibly imagined, swept through him. Tears formed in his eyes. In all of ten seconds, she'd completely stolen his heart. How was that possible?

After all, she wasn't even his child.

"What did the boys think of their new baby sister? You were concerned about sibling rivalry, especially from Will."

She grinned. "I needn't have worried. Both of the boys are thoroughly smitten with their little sister. Emmitt was excited to hold her and Will wouldn't stop kissing her head."

"I can certainly understand that," he replied, snuggling the baby a little closer. Smitten. That's what he was, all right. Not just with this precious baby, but with her adorable big brothers, *and* their amazing mother as well.

Reluctantly, he handed Andrea back to Emma. "I think she's wanting her Mama."

"Time to eat. Can you hand me the quilted nursing cover, please?"

Instead of returning to his perch on the edge of her bed, he chose the couch along the wall to give her a bit more space. And privacy.

It seemed a bit odd to be sitting in the room with her while she nursed the baby. He wasn't the husband. Wasn't little Andrea's father. And nursing seemed like such an intimate act. He stole a glance at Emma's face and saw her gazing tenderly at her daughter. She seemed nonplussed. Almost as if she'd forgotten he was even in the room.

Despite the events of earlier this morning, and the exhaustion she had to be feeling following the delivery, her face was absolutely radiant. He sucked in a few fortifying breaths, overcome suddenly by the powerful urge to pour out his heart to her. To lay bare all of his desires where she was concerned.

And to hear that his affections were returned.

It was time to go. Before he did something he'd only regret later.

He moved from the couch and stood next to the hospital bed. "I'd better get home, Emma. You need to have some time alone with your baby, and I'm sure you are probably worn out."

"You'll be back tomorrow, though, right?" she asked, a strange twinge piercing her heart at the thought of him leaving.

"Of course. Although I'm not sure how much time I'll get to spend with my beautiful girls with Beth here."

She blushed at his comment. "I'm so sorry about the way she's treated you, Justin. It isn't right."

"No, but it's understandable. At any rate, I'll come back tomorrow night after work when visiting hours are over. That is, if you want me to." *Please say you want me to*, he thought.

She reached out and took his hand. "Of course I do. You're my friend. My best friend, these days," she added softly, glancing down quickly to avoid his gaze.

He frowned momentarily at her lowered head before forcing a grin for her sake. "It's settled then. Try to get some rest, Em. I'll see you both tomorrow."

Pressing a kiss to his fingers, he lightly touched the baby's head, covered with the blanket. Then, he swept back Emma's bangs and kissed her forehead. "'Night."

"G'night, Justin."

While his heart thrilled at the realization that their relationship had grown and flourished in the last nine months, the very last thing he wanted to be was her best friend. That was Noelle's role, not his.

He longed to be someone infinitely more dear to Emma than simply the best friend.

He longed to be her husband.

Grace believed that her daughter's heart was already turning toward him. While he wasn't as sure, he recognized that he was too close to the situation to be able to accurately see things as they really were.

So what if she was right?

What if everything he'd longed for was about to come true?

Please, God.

The last thing he wanted to do was scare her away.

So, he'd keep doing exactly what he'd been doing. Spending time with her and the children. Looking out for her. Praying for her. Loving her quietly.

And perhaps one day, in her own time, she'd recognize his actions for what they really were.

Chapter Twelve

June

The crunch of tires on the gravel jolted Emma from her reverie. Opening her eyes, she took in the flowers freshly planted in front of Andrew's gravestone. Had she only planted those this morning? After her quiet hour spent reflecting on all that had passed during the last year, it felt much longer. Hearing a car door slam close to where she was sitting, she glanced up and saw Justin's Corvette parked just behind her minivan. Their eyes met and her heart slammed into overdrive. Just as quickly, a wave of guilt swept through her. What kind of wife was she? Here she sat - at her husband's graveside - and she was excited to see another man. Wasn't that disrespectful to Andrew's memory? It's not like she envisioned remaining single forever--she was under thirty, after all. But to be so strongly attracted to Justin after only a year of widowhood? But wait. It was less than that, actually. She'd been having these feelings for awhile now. Yes, there was history there. However, it was still way too soon. Wasn't it?

He strolled toward her, carrying a cluster of lilacs - Andrew's favorite flower - their scent filling the air. He bent and pressed a light kiss to her forehead before placing the flowers next to the marble box. "I thought you might be here."

Emma nodded at the flowers, smiling in appreciation. "It was sweet of you to bring them, Justin," she said, rising from the ground and sitting on the bench, leaving enough room for him to join her. When he did, her heart rate tripled. With their knees, arms, and shoulders touching as they squeezed together on the tiny space, excitement raced through her body. What in the world was *wrong* with her? *Stop it!* she commanded herself.

He took her hand in his, rubbing it gently with his thumb. "You okay?"

Despite the giant sparks of electricity shooting up and down her spine at his soothing, innocent touch, she was determined to focus on Andrew today. No matter that her feelings for Justin were beginning to intensify, she owed it to him. "I can't believe it's been a year already. A whole year without my husband, without the kids' Daddy."

Justin eased his arms around her, longing to provide her with the slightest iota of comfort. She immediately responded by turning and wrapping her arms around his waist, snuggling deeper into his broad chest. He forced himself to take several deep breaths in an effort to slow his pounding heart. Lately, it seemed like her feelings for him were changing from friendship to something more. But he worried that it was still too soon. To that end, he made every effort to rein in his emotions when around her. If anything happened between them, he wanted it to be at her pace, not his.

"I was thinking about that day. About all the good memories I have of our last day together. I wish the boys could remember. They've already forgotten," Emma admitted in the barest of whispers.

He squeezed her tighter. "You'll always have those memories, Em. And the boys have the pictures you took, even if they can't remember that day themselves."

She nodded, relieved that she'd finally managed to get control over her crazy emotions. "We didn't normally have the camera with us--I've always been horrible at remembering it. Even to this day, the main reason we have any baby pictures of the kids is because they have two Grandmas who are picture-taking nuts. But for some reason, on that day, I remembered."

"I think God prompted you to remember, knowing what was coming and that you'd need the reminder of a good family memory."

"I hadn't thought of that," she replied softly, wonder and relief evident in her voice. "Thank you, Justin."

They were quiet for awhile, each content to hold the other in silence.

After several minutes, Justin pulled far enough away to be able to look into her eyes. "Did I ever tell you that I talked to Andrew before he died?"

Emma shook her head in confusion. "I thought he was unconscious when he was brought in."

"He was. And then while we were prepping him for surgery, he awoke for a few minutes, just long enough for us to talk."

"What did he say?"

Justin took her hand in his once more and stroked it. "I think he knew...." he started, allowing the rest of that thought to taper off. No need in stating the obvious. "He wanted you to know how much he loved you and the boys, and how grateful he was that you'd married him."

She closed her eyes, a few tears slipping through her closed lids.

How he longed to kiss those tears away, but squeezed her hand instead. Should he tell her the rest? If he did, how would she react? Would she finally vocalize what he'd seen in her eyes a few moments ago? His gaze wandered to the gravestone a few feet from where they were sitting and his heart sank. Of course she wouldn't. Not here. Not today.

"Is that all he said?"

He frowned. Under no circumstances did he want to lie to her. On the other hand, he knew this wasn't the time or place for her to hear the rest. Instead of answering, he gathered her back into his arms and embraced her.

Enfolded in the warm cocoon of his arms, Emma lost all rational ability to think. She'd just asked him a question...but what was it? She couldn't remember. At this moment, she could only feel. Confused by her feelings and desperate to get away from him, she pulled away and jumped to her feet. "I've got to get home--it's almost time for Andrea's feeding."

Relief swept throughout Justin's body. He'd successfully evaded the question. *Another time, my darling. Another time.*

He loaded the gardening tools into the back of the van while she climbed behind the steering wheel. After shutting the back hatch, he strolled over to the driver's side door and leaned his arms on the lowered window. "Give the boys and little Andrea a hug from me, please." He purposely refrained from using the title Andrew's mother had grudgingly given him--Uncle Justin. His desire was to eventually become the children's new father, so the last thing he wanted them calling him was "uncle". But he knew that title was Beth Darcy's way of placing the special bond he shared with Emma's children in an acceptable category. She'd never been overly thrilled with his presence in their lives. She reasoned that perhaps if the children viewed him as just another family member, they wouldn't ever think of him as a potential Daddy. And unfortunately, this ploy seemed to be working.

She nodded. "Are you coming over for dinner tonight? Beth is cooking a lasagna for us to enjoy even as we speak. Not that she's gonna be there," she quickly added, not wanting him to think it would be a family dinner.

He looked away and smirked. Somehow, he doubted Beth would be thrilled with him savoring the dish, commonly known as her personal specialty, with Emma and the kids. If she didn't approve of his relationship with the children, that went double for his relationship with their mother. He knew that the very last person she wanted Emma spending time with was him. Every day, but especially today. "As tempting as that sounds, I can't. I'm working tonight."

"I thought you were off this week," she stated, confused.

"Yeah, I was. But honestly, Em, I figured you'd want to be alone today. So when Dr. Walker's mother died, I agreed to take her shifts for the next couple days. This way you can have some time with the kids and I won't be sitting at home worrying about you. Instead I'll be at the hospital worrying about you," he quipped.

Emma patted his arm. "At least you'll be busy."

"I'll let you get home. Would you mind if I hung out with you and the kids Thursday night?"

"We'd love you to," she assured him with a smile. "See you then."

He smiled at her in return, then leaned his head in the window to kiss her cheek. However, at that same moment, she turned slightly to do the same and his kiss landed square on her lips. Both of them jerked backward in surprise.

His heart pounded in his chest. Had he imagined it, or he had he just kissed her? He mumbled a half-hearted apology, knowing that he wasn't really sorry. Knowing full well that he'd do it again if given the chance.

Emma's face was scarlet with embarrassment. Justin had just kissed her! Inadvertently, of course. He seemed so disappointed that she was instantly crushed. Of course he was disappointed. He didn't have feelings for her and hadn't meant it to happen.

Her refusal to look at him cut him to the quick. He must've been imagining the tenderness in her eyes all these weeks. Heart aching, all he wanted was to get away before she saw how hurt he was. "See you Thursday, Emma."

The glance she briefly tossed his way revealed tear-filled eyes. His heart was pierced anew. He certainly hadn't meant to kiss her, but did she know that? He wasn't sure. Justin stepped back and watched as she drove away before walking back to his own car.

He'd originally wondered if Thursday would finally be the day. His heart had misled him into believing it was time, that she was ready to hear how much he loved her, while his brain kept insisting it was still too soon. After today, it was clear. She didn't seem him as anything other than a friend.

A part of him thought of their time on Thursday with nothing but dread. But strangely, the largest part of him looked forward to it with great anticipation.

Not only was he a fool, he was also a glutton for punishment.

Emma sat at the breakfast bar and wrapped her hands around her coffee cup, desperately trying to absorb some of the warmth into her chilled skin. She was still in shock over what had happened that afternoon. How in the world was she going to tell Justin? *Should* she even tell him? She worried it would freak him out---indeed, it freaked her out just a little bit.

Her youngest son had called Justin *Daddy*!

All morning he had been asking for Daddy, and each time she had gently, but lovingly, reminded him that Daddy was with Jesus in Heaven. Each time he would frown in confusion.

Following his afternoon nap, he'd asked again. "Mama, where Daddy?"

Emma squatted on the floor in front of her son and caressed his cheek. "Sweetheart. Daddy is in Heaven. Remember? You and Emmitt helped me pick out some flowers to plant at his grave."

Will stomped his foot in frustration. "No!" Reaching into his pocket, he pulled out a picture he'd brought in from his room. "Daddy! Where *Daddy*?"

She took the picture and froze, her face ashen. It wasn't a picture of Andrew she was holding. It was a picture of the boys and....*Justin*. Her legs suddenly weak, she collapsed backward onto the floor and just stared at the picture, trying to grasp what had just happened. Her son thought Justin was his father. Her heart thrilled and ached all at the same time. The thought that someone else was replacing Andrew in her young son's heart was heart-wrenching.

And yet....

This was yet another sign that life had returned to her small family. Even as the tears flowed, her heart soared.

When his mother still hadn't answered him, Will climbed up in her lap and snuggled against her chest. "Mama. Where Daddy?"

She wiped her eyes with the back of her hands. Then, cuddling her son closer, she replied, "Do you mean Justin?"

He nodded.

"Well, he's had to work at the hospital the last couple of days." She grasped his small shoulders and held him so that she could see his face. "Will, Justin is not your Daddy, sweetheart."

His eyebrows puckered in confusion. "But he here evwy day, Mama. He pways wif Emmitt an' me. He hugs you."

Emma frowned in consternation. He had her there. "Yes, son. Justin does come to see you every day. He does play with you and Emmitt, and hold your baby sister. And yes, he *does* give Mama hugs. But he is our friend. Those are all things friends sometimes do."

Thankfully for Emma, he'd been content enough with that answer to climb off her lap and run into his room to play.

Now she sat trying to figure out what to do. The Daddy thing today. And that kiss... Even after several days, her body instantly warmed with just the thought of Justin's kiss.

She sighed in frustration. How silly she was being! For goodness sake, it wasn't even a real kiss. Nothing like the few times he'd kissed her all those years ago. And yet. The briefest touch of his lips the other day had stirred more emotion in her heart than she'd felt in a long time. She'd played and replayed the event over and over in her head the last couple days. Initially, she'd believed the look on his face to be disappointment. But what if it wasn't? What if she'd misread the situation? What if he was just trying not to hurt or rush her? The possibilities filled her with nervous excitement.

A knock on the door signaled Justin's arrival for dinner. Taking a deep breath in an attempt to calm herself, she smoothed her hair before opening the door. She allowed her eyes to roam over him, a huge smile spreading across her face. Dressed in a navy cotton t-shirt and a pair of trendy jeans, with his stylish hair a bit windblown from driving around with the convertible top down, he looked irresistibly handsome. Suddenly a bit weak at the knees, she leaned on the door jam for support. "Hi," she whispered, finally meeting his gaze.

"Hi," he returned, more than aware of her perusal. His heart pounded in his chest. He'd expected her to be distant. But she wasn't. Had she been thinking about that kiss as much as he had? The sudden urge to pull her into his arms and give her a proper kiss seized him. With great restraint, he grasped her elbow with one hand, inched toward her, and placed a kiss on her check, just to the side of her mouth.

Her stomach flopped and her palms began to sweat in anticipation. Her senses swam. His cologne teased her nose tantalizingly, reminding her of time spent alone a lifetime ago. The skin of her elbow where his hand rested was tingly and alternately hot and cold. She didn't think she could take much more.

After lingering for a few heartbeats - as if he might do it again - he straightened and bestowed a killer smile upon her.

Once he was inside, she shut the door and then leaned on it, watching him head down the hallway to find the boys. Something had changed. They'd only spoken one word to each other, but volumes more were silently being said between them during those few minutes at the door. She thought she'd interpreted the look in his eyes as longing.

Emma picked up a magazine from the coffee table and began swiftly fanning herself.

It was going to be an interesting night.

They made it through dinner without any awkwardness, mainly because by some silent agreement they each strove to keep their conversation neutral. Emma and the boys told him what they had done over the last few days, and Justin shared several funny anecdotes about some of the people he worked with at the hospital.

Emma was struck by how normal sharing a meal together had become. It was almost as if they'd become a family over the last year, happening little by little over the months. The proverbial frog in warm water.

After dinner, Justin took his glass of water into the living room and entertained the boys while Emma fed Andrea in the nursery. Over the sounds of the boys' play, he was able to hear her singing to her daughter. With a chuckle, he reasoned that either she'd forgotten the baby monitor was on, or else she'd grown comfortable enough with him to sing around him, as she was painfully self-conscious about her singing voice.

Will suddenly got up and raced out of the room. Justin wasn't surprised when a moment later he heard him talking to Emma in the nursery. Since Andrew's death, the young boy had at times been very clingy, often stopping whatever he was doing long enough to make sure his mom was still there.

With Will out of the room, Emmitt was strangely quiet. In the silence, Justin could distinctly hear every sound over the monitor, almost like he was right in the room with them. He could even occasionally hear the baby loudly slurping as she nursed.

"I think your sister was hungry," he remarked to Emmitt with a laugh.

Emmitt shrugged. "She's always hungry," he replied.

He heard a loud burp and knew Andrea was halfway through her feeding. Emma would switch sides, change and dress her daughter for bed, and then it would be his turn. It was his job to rock her to sleep each night, something he enjoyed immensely. There was nothing quite like feeling that warm little body snuggled against his chest, or the powdery scent of her hair close to his face. Truth be told, he'd spent so much time with her, had been with her from the very beginning, that he didn't think he could love her any more if she were his own daughter.

"Andrea's almost finished eating. If you'd like me to read that bedtime story, you'd better get it now so that I can read it to you before Mama says it's time for bed."

"Okay!" Emmitt ran to his room, where the boys' books were neatly stacked on a small shelf.

Silence descended again until, over the monitor, he heard Will ask, "Mama, I have juice?"

"Yes, love. If you'll wait a few minutes, I'll get you some."

Justin picked up his empty glass and started toward the kitchen for both a refill and to get Will's juice.

"Daddy get it?" A few steps away from the sink, he froze.

"You mean Justin?"

"Yes--Daddy."

He was so shocked at what he'd heard that he barely noticed when the glass slipped from his hand and shattered on the tile floor.

"Justin?" Emma called. "Is everything all right out there?"

He gulped, trying to remember how to breathe. "Yeah," he called, his voice surprisingly steady. "Don't let the boys come in the kitchen--I need to get this broken glass cleaned up."

"Okay!" she called back.

Then, the conversation with her son continued. Justin strained to hear every word even as he quickly swept the floor.

"Will, we talked about it earlier, remember? Justin is not your Daddy. Your Daddy is in Heaven with Jesus."

He realized two things simultaneously: one, Emma most certainly did *not* realize that the baby monitor was still on; and two, he wanted more than anything to hear Will call him Daddy. Permanently.

"But I wuv him, Mama."

"I know you do, sweetheart. So does Mama---" she cut the sentence short, as if suddenly realizing what she'd said.

In the kitchen, Justin was so stunned by what he'd overheard that he abruptly stopped sweeping and leaned on the counter for support. She *loved* him? Please, God, let it be so! In a daze, he slowly made his way back to the couch and gingerly sat down. She *loved* him!

Emmitt reappeared with his favorite book and climbed into his lap.

"Shall we wait for your brother?" he asked absently. Although he was still trying to wrap his mind around what he'd heard, he knew the little boy on his lap deserved his full attention.

The four-year-old shrugged his little shoulders and eyed Justin intently. "I dunno. He's talkin' with Mama right now."

"Yes, I know."

Just as he was about to open the book, Will reappeared. Justin waited with baited breath to see how he would be addressed. But for some reason, Will just climbed up onto the couch next to him and pulled Justin's arm around his small shoulders. His signal for Justin to begin.

With a long sigh, he opened the book and began to read.

Toward the end of the book, Emma emerged, cradling a sleepy Andrea in her arms. Taking one look at her sons cuddled up to Justin, her heart fluttered and warmth spread throughout her entire body. He was so good with her children. And it appeared as if he truly enjoyed being with them. A Mommy friend of hers had made the comment recently that there was nothing sexier than watching the man you loved enjoy fatherhood. She'd always found that to be true of Andrew. Justin certainly wasn't their father, although he had apparently replaced Andrew in Will's heart; there were still many nights, however, when Emmitt cried out in his sleep for his Daddy.

Still, she'd watched Justin's interaction with her children over the last months and had to admit that it was true of him as well, father to her children or not. A man who enjoyed being around children *was* sexy. One of the things that drew her to him the most was the tenderness he consistently showed Emmitt, Will, and Andrea. A wave of longing swept through her and she pressed a kiss to her baby's head in an attempt to drag her thoughts away from the delectable man before her.

When Justin briefly raised his eyes to hers, the smoldering look in those beautiful dark orbs nearly took his breath away and he paused, allowing a longer glance. It was nearly his undoing. Taking a ragged breath, he began again, but concentration was a struggle. Finally, after great effort on his part, he finally finished the book and hugged the boys, trying desperately to act as if nothing out of the ordinary had occurred. As if he hadn't heard the conversation in the nursery. As if he hadn't seen the love and desire in her eyes when she'd looked at him just now. "Night, boys. See you tomorrow." He held his breath once more, curious to see how Will would respond. But when the toddler merely gave him a little wave before heading down the hall toward his bedroom, he was disappointed.

"She's almost asleep, so I don't think you're gonna get much snuggle time tonight, Justin. I'm sorry," Emma informed him, gently placing her daughter in his arms. Their arms brushed, and her entire body tingled. She refused to meet his eyes again, a little off balance by the intensity she'd seen in his expression moments ago. Risking a tiny glance, she was ensnared and nearly scorched by the heat she saw. Pleasurable chills raced up and down her spine and she shuddered.

"That's all right," he finally answered. And this time, it was his turn to press a light kiss to the top of the baby's head in an attempt to rein in his thoughts. "She and I can snuggle any time. I was actually hoping to spend a little time with her Mommy tonight, if that's all right with you," he added, piercing her once more with his gaze.

"Um, sure. Let me just get the boys in bed and I'll be back," she said over her shoulder as she practically ran out of the room.

"Well, little girl. It's just you and me."

Once in the dimmed nursery, he sat in the glider rocking chair and stretched his long legs out, crossing them at the ankles. Then he gently placed Andrea against his shoulder, snuggled into his neck, and began to softly rub circles on her back as he rocked. In no time at all, she was completely limp. He turned his head slightly and inhaled her delightful baby scent. He'd never known how good babies smelled! Well, most of the time anyway, he amended with a grin.

Normally, he looked forward to his snuggle time with sleeping beauty. But tonight, he was anxious for some time alone with her mother. With that thought in mind, he stood and made his way slowly to the crib, rocking her in his arms for a few minutes to ensure that she was, in fact, asleep.

After tucking the boys in bed, Emma decided to peek in the nursery. Justin was standing with his back to the door, slowly swaying back and forth with Andrea asleep on his shoulder. As he started quietly humming to her sleeping daughter, her heart swelled within her. *I love you.*

He visibly jerked and stopped swaying.

Horrified, she realized she'd actually said those three little words out loud. Out. *Loud*! She desperately wanted to run from the room, thoroughly embarrassed at what she'd inadvertently let slip. But she was rooted to the floor and could not move.

Although every nerve in his body was screaming with the longing to pull Emma into his arms and give her tangible evidence of his love for her, he forced himself to calmly lay the baby in her crib. The woman of his dreams had just told him she loved him; the very last thing he needed was to drop her baby.

Finally, he turned and faced her. She was as white as a sheet, her hands clamped firmly over her mouth, eyes wide in fear and uncertainty.

Emma took one last look at him and bolted down the hall to the living room. Throwing herself onto the couch, she grabbed a lap quilt and pulled it over her head. What had she done? She knew he cared for her...but love? It was too much to hope that he actually loved her in return.

It finally began to sink in that she was in love with Justin. With her husband of six years gone barely a year, she was in *love* with another man! Conflicting emotions overpowered her. The rush of falling in love again. The shame that it had happened so soon. After all, she doubted anyone - even her mother-in-law - expected her to remain single for the rest of her life. But shouldn't she grieve her husband for longer than a year before falling in love? Like a bucket of freezing water splashed in her face, she had the bracing realization that it had actually been *less* than a year before she'd developed romantic feelings for a man not her husband.

She was scum of the earth.

Justin had purposely remained in the nursery for a few minutes, giving her some time alone. He took his time straightening up, making sure Andrea's diapers and wipes were readily available for her late-night feeding. Then, he switched on the nightlight and turned off the dim light next to her crib. Hoping he'd given her enough time, he quietly closed the door to the nursery and made his way back into he living room. As he neared the couch and heard her gut-wrenching sobs, his heart ached for her. He could guess why she cried. Understand why she cried. But that didn't make it any easier for him to hear. He wished she weren't so tormented by her mixed emotions. Falling in love should be a joyful, exciting time. Not something to be ashamed of. He cautiously sat on the couch next to her and hesitantly touched her shoulder.

She loudly sniffed and then sat up, shooting daggers at him with her eyes. His face wrinkled in surprise. He couldn't figure out for the life of him why she was so upset with *him*, when *she* was the one who'd made that admission of love.

Until he realized what she was holding in her hand.

The baby monitor.

"You heard, didn't you!" she accused, waving it in his face. "You heard Will! And you heard what I said!"

"Yes," he replied slowly, still not understanding why she was so upset. After all, hadn't she herself admitted that she loved him?

She was so furious she could hardly see straight. Why, she really didn't know. But she imagined using the monitor as a missile against him and actually drew back her hand, preparing to launch. Through the red haze of anger, she saw him wince and hold both of his hands up in defensive surrender, confusion marring his handsome face. What was she doing? Why was she acting like this was all Justin's fault, when she really had no one but herself to blame? There wasn't anything to be angry with him for. Her arm slowly sank, the monitor falling to the couch next to her. Once more, she dissolved into wracking sobs.

Tentatively, Justin laid his hand on her leg. At his touch, she sat up and launched herself into his arms, desperately seeking comfort. Self-control vanquished, his longing to hold her seized control. With a groan, he pulled her sideways onto his lap, tugging her tightly against his chest. Emma clung to him, enveloped in his strong arms, her tears soaking through the thin material of his t-shirt. He gently rubbed her head and back, rocking her in his arms like he'd done earlier with the baby.

All evening, he'd desperately fought his desire to kiss her, but when she looked up at him with sorrow-filled eyes, the battle was lost. Framing her beautiful face with his palms, he brushed away the tears with his thumbs and swept a kiss across her forehead. Her chin. Each cheek. Then finally, her lips.

Neither could've imagined the roaring flame that was ignited with such a gentle kiss. She wrapped her arms around his neck, straining closer, even as the tears continued to fall. He pulled her even tighter, twining his fingers in her silky hair as he kissed her deeply.

Just as his last shred of control was seeping away, a tiny voice from deep within him screamed at him to stop.

Suddenly, the salty taste of her tears registered and he abruptly pulled away. Passion's fog lifted, bringing with it a realization of the kiss they'd shared.

Ashamed and horrified, Emma flew off of his lap and ran into the bathroom, slamming the door behind her.

Justin mentally cursed himself for losing control. Head in his hands, he groaned. This is not at all how he'd planned the evening to go. After spending the last three days dreaming of their inadvertent kiss---and remembering the brief, but sweetly passionate kisses they'd shared as teens, he'd hoped there would be a goodnight kiss to look forward to. But certainly not a hot and heavy make-out session on her living room sofa, as if they were a couple of horny teenagers. He'd messed up. Big time. This was much more characteristic of the old Justin. Not the man of God he'd become. *Lord, forgive me. I want to honor You in our relationship. Honor her. Help me to do that.*

The bathroom door opened, and in a moment Emma was standing at the perimeter of the room, eying him. She'd run a brush through her hair - the hair that only minutes ago he'd combed his fingers through - and secured it in a low ponytail at the base of her neck. She'd also smoothed some powder over her cheeks, somewhat covering the tear streaks. Without a word, she headed into the kitchen and flipped on the burner underneath the kettle. "I need some tea. Would you like some?"

He took that as the invitation it was and folded his tall frame onto a stool at the breakfast bar. She set out two mugs with a tea bag in each on the counter in front of him, then filled them with hot water. Before joining him, she added the creamer, a pretty porcelain sugar bowl, and two spoons. Shooting him a glance, she purposely chose the stool across from him. So they weren't touching. It was just as well, really. Each of them remained silent while doctoring their tea according to individual tastes--his with just a little sugar, hers with cream and sugar. She distractedly stirred her tea, the occasional sniff escaping.

Those sniffs further pricked his conscience. He stretched his hand out to touch hers, but she pulled away and wrapped her hands around her mug instead.

It was going to be a long night.

Chapter Thirteen

Emma hadn't meant to hurt his feelings by shying away from his touch. However, she could see by the frown on his face that she had. Couldn't he understand why? His slightest touch turned her brain to mush. She couldn't afford to lose her mental faculties. Again. She'd enjoyed their kiss much more than she'd ever imagined she would. How was it possible to love two men, so different from each other, so passionately? The fact that Justin brought out feelings in her that only Andrew previously had, confused and shamed her. Right or wrong, she felt it called into question her commitment to her husband.

Finally, Justin could endure the silence no longer. "Emma, I am so sorry." He reached once more for her hand, his eyes silently pleading for her to take it. When she did, albeit reluctantly, he sighed with relief. "You needed a friend and I allowed my love and desire for you to take advantage of that."

Her eyes whipped to his, shock written across her entire face. Sucking in a deep breath, she shakily whispered, "Love? You *love* me?"

He squeezed her fingers and smiled. "I do. I love you, Emma Joy Darcy."

Her eyes slid closed over a few tears that had managed to escape. "I didn't know. I was afraid..."

He squeezed her fingers again. "You were afraid I didn't love you back?"

She nodded. "Before, I did... And you didn't..." Although, truth be told, she'd *never* felt this way for him before. What she'd thought was love as a girl was nothing but infatuation.

"Oh, but you're mistaken."

She peered at him questioningly, confusion wrinkling her forehead.

"I think I've loved you for a long time, but I was too stupid and immature to realize it. When I told you at the reunion that you were one of the reasons I'd returned to Cancun, I meant it."

"So, even then..." She couldn't finish that thought.

"Yes. Even knowing you were happily married. Knowing that there would never be anything between us other than friendship. You are more important to me than you'll ever know."

Her mind just couldn't begin to comprehend what was being said. Justin loved her! It was all so surreal.

She looked down into her tea, then glanced up at him again. "I'm sorry I was so angry earlier. Truth is, I wasn't even angry at you, but at myself."

He rubbed his thumbs over her fingers, waiting for her to continue. But how could she when that simple action caused her heart to pound and her body to tingle? "Can you please not do that?" she asked raggedly, thankful yet disappointed when he quickly obeyed.

He grinned at her obvious disappointment. It was reassuring that they were in this particular boat together. "Go on, sweetheart," he gently urged when she remained silent.

Emma inhaled deeply and let it back out in a long sigh. "It's only been a year, Justin. And since my feelings didn't change overnight, it means I began falling in love with you before my husband was gone even a year."

His suspicions were confirmed. Unfortunately, he didn't know exactly what to say to allay her fears or guilt. "Emma, everyone knows how much you loved Andrew. *Still* love Andrew. The last thing I want to do is to take his place, or make anyone forget him."

She brushed a few tears out of her eyes before meeting his, giving him a watery smile. "Thank you. You don't know how glad I am to hear you say that. But it's already happening."

"Will," they responded in unison.

"I know we've only just expressed our true feelings for each other, Emma. However, I want to lay it all on the table now so that there are no misunderstandings. I love you. I love the children. I know we have a long road ahead of us. But in time, I want to marry you. Be a father to your children. And, God willing, have more children with you."

Her face and neck turned pink at the mere thought of all that entailed. If tonight's passionate kisses were any indication, becoming his wife would indeed be something to look forward to.

He found her sudden shyness endearing. Especially since she'd been in a very passionate marriage for six years. Not that she'd ever mentioned as much. But he had eyes. And of course, the family picture gallery marching down the hallway spoke volumes.

At her quiet, "I want that, too," desire swept through him anew. *Lord, help!* It was a good thing they were separated by the breakfast bar. It was better not to touch her right now--even an innocent touch like holding hands across a table.

"Emma, if I thought either of us were truly ready for that next step, I'd kneel down and propose this minute. But I'm not convinced that the timing is right. I'm not a fool; I know that there are family members - probably even some friends - who are not going to be happy about us being together. They might deem it far too soon." At her dejected expression, he quickly added, "Let me reiterate. *I* don't think it's too soon. You grieved for your husband. All of us saw it. I don't think anyone can say you did not. And I don't think anyone would disagree that you deserve to be happy. To remarry. But that it's *me*, given our past history, and that we've spent so much time together over the last months, is what some might take issue with."

"Like Beth," she softly replied.

"Yes, like Andrew's mother. And there are probably others. Even though Will has decided to call me Daddy, I have no way of knowing how he'll react to me actually *becoming* his Daddy. Nor do we know how Emmitt feels about it," he added, his voice thick with emotion. "Anyway, I don't want to take anything for granted. I want to take things slowly in order to give everyone time to fully accept how we feel about each other. I also want to make sure *you* have had enough time to fully grieve your husband and are ready to become a wife again."

She nodded in understanding. "So, where do we go from here?"

"I'm not exactly sure. I know that I want to spend the next sixty years or so with you as my wife. But I'm not really sure how to get there."

"Perhaps we should start by telling our friends and family members," she suggested, although her face clearly revealed how she felt about that idea.

He smiled affectionately. "As much as I'd enjoy nothing more than to shout to the world that I'm in love with the most beautiful, wonderful woman in the world, can't we just let this marinate awhile?"

She laughed merrily. "*Marinate*? So you're a chef now, huh?"

"Yes, marinate. Roll with it, babe."

Suddenly, her expression sobered.

Confusion lit his face. "What?"

"Andrew used to call me 'babe'," she responded quietly.

With one word, the joy of the moment was dimmed. Would it always be this hard, he wondered? Would the littlest things serve as stark reminders that the man she'd planned to grow old with was gone? The difficulty of their up-hill battle suddenly overwhelmed him.

Without a word, he circled the breakfast bar until he was standing next to her. Pulling her into a brief embrace, he then led her to the couch. Gently, but firmly, he pushed her onto it, dropping down to sit next to her. He held out both of his hands and waited expectantly for her to place hers in his. Closing his eyes, he leaned his forehead into hers and began to pray.

"Lord Jesus, we may not understand why You chose to take Andrew Home. But we are thankful that You have helped Emma, the children, and their friends and family members through this time. Continue drawing them to Your side, Lord. Jesus, we believe that You have brought us together for a reason and that this relationship is from You. We ask that You help us to use it to bring You honor. Help us to keep our thoughts and hearts pure before each other and before You. Lord, we're not exactly sure how to proceed from here. We know there very well may be people who do not understand or are hurt by this relationship. Help us to be sensitive and to take things slowly and with great patience. Soften hearts to Your will, Lord. We invite you to be a part of this relationship, Father, because only with Your help will it succeed. Thank You once again for Your blessing and loving mercy in our lives. We love You and seek only to do Your will. It is in Jesus' precious name that we pray. Amen."

"Amen," she repeated. "Thank you, Justin."

He continued to hold onto her hands, but instead of remaining seated, knelt at her feet. "I meant what I said, Emma. I want to marry you. But I also want to honor you before God. What happened tonight should not have happened, and I take full responsibility." When she started to argue, he placed his fingers against her lips to silence her. "The blame is mine. You were distraught. A gentleman does not take advantage of the situation, regardless of how he feels about the lady. With God's help, I promise you that it will not happen again. I - and I'm sure, *He* - will not allow it. Regrets are very powerful things. Eventually, you will be mine and I, yours, Emma, and I don't want to begin our married lives with any regrets between us. I want us to be able to look forward to our wedding night, knowing we waited for each other."

"But, Justin. Neither of us can say that. I was married. I have three children. And you and Lisa lived together..." She didn't have the heart to finish the sentence. He'd always bear the emotional scars from the loss of his child.

"Not in the technical sense, no. But there's not been anyone else for you but Andrew. And, Emma, I promise you there hasn't been anyone else for me but Lisa."

She'd always wondered about that. Hearing that he'd lived with a woman had been a shock to her all those months ago. A part of her had always wondered if there'd been more after his first. After all, if he'd slept with one woman, the odds were great that he'd slept with more.

"I wish I could tell you that I turned back to God after my child died. But I didn't. I went wild. Honestly, it's a miracle I even managed to graduate and become the charmingly successful doctor I am today."

A giggle escaped her.

His face became serious again. "No matter how I strayed, the last thing I wanted was for someone else to have the chance to hurt me like that again. And so I never let any other relationship get that far. Never let another woman that close again. Then, after my brother was killed, I lost all will to live. Emma, I'm not proud of this, but I came so close to taking my own life. I had another doctor write me a prescription for sleeping pills. I actually had them in hand, ready to swallow them. And then Matt's friend Ryan found me and slapped them away before I could take them. He saved my life. Oh, I wasn't happy about it at the time. I raged and cursed at him something fierce. But he refused to let me give up. He stayed by my side for a week, praying over me. Reading Scriptures to me. And finally, kneeling beside me and praying with me as I accepted Jesus as my Savior.

"God showed me something, my love. He showed me what I'd thrown away by walking away from you. And that I'd been comparing every woman I met to you. I knew then that my feelings for you weren't what I'd always professed or believed them to be. I even had this fantasy that I'd return home one day, a surgical success, and find you waiting for me."

Her heart went out to him, realizing how he must've felt upon discovering that she'd married Andrew.

He snorted in derision. "I think we both know how that turned out."

"Yes, we do," she smiled, laying her hand tenderly on his whisker-roughened cheek. "It's been difficult, my darling, and we certainly have a hard road ahead of us, but look where we are."

He returned her smile, resting his palm over her hand. "I love you, Emma."

"And I love you, Justin."

Very cautiously, he cupped her chin and lowered his lips to claim hers in a sweet kiss. This time, he kept it chaste and brief. While neither of them were left completely satisfied with it, he was determined to keep his promise to honor her. And ravaging her lips on the living room sofa with her children in the next room was not the way to do it.

He glanced at his watch. "It's getting kinda late. I'd better go."

"We have lots to talk about in the days to come, don't we?"

He nodded in agreement. "Do you still want me to come over in the evenings after work?"

"You'd better," she scolded, wagging her finger at him playfully. "I think the kids would be angry with me if I said you couldn't."

He wrapped her in another embrace and kissed her one last time, briefly, before turning to go.

"Sweet dreams," she murmured lovingly.

"Only if they're of you," he answered with a wink. "See you tomorrow, my dearest."

Even after he was long gone, the smile refused to leave her face. Emma knew that their journey had only just begun. There were still many trials yet to face. Yet, tonight, she was content in the knowledge that she was in love.

And more importantly, Justin loved her in return.

It was a miracle.

Looking back over the last months, his feelings for her were painfully obvious. The way he took such tender care of her. The strength of his embrace, so willingly offered. That fleeting intensity in his expression she'd glimpsed from time to time. It's little wonder Beth was in such a dither about their time spent together. How had she missed it?

If Justin's feelings for her were so blatantly obvious to everyone, were hers for him as well? A frown marred her features briefly. They'd just have to be careful when around other people.

Because as much as she relished the thought of being in love again, she most certainly was *not* ready to announce it to the world. Surely Justin would be patient enough to wait awhile before making their relationship official. He'd waited this long, hadn't he? What was another few months of waiting?

Chapter Fourteen

The next morning, when Allie dropped by for a visit, Emma had to bite her tongue to keep from mentioning her joyous news. While her sister-in-law spent a few moments with her nephews in their room, she took the time to clean up the breakfast dishes and to start water boiling for some tea.

Although she knew that it was too soon to tell everyone about Justin - was indeed extremely nervous about how others would take the news - her heart just couldn't keep quiet. Before long, she found herself softly singing a love song. And the huge smile that had seemingly taken up permanent residence across her face would not go away, no matter how strongly she willed it to.

Behind her, Allie stepped into the kitchen and leaned on the door frame, her arms folded at her chest and one leg crossed over the other at the ankles. "She's singing, ladies and gentlemen."

Emma spun around, feeling slightly guilty about being caught. "Oh, you know. When the mood strikes or you get a song stuck in your head."

"I hate when that happens. Unless it's a good song, anyway. Which, let's face it, usually it's not."

The women took their places at the breakfast bar, the tea things placed within easy reach. While they each fixed themselves a cup and enjoyed the first sip, Emma decided to let her sister-in-law lead the conversation. She was still trying to figure out how to keep a lid on the pot of her feelings.

"As much as I love playing with the kids, there was actually a reason I stopped by today," Allie began, excitement building.

"I suspected as much by the look on your face," Emma teased. She had a good hunch just what Allie was so excited about, too.

"He asked me out! Devon actually asked me to dinner tomorrow night!" she exclaimed, wiggling in happiness in her chair.

"That's great, Al! I'm so happy for you. So where's he taking you?"

"Rosetti's. It's this new little bistro just outside of town, overlooking Smithton Lake. I've been just dying to go, but it's been booked solid ever since it opened."

"Then, how did he get reservations on such short notice?" Emma queried.

"His best friend Tony is the chef. So he's got standing reservations any time he wants them," Allie replied.

And a playboy like Devon Hunter probably put those standing reservations to use quite frequently, Emma mused. She hoped that Allie wasn't in for a disappointment.

"Now, I know what you're thinking, Em. I know he's got quite the reputation around town. Don't worry, I can handle it."

"As long as you know what you're doing," she answered warily. "I'd hate to see you get hurt."

The pair were silent for several minutes, each enjoying their tea. Despite the fact that her heart was somewhat concerned for Allie's, the smile would just not leave her face. She ducked her head in an attempt to hide it.

"Just what is *with* you today, Emma? First the singing. And now you look absolutely lit up inside."

"It's just been a good day, that's all," Emma replied with a shrug. "God's been good," she added, hoping it would be enough to appease Allie. The last thing she needed was for the girl to mention it to Beth, who was already hyper-suspicious about Justin to begin with.

Allie reached across the counter and briefly squeezed her hand. "I'm glad to hear that, Em. I don't think my brother would want you mourning him forever."

"Oh, I know," she sighed, desperately trying to tone it down a bit.

"He once told me that if anything ever happened to him, he wanted you to remarry," she casually mentioned, peering at Emma over the rim of her teacup.

"Well, sure. A long time from now, I'd imagine."

She shook her head vehemently. "Not at all! As much as he loved you, Em, he didn't want you to be alone. He didn't want you having to raise the kids on your own, either."

Emma quietly mulled this information over for a few moments. Andrew had wanted her to remarry sooner rather than later? She had to admit that this surprised her just a bit. After all, if the tables had been turned, would she be able to say the same about him with perfect equanimity? She wasn't sure.

"It's been a year, sis. I think it's high time for you to at least *consider* getting back out there."

"'Getting back out there'?" she parroted.

"Yeah. You know, go on a date."

"And with whom do you suggest I go on a date?"

"Oh, I don't really know. Aren't there any single men in your church? Or, you can go online. Several friends of mine have met their spouses through sites like eharmony.com."

"Allie! I'm hardly looking for a new spouse!" Emma cried, guilt tingeing her conscience just a bit. She wasn't actually looking for a new spouse because she'd already found one. Well, a future spouse, anyway. So it was technically true, even if a bit misleading.

"Goodness, Emma, I wasn't suggesting you get re-married tomorrow, you know," she retorted, chagrined.

After several moments of silence, the conversation seemingly dropped, Emma sighed in relief.

Just as she took a sip of her tea, Allie's face lit up and she snapped her fingers. "I have it! What about that doctor friend of yours?"

Emma nearly choked on her tea. "Justin Bennet???" She clarified, quickly setting her teacup on its saucer lest she accidentally drop it. With both hands, she reached out and steadied herself on the counter. If Allie noticed her odd behavior, she certainly didn't say anything.

"Yeah, that's him! He's single. Well, at least I *think* he is. And he's *smokin'* hot."

"Yes, well," she said, completely flustered. If she wasn't careful, Allie would have a whole lot more to report to Beth by the time they were through.

When Emma didn't respond, Allie sighed and added, "Although, come to think of it. A guy like that probably already has a girlfriend."

"They always do," she agreed, even while her heart gave a little leap. *That would be me, the girlfriend.*

"Oh, shoot! Look at the time! I promised to meet Lily at the mall."

"And what does *she* think about you going on a date with her twin brother?"

"She's even more excited than I am. I think she's hoping that we'll become a couple and eventually get married."

"Just be careful, please. I don't want to see you get hurt," Emma admonished her sister-in-law.

After hugging the boys and kissing her sleeping niece goodbye, Allie left Emma alone with her thoughts.

So she'd thought to set her up with Justin, eh? Maybe this wouldn't be quite as bad as they'd originally thought. For the first time, Emma realized that she really could become a wife again very soon.

While the thought still brought a touch of sadness to her heart, she had to admit that she was looking forward to becoming Mrs. Justin Bennet.

Later that night, Justin lay a sleeping Andrea into her crib with a huge grin. Just twenty-four hours ago, his entire life had changed. Emma loved him! Had actually spoken those words out loud! He still couldn't believe it was finally happening.

Never again would he have to hide his true feelings from her. He could let all the love in his heart shine forth without fear of discovery. Er, at least when they were alone.

That thought was enough to tamp down some of his exhilaration.

Naturally, they'd only just voiced their true feelings for each other, so he couldn't expect she'd be ready for anything more serious. But surely she wouldn't expect him to wait a long time before telling the world about their love for each other, would she? Hadn't he waited long enough as it was?

He was practically busting at the seams to share his news with *someone*. Anyone!

After her sister-in-law's visit this morning, Emma had called and shared bits of their conversation with him. That Allie found him 'smokin' hot' amused him greatly. Of course, he didn't give a katy what other women thought of him. Only one woman's opinion mattered. He was morbidly curious what her response to Allie had been, but she'd been silent on the matter. He wasn't a particularly vain man; he just craved the reassurance that she found his features as appealing as he did hers. Not that looks really mattered, of course. He loved Emma for the woman she was inside. If she happened to have long, sexy legs, lustrous locks, and piercing brown eyes he longed to immerse himself in, so much the better. Like sumptuous icing on an already decadent cake.

He shut the door to the nursery and found Emma washing the supper dishes. "Sleeping beauty's down for the night."

She glanced up at him with a smile. "And will she remain asleep until her very own prince comes to wake her with a kiss?"

He narrowed his eyes. "If the prince were a wise man, he'd leave her asleep. I don't want any other princes in her life but me at the moment."

"Well, then I guess she's out of luck. You've already got a princess."

He bent his head and kissed her lips briefly. "You've got that right."

"I'm almost finished here. Why don't you relax for a bit in the living room and I'll be right in?"

He pouted. "I'd rather stay in here and watch you."

"Justin," she said, exasperated. "Good grief, honey. You know I can work much faster without you watching me."

"All right then. Don't be long."

Once she was finished in the kitchen, she joined him on the couch, careful to leave some space between them. She really did appreciate his desire to keep their relationship honorable before God. As strong as he was, she knew it was important to do her part in helping him keep his promise.

Justin reached across the empty cushion between them and took her hand in his. "You didn't finish telling me about your conversation with Allie." So, okay. He was shameless.

Her brow wrinkled in confusion. "Didn't I? I thought I did."

Are you really gonna make me ask? he thought. "Nope, I don't think so."

She suddenly realized what he was fishing for and laughed. "Oh, Justin. You're incorrigible."

He wriggled his eyebrows at her. "Worse has been said about me."

"Well, since you're so obviously dying to know what my response was, I'll tell you. I didn't say anything back to her---"

His face fell.

"---but what I thought was, 'O, yes, he certainly is smokin' hot.' Lest anyone get any ideas, you're *my* smokin' hot man," she added fiercely. "I don't know how it's possible, Justin Bennet, but you're far more handsome now than you've ever been. There. Have I embarrassed you enough now?"

He winked at her. "And you, my dear, absolutely take my breath away. Your physical beauty is enough to set my heart pounding. But what I love most about you, what is most beautiful about you, is your sweet devotion to those you love. Especially those little gifts from God sleeping in the other room."

"Justin..." she whispered, pressing a kiss to his lips. "I love you."

"And I love you. Forever," he responded, returning her kiss.

That evening began the first of many evenings spent in a similar fashion. After dinner, they would take turns putting the kids to bed while the other cleaned up the supper dishes. Then, they would sit at the breakfast bar, lingering over coffee and dessert, talking and dreaming about what their future would look like.

After about a week, Justin brought with him a couple's devotional book, which they began to read together each night as well. While they grew deeper in love with each other, it was his intention that they grow closer and closer to God both as a couple and individually. Emma still stubbornly held onto anger towards the men she deemed responsible for her husband's death, and this greatly concerned him. He prayed constantly that God would break that shell around her heart, whatever it took.

They continued to keep their relationship a secret from their friends and family. Well, most of them, anyway. Emma's parents and brother knew, of course, so Justin decided to share the joyous news with his mom. Even though she'd met Emma a few times as a young girl, he wanted her to know the amazing woman she'd become. The woman he loved with all of his heart.

They left the kids with Emma's parents and met his mom for brunch one Saturday at her small cabin on the outskirts of Denver. Their time together was brief, yet sweet. In just a short time, it was evident the two women he loved most would have a wonderful relationship. How blessed they both were--no horrible mother-in-law clichés for them!

Except for the fact that they were hiding their love from Emma's friends and in-laws, something that nagged his conscience, life was perfect. He prayed they would be able to be open with everyone very soon. After waiting for so long to get where they were, he didn't know how much longer he could continue without making things more official.

Soon. Surely, soon she'd be ready to reveal the truth of their relationship.

Chapter Fifteen

July 4

Justin added the remaining ingredients to his secret recipe potato salad while Emma finished cutting thick slices of watermelon across the breakfast bar from him. Her entire family - Darcys *and* Johnsons - were having a cookout at Smithton Lake. They were to arrive a little after 3 PM for the annual family beach volleyball match on the warm lake shore. Afterward, the feasting would begin and would continue all the way up to 9 PM, when the Cancun city fireworks display, annually shot from the less populous shores across the lake, would begin.

They'd been working together to prepare their offerings for the gathering, his potato salad, her dessert and watermelon slices. While they worked, he occasionally caught her peering at him. Each time, a deep blush would stain her lovely cheeks. It was the strangest thing, really. Over the last couple of days, her behavior toward him had changed somehow. She was more hesitant in her displays of affection and acted increasingly more shy around him whenever anyone else was with them. Especially Emmitt. And he was beginning to worry.

Two weeks ago, when she'd first invited him, they'd discussed talking about their relationship with their families. A few days ago, since there had been no further discussion about it, he had initiated a conversation with Emma regarding their tentative plan. To his great surprise, she'd abruptly changed the subject and had refused to talk about it. Part of him wanted to do something to force the issue. The other (wiser) part of him warned that it was a recipe for disaster. At the moment, the more foolhardy side of him was winning.

As patient as he had been for so long, and at a time when he should've been exercising the utmost of caution, an inexplicably stubborn streak was growing in his heart. He was tired of hiding his feelings for her. Tired of her acting like he was just a friend around everyone--even her children. He was ready to bring their relationship out into the open.

And tonight seemed as good a time as any to do it.

For the millionth time since their arrival at the lake, Emma wished Justin wasn't being quite so obvious about their relationship. He seemed to be going out of his way to proclaim to the world that they were a couple with each touch of his hand to her lower back and with each smoldering look---even in the way he sat just a bit closer to her than others might deem appropriate. And he appeared to be completely oblivious to the glares thrown his way by Joe, Beth---even Emmitt.

But she wasn't. With each subsequent glare, she cringed inside. This was not at all how she imagined this moment to feel. Shouldn't she be more joyful about this?

The longer the evening progressed, however, the angrier and more resentful she became. Why was he so intent on this? Didn't he realize her family wasn't ready? *She* wasn't ready? He'd been so patient with her all this time. Had been willing to take things slowly.

So why was he now plowing ahead full steam when that's the last thing she wanted?

As the evening grew, Justin's heart fell more and more. Something was *definitely* wrong. With each simple touch he gave her, she would shrink away from him as if he'd burned her.

As if she were still married and he was putting the moves on another man's wife.

That thought alone hurt more than anything. He'd finally realized what the problem was. She wasn't ready and he wasn't sure if she ever would be. She claimed to love him, yes. But did she really? There was only one way to find out.

And so he continued to push. To make his feelings known. It wasn't a great idea, he knew, but it was the only one he could think of. Maybe if he pushed her hard enough, she'd have to finally admit she loved him...or admit she wasn't ready for a relationship.

The fear that he could push her to the latter scared the life out of him. But then either way, he'd finally know. And he wouldn't have to hide his feelings from a dead man's family. Like he had something to be ashamed of.

Determination arose within him anew. Before God, he had absolutely nothing to be ashamed of. There was *nothing* bad or sinful about their relationship or either of their feelings for the other. In fact, he firmly believed they were *from* God.

And if this was the only way to make her realize what they stood to lose....

So be it.

If, after all, he was right and this was from God, He would make them a couple in His time. And if not... Well, the not knowing was killing him.

The fireworks this year were the best she'd seen in a very long time. It was fun watching Will's reaction to them. Last year, none of them had felt like watching fireworks, so this was his first time seeing them. He oohed and ahed with every colorful explosion in the sky. Justin held the excited little boy on his lap while she held Andrea. For some reason, Emmitt had wanted to sit with his Aunt Julia, seated clear across the group from where they were. It was the first time all day Justin had been content to give his attention to someone other than her. After all the glares, she was relieved to have a reprieve. The constant glares and icy conversations had charged the air--for her the fireworks had begun long ago. And at the way things were going, they were likely to end in a big explosion as well. She almost wished she could just scoop up her children and go home. But not for anything would she put a premature end to their fun.

Even if it meant prolonging the friction.

The fireworks' big finale signaled the end of the evening. Emma began gathering up the kids' belongings and her serving containers, stacking them neatly on a table for Justin to carry to the van.

She was just packing the last of the baby's toys into her diaper bag when he slid his arms around her waist from behind and pulled her closer. "Happy Independence Day, my love," he stated. Then, before she could so much as breathe, he turned her in his arms and kissed her.

In front of her gaping family.

She brought her arms up against his chest and pushed until he released her. In his eyes showed love, longing, and regret.

In hers, however, was only anger. In that moment, he knew. And his heart ached. He had only himself to blame.

She turned abruptly on her heel and stormed away from him, too angry and mortified to speak.

Emma didn't pay attention to where she was walking. All she knew was that she had to get away from Justin before she did or said something they'd both regret. She'd been careful all night not to give Beth or Joe any ammunition to use against her. He may have raised their hackles with his actions today, but, prior to that declaration and kiss, they'd had no *proof*. But now...

Now there was no doubt whatsoever what his intentions were toward her.

"Emma, wait!" he called, grabbing hold of her arm to stop her.

She jerked away from him and faced him in one swift movement. "Why did you do that? What did you think to accomplish, Justin?"

He set his jaw. "I thought we'd decided it was time to bring our relationship into the open."

"*You* decided that!"

"I know you're angry with me for outing us, Emma, but we *did* talk about it. Remember?"

"We talked about it yes, but we never came to any definite decisions. And now there's no going back, is there?"

"Is that such a bad thing?"

She bit her tongue to keep from answering. They were on the edge of a cliff here and one small breeze would knock them off.

He laughed bitterly. "So that's your answer."

"I didn't say anything, did I?"

"Your lack of response speaks volumes, my dear."

She let out a huff, angry tears cascading down her cheeks. "Things were fine just the way they were. Why did you have to go and ruin it?"

"Ruin it? Admitting to the world that I love you is 'ruining it'? Just how much longer did you think we could keep things quiet? Emma, I love you. You said you loved me. Why should we hide that?"

"Because people would think I wasn't faithful to Andrew!"

"Andrew has been dead for over a year, Emma."

"I know! *Only* a year! That's what they'll say."

"And if they do? Where is it written that you have to remain a widow for more than a year before you're allowed to fall in love and remarry? Nowhere. Why are you letting other people's opinions dictate our relationship? Or is it all an excuse, Emma? Are you hiding behind Joe and

Beth because you can't face the fact that you didn't follow everyone's idea of the proper grieving period? Because you can't face the fact that *you* aren't ready?"

Her eyes widened in shock and she jerked as if slapped.

"That's quite enough, Justin!" roared an extremely angry Joe, yanking Justin away from her.

"Stay out of this, Joe!" he yelled, shoving back.

Just before the two came to blows, little hands hit Justin's stomach and a small voice cried, "You stop making my Mama cry!"

Both looked down in surprise to see little Emmitt standing in front of Justin, hands on his hips, his little face drawn in anger.

Justin knelt in front of the little boy and tried to draw him into his arms. "Buddy..."

"No!" he cried, pulling away and standing just in front of Emma. "You don't ever hurt my Mama!"

"That wasn't my intention, buddy. I didn't mean to hurt your Mama. I love her and want to marry her."

"*No*! You stay away from my Mama!"

Justin's face whitened. Now, he was the one who looked like he'd been slapped. He stood and dejectedly reached a hand out to Emma. "Em, I'm sorry..."

"I think you've said enough, Bennet," Joe snarled, taking a hold of Emma's arm and leading her away.

She glanced back only once. The look on his face told her that his heart, like hers, was breaking. And she hadn't the faintest idea how to make things better. What he'd said... Well, she wasn't any more prepared to face it than she'd been prepared to come clean to her family about their relationship.

When her young son reached out and took her hand in his, her heart broke anew for Justin. What that must've been like to hear... She'd known for a week that Emmitt was angry about their relationship. Unbeknownst to Justin, he'd caught them kissing late one night when they thought the boys were asleep. It had been a briefly passionate kiss that had completely terrified the little boy. She still couldn't understand exactly why. But after Justin had left for the night, she'd stepped into the boys' room and had found Emmitt awake. And seething. Since then, she'd tried to be very careful how she acted around Justin, wanting to give him some time to accept the relationship.

But after tonight, it seemed like he'd never accept Justin as her new husband. As a new father. If that was the case, maybe what happened tonight was for the best. A clean break, while painful, would be easier to recover from in the long run.

She'd learned to live without Andrew. She would just have to learn to live without Justin as well.

Chapter Seventeen

To Emma, the following two weeks felt like they lasted an eternity. If moving on after Andrew's death had been agony, getting over a very-much-alive Justin felt like torture. Knowing he was within reach - just a phone call away - yet she couldn't have him. She'd really made a mess of things.

The first few days when he didn't come by, Will cried and cried, asking after him over and over. But when Emma explained that Justin wouldn't be coming over again for awhile, she wasn't prepared for her little son's anger.

And boy, was Will angry with his Mama! He'd only just started speaking to her again within the last couple days.

Ironically, the one person for whom she'd distanced herself from the man she loved, had only last week - merely one week after that horrible night - had a change of heart. Emmitt had actually *apologized* to her for his attitude and for hurting Justin!

This morning, she'd left the kids with their Aunt Allie so she could take her time at the grocery store. Who knew that after children, a trip to the grocery store alone could feel like a mini vacation?

She was wandering mindlessly up and down the aisles, not really paying too much attention to those around her, when she heard someone call her name. She snapped to attention and threw a glance at the people around her--her gaze landing on the priest from the hospital. What was his name?

"Mrs. Darcy, it is you. You look very different than you did the last time I saw you," he said warmly. "How have you been doing since your husband's death?"

Tears instantly started pricking the backs of her eyes and she swallowed, desperately trying to keep control.

"About as well as you could expect. Perhaps the biggest change for me is that I had a daughter in February."

His eyebrows rose in surprise. "That must've been quite a shock. To find yourself newly widowed and pregnant as well?"

The burning intensified. "You have no idea, Father." What was this guy's name?!

"Please, call me Ben."

"All right, then."

"And the rest of your family? How are they adjusting to a new family member?"

At the mention of a new family member, even though the priest clearly was referring to the boys' sister, Emma completely lost control. Tears rained down her cheeks in torrents. Right there in the middle of the dairy aisle.

Ben eyed her with concern, acting as if speaking to a weeping woman standing in the middle of a grocery store aisle were commonplace. In his line of work, maybe it was.

After several moments, Emma tried to regain control of her emotions. "I'm so sorry, Father. It's just been a rough few weeks, that's all."

"Oh? Anything you care to share?"

With very little encouragement, she blurted out the whole story, occasionally dabbing her nose with a napkin she'd found stuffed in her purse.

"Perhaps you'd like to come to my office tomorrow and talk about this further. It sounds like you've been keeping a lot inside lately. It would be very good for you to get some of that off your chest. Here's my card with my office phone number. Why don't you call me tomorrow morning and we'll see what we can do?" he added, patting her hand as she took the card from him.

She nodded. "Thank you, Father."

"Ben, remember?" he reminded her gently. "Less formal that way. Until tomorrow then, Mrs. Darcy."

"My name is Emma."

He smiled. "I hope the rest of your day is better, Emma."

As she watched him walk away, a peace stole throughout her and she sighed. Maybe he was right. Perhaps it *was* time for her to get some things off her chest.

For the next week, Emma met with Father Ben every morning. Between the various members of her family, she always managed to find someone to stay with the kids. But not one of them knew what she was really doing. To a person, they believed she was job hunting. The insurance money from Andrew's death had paid for the house, but she was quickly running through their savings on everyday expenses--something she knew was unwise. Especially in this market. And so, she'd decided shortly after the breakup that she needed to find a job. The thought of being away from her children was extremely painful, but as both mother *and* father, it was also necessary.

What her family was unaware of was that she already had a job lined up. Noelle had helped her get a position doing clerical work at her sister Adrienne's travel agency. She was to start the end of August. Damaged in a heavy wind storm last month shortly after the holiday, the building had needed some major repairs done before the agency could reopen. While she didn't necessarily feel comfortable about the lie, she reassured herself she'd tell them about the job after just a few more counseling sessions.

She and Father Ben had discussed many things during their discussions. From her shock about the pregnancy to her relationship with Justin. The last couple sessions had grown increasingly uncomfortable as he'd asked her some rather pointed, probing, questions.

Particularly about her feelings for Justin and an unresolved guilt he believed she still harbored.

Questions better left unasked, as far as she was concerned.

To her chagrin, however, he picked up the threads of their last unpleasant conversation and began again. "Are you praying?"

"Am I praying? What kind of question is that? I'm a Christian, Ben, of course I pray."

He eyed her for several seconds, his brow furrowed. "I'm talking about more than 'bless this meal' or 'be with my children today' kind of prayers, Emma."

She frowned. "What kinds of prayers are you talking about then?"

"The kind where you talk to God about your anger and unforgiveness."

"Unforgiveness?" she whispered. Where was he going with this?

"Yes, unforgiveness. Dear one, have you ever forgiven the men for their part in your husband's death?"

"For their part in my husband's death?" she repeated vehemently. "They are the *reason* he is dead!"

He steepled his fingers, peering at her over the tops of them. "I'm going to take that as a no."

"You're darn right I haven't forgiven them!" she exclaimed angrily, forgetting for a moment whom she was talking to. Remembrance flushed her face scarlet. "Sorry."

"Are you happy, Emma? Do you have true joy in your heart and life?"

His abrupt change of direction caught her off guard. What kind of question was that? Was she happy? Of course not! Hadn't he been listening over the last week?

"How can you expect to be happy if you stubbornly cling to the anger in your heart? It's like a cancer in the body, my friend. God wants to fill your heart with His joy and peace. But you have to let Him. He can't put joy in an angry heart. He can't put peace in a hard heart full of unforgiveness. I believe the best way for you to find peace and joy is to let go of your bitterness and forgive the men who are responsible for Andrew's death. And this may sound extreme, but I believe God would have you do this in person."

Her eyes widened in shock and her face drained of all color. Without a word, she jumped to her feet and raced out the door. In the parking lot, she sat behind the wheel of her van for several minutes taking deep breaths to calm her racing heart. The mere suggestion of seeing the men again stimulated a major adrenaline rush throughout her body and she had the strongest urge to run.

But actually *forgiving* them?

He asked the impossible.

Chapter Eighteen

For the next ten days, Emma thought of little else than Father Ben's suggestion that she go to the prison and forgive the men responsible for her husband's death. She tried desperately to think of another way to get that promised joy and peace, as peace was seriously lacking in her life at the moment.

Besides the priest's ridiculous suggestion, her boys were in anguish over Justin's departure from their lives. Emmitt had truly believed his apology would make everything the way it was before and his beloved friend could return to them. If only it were that easy. When the days stretched on with no calls or visits from Justin, the boys became increasingly despondent. Only last night, her oldest son had wailed at bedtime that it was all his fault and that Justin wasn't there because he was angry with Emmitt. She'd tried repeatedly to explain that neither of the boys had done anything to drive their friend away, but they couldn't seem to get the idea out of their heads.

It was all reaching a head for her. Something had to change soon or else she would bust.

"Okay, God. If I go to the prison will You leave me alone?"

My daughter. I know you by name. I numbered the hairs on your head and the days of your life. I have ordered your steps if you will but follow Me. I will never leave you alone.

"I'm so tired of running."

My yoke is light. Seek after Me, my daughter, and you will have rest.

She broke down and cried. In her mind, she pictured a giant boulder rolling off her shoulders and she felt more at peace than she had in months. She also knew just what she needed to do next.

The next morning, she called Joe. His response, while exactly what she'd expected, only made her strangely more determined.

"You're not family, Emma. And as such, you can't just go to the prison and expect them to let you see the men. There are steps involved. Time-consuming steps," he added angrily.

"Listen to me carefully, Joe. This isn't just a whim. I didn't wake up this morning and say, 'Hey, I think I'd like to visit the men who killed my husband.' I wouldn't be doing this in the first place if I didn't feel strongly led to. And if God really *is* leading me to do this, don't you think He can clear away any red tape in front of me?"

There was a pause and then a long, frustrated sigh. "If you are bound and determined to do this, Em, I suppose I could make some calls. I happen to know the judge who heard the case. Maybe he can grease some wheels for you. I'll get back to you later, okay?"

"Thank you."

"I still think this is a bad idea."

"I know. And I appreciate you helping me despite your misgivings."

He snorted. "Misgivings, indeed," he muttered under his breath and hung up the phone.

Two hours later, he called back. She had miraculously been cleared to visit the younger of the two men--the accomplice. The other one, when asked if she could see him, had been belligerent and had flatly refused. The visitation was scheduled for first thing the next morning.

Emma was still petrified at the thought of facing even this man. But now that the visit was a certainty, she continued to feel an overwhelming peace filling her heart and mind.

What would she say to the man? She never imagined she'd be in this situation to begin with. As she'd said to Joe, if God was leading her to do this, He would have to give her the words to say.

Because she was in completely uncharted territory.

The next morning, Joe surprised her by showing up at her door just as she was about to leave. Noelle had offered to baby-sit, as Emma hadn't wanted to tell her family members where she was going, or what she'd be doing, quite yet.

"So you're still determined to do this, huh?"

She nodded.

"Then I'm coming with you," he stated, taking up a stance in front of her, feet spread apart and arms crossed at his chest--a position she and Noelle had nicknamed the policeman stance. Thick sunglasses blocked his eyes from view, but she could only imagine what they'd express to her if she could actually see them.

"If you insist," she conceded with a shrug. Truth be told, she was actually relieved to have him along. Not that anything would ever happen, of course. Regardless, even unarmed, *nobody* messed with Joe---who, prior to becoming a policemen, had served in the military. He was massive. She always felt like a tiny bug in comparison to him.

They made the drive to the small prison on the outskirts of town without speaking to one another. To fill the silence, Joe played 80s rock music to the point of blaring in loudness. The hard beat jarred, but considering his present mood, it was far better than receiving a lecture, something she knew he was just itching to do.

A guard was awaiting their arrival, and he quickly led them through many locked doors to a small visiting room, currently empty of other people. Emma hadn't known quite what to expect. But picnic tables spread throughout the room was not it. Her only exposure to prison was what was shown on television. The guard indicated that she choose one of the tables and sit down, which she did. Joe immediately moved into place just behind her, so close that she could've leaned back into him if she'd wished, and resumed his policeman stance.

She'd barely had a chance to school her thoughts when a door to her right opened and two more guards brought the man in. They seated him at the table across from her, then chained his arms and legs to special slots on the table. This action momentarily terrified her and, in a panic, she rose and looked at the door she'd come through.

That's right. He's clearly too dangerous. Think of your children--what if something happened? You really should go.

The other voice was back, making perfect sense as usual.

She threw one leg over the bench seat, thoroughly intending to leave. Joe grasped her elbow in assistance.

Wait, My daughter! Look at this man chained to the table. What can he do to you when I am near?

She froze, one leg on either side of the bench, and, seemingly against her will, felt her eyes drawn down to the man before her.

His head bowed low, shoulders stooped in defeat. Just at that moment, he raised his eyes to meet hers. She peered into their hollow, empty depths and her heart broke. Mirrored within this man's soul, she could see a glimpse of herself and how empty she'd become over the last year.

It was then that she recognized the other voice for who and what it was. Satan's. He didn't want her to find joy or peace--didn't want to bring either of those things to this man in front of her. Suddenly, she knew exactly what to say.

With fresh determination, she turned and regained her seat. Without a word, Joe resumed his former position at her back, but this time, he lightly rested a hand on her shoulder. As if to make clear that no one would be allowed to hurt her as long as he was there.

"What is your name?" she asked.

He looked down again, refusing to meet her eyes. "Zach. Zach Nicholls."

"Before, I wasn't quite sure what I would say when I saw you. But now I know."

He flinched as if expecting the worst.

"May I tell you a story, Zach?"

He nodded, eyes still lowered.

"I was very angry with you and your friend for the longest time. There were quite a few things I wanted to say to you both at the trial, but it seems God wouldn't let me. At the time, it only frustrated and angered me more. But now...well, I think I understand why. I would've poured out my anger and hatred on you both for your part in my husband's death. Instead, God wants me to tell you how much He loves you. That He's been watching you throughout your whole life, waiting for you to turn to Him. Even now, after what you've done, He still loves you and wants you for His own. Our government has decided it's right that you pay a price for your crimes. But He wants you to know that His Son paid the ultimate price for your sins, through death on a cross. He who had done no wrong willingly paid the price for those of us who have.

"We - you, me, all of us - rightfully deserve to die for our stubbornness and selfishness. For our sins against a Holy God. Yet His Son, Jesus, paid that price for us so we might be free. He is willing and waiting to forgive you for your sins against Him. All you have to do is ask.

"Zach, God also wants me to say this as well," she paused, reaching out and touching his hand. At her gentle touch, his eyes shot upwards to hers. "I forgive you for your part in my husband's death."

For a split second, there was complete silence in the room. The guards as well as Zach were clearly shocked by her freely spoken forgiveness. Then, the convicted man bowed his head again as great, heaving sobs tore through his body. Never before had she seen another man cry like that. He cried as if his very heart were being ripped in two.

Once the words were spoken, joy unspeakable filled her heart to bursting and she felt the greatest peace that she'd ever felt before in her life.

Thank You, Lord, for filling me with Your peace and joy. Forgive me for my stubbornness and angry heart. Forgive me for refusing to obey Your leading sooner. And above all, Lord, forgive me for putting others before You. I see now that You are all I need.

As you did for this man, my daughter, so I do for you. You are forgiven, and I will be with you always.

Just before she and Joe left, the young man met her eyes once more and whispered a broken "Thank you". It was enough.

Later, as she talked about the morning with Father Ben, she couldn't help wishing Justin were there so she could share it him as well. It was the one negative part of the experience for her. More than ever, she found herself missing their friendship, wishing she could talk to him.

But that was clearly not to be. Her boys may have accepted him into their lives, but Joe and Beth definitely hadn't. Despite her newfound relationship with God, or maybe because of it, she was unwilling to stir up strife within her family in order to pursue a relationship nobody else wanted.

No, now it was time to focus on her family and her new faith in Jesus. If she and Justin were meant to be together, God would have to bring it about in His own timing, for she was too battle weary to continue fighting for something that brought so much pain to others.

Even if that meant sacrificing her own heart and staying away from Justin.

Chapter Nineteen

Mid-August

Once the children were in bed, Emma realized that she could no longer put off the one task she'd been avoiding for some time. As much as she dreaded it, and as tempting as the thought of lounging in front of the TV was, she knew it was past time to put some semblance of order to the corner of her closet where she'd stashed Andrew's stuff. She was quickly running out of room and was heartily tired of piling her own things on chairs around the room. Especially when there was perfectly adequate closet space to use. *If* she moved his things to the garage, that is.

She worked for about an hour, boxing up the clothing to be given to Goodwill. Next, she pulled out the three boxes of papers and documents she'd removed from his office at the high school. Most of it could be thrown away or recycled.

At the bottom of the last box, she discovered an envelope with her name printed in Andrew's neat handwriting and frowned. How had she overlooked this? She waited for the familiar ache at the sight of his writing, but it didn't come. Her counseling sessions with Father Miller had really been helping her work through the lingering guilt and depression.

May 16

My Darling Emma,

It may seem a little strange that I'm writing this now. But, for some reason, God has really been speaking to me about this for the last couple weeks. I'm not entirely sure why, as I don't plan on leaving you and joining Him anytime soon. We both know, however, that we don't always get to decide when He brings us Home, do we?

And so, my darling, I wanted to take this opportunity to tell you just how much you mean to me. You are my best friend and have always been. The day you first told me you'd fallen in love with me, I felt like the luckiest man in the world. Even after all this time, I still can't believe that such a sweet, loving, intelligent, and gorgeous woman could ever love me.

Emma, I will never forget how beautiful you looked on our wedding day. Your lovely face was radiant, as if you'd swallowed the sun. You absolutely took my breath away, and still do to this day. I love to hold you in my arms and watch you sleep. You are beautiful, my love. Both inside and out.

The boys could not ask for a better mother. You are tender and gentle with them. It is obvious to one and all that you are in love with your precious babies. One day soon, I hope to give you the one thing you've been wanting, a little girl. Until then, I guess we'll just have to keep trying. And babe, the trying part is something I look forward to with great anticipation.

Emma, my darling, if something happens to me, and we're not able to grow old together, I don't want you to remain alone. It breaks my heart to think of you suffering. Alone. Trying to raise our children by yourself. You were meant to love and be loved. Therefore, please promise me that, no matter what anyone else thinks, if you're able to meet and fall in love again (regardless of how soon this occurs), you'll let yourself love again. Don't worry about what our families and friends say. As long as you and the boys are ready to move on, please promise me that you will. You know you don't owe it to me to remain single, and you don't need to follow anyone else's idea of a proper grieving period, either. If your heart says you're ready, and God leads you to a man who will love you and our children as much as I do, then I give my blessing. Wholeheartedly.

197

If this happens, Emma, and our families give you any grief about it, please let them read these words so that they know you are acting according to my express wishes.

God willing, this will never be necessary, and this letter will remain with the other information in my will. But if He wills it otherwise, I want you to be happy and loved.

All my love,
Andrew

Emma glanced briefly at the date of the letter and gasped, the sheet of paper fluttering out of her hands. He'd written it on their wedding anniversary! The pieces came together in a rush. The week before their anniversary, he'd been more distracted than ever. At the time, he'd seemed almost...sad as well. Could it be? Could it be that he'd somehow sensed what was coming? It certainly explained the tenderness he'd shown her from the day of their anniversary through the day he'd died. With his busy school schedule, both at the high school and with his Master's work, they'd not had much interaction as a couple, having instead become roommates merely sharing space in the same house.

But since then, it had been more like their newly married days all over again. Even now, she cherished the renewed intimacy they'd found. After all, Andrea was a product of that intimacy.

She stretched out on the bed and reread the letter, appreciation for her compassionate husband swelling her heart. He must've placed it in his desk drawer, intending to bring it home and place it with the other paperwork, but forgot.

With a jolt, she lurched to a sitting position. Andrew had meant for her to find this *months* ago! Not a year after this death. If she had found this when he'd meant her to, things might've gone differently with Justin.

All of her reasons for staying away from the man she loved melted away like ice cream left in the sun. Emmitt's despondent behavior without Justin the last month was a confirmation that the little boy had certainly had a change of heart and was ready for the man who'd won all of their hearts to become a permanent member of the family.

And those friends and family members she was afraid wouldn't approve? Most had expressed an interest in seeing her enter the dating world again. As for Joe and Beth... Well, she was not naive enough to believe Andrew's best friend and mother would readily accept Justin in Andrew's place, at least not for a long time to come. Was it really worth staying away from him for just a couple people? Especially knowing what Andrew's wishes were on the matter?

Determination propelled her off of her bed and down the hall to find her cell phone. It rang just as she located it.

It was Aaron.

"Em, what are you doing?" her brother asked breathlessly. Due to the racket in the background, he was practically yelling into the phone to be heard.

"What? Aaron, what kind of greeting is that? Where are you, anyway?"

"Denver."

"What are you doing there? Are you and Jules on a date or something?"

"Is there someone you can call who will come stay with the kids for awhile?" he asked sternly, ignoring her questions.

"You're really starting to scare me, Aaron. What's going on?"

"I don't have time for this, Emma! Is there someone you can call or not?"

"Yes. I-I guess I can call Allie or Beth. Or mom. Why?"

"There's been an accident. You need to come to the hospital here right away," he said flatly.

Dear God, not again! "Who?" she asked, although in her heart, she knew. *Justin.*

"It's Justin," he confirmed, forcing a gentler tone into his voice.

Hearing him say the words sent her heart plummeting. Sheer terror began to take hold. "I'll call you as soon as I'm on the way."

"Are you sure you should drive? Maybe I'd better send a cab for you."

"Aaron, I'll be careful. I promise. I don't want to wait for a cab."

She didn't even wait for a response before disconnecting and pressing the speed-dial button for her in-laws' home. Once assured that Beth was on her way, Emma collapsed on the couch, tears streaking down her cheeks.

What if.....

God, not again. I can't do this again. Please don't take someone else away from me that I love. I need to tell him how I feel. That I don't care any more what people think. All I want is Justin, Lord. I want him to be my husband. I want him to be the kids' Daddy. Please protect him.

Be still and see what I shall do, daughter.

Peace flowed through her body like a warm blanket. She sighed, releasing any remaining tension. Somehow, no matter what happened, it would be all right. Finally, after a year of agony, and largely through her counseling sessions with Father Miller, she'd learned that whether or not she had a future with Justin, God was enough. She could lean on Him and no one or nothing else. Tremendous growth had come from their time apart. She'd recommitted her life to Christ, and had learned the freeing power of forgiveness in the most profound way that she longed to share with Justin. He just had to be okay--there was so much to say!

After repeated checks to the window, Emma finally saw lights flash through from the driveway. Beth was here.

Purse slung over her shoulder and keys in hand, she opened the door to a slightly frowning Beth. "Thanks for coming over, Beth," she gushed, jumbling the words together in one breath.

Instead of allowing her to pass, her mother-in-law gently grabbed her arm and halted her. "Just a minute, Emma. Do you really think this is a good idea?"

Emma just stared at her, desperately trying to choke back her anger. "As a matter of fact, Beth, I do. Now, if you'll excuse me, I need to go. The kids are down, and since Andrea's been sleeping through the night the last few days, I doubt she'll need any further attention. If she does, there are some bags of breast milk in the freezer you can thaw and warm up for her. And the box of baby cereal and jars of baby food are in the cupboard to the right of the sink." For the first time, Emma was glad for the part-time job she'd soon begin. In preparation for leaving her baby with the sitter, she'd been pumping her extra breast milk for the past few weeks. Of course, since she'd introduced Andrea to baby cereal last month and to simple baby foods this month, her daughter hadn't been nursing quite as often.

Once again, Andrew's mother prevented her from leaving. "Wouldn't it be better if you stayed here? I'm sure Justin's family is there already. Surely they don't need you as well and would understand you waiting for news here."

Emma yanked her arm out of Beth's grasp and ran down the hallway to retrieve the letter. At the door, she all but forced it into her mother-in-law's confused hands. "This is a letter I found today in Andrew's things. Read it," she pleaded, softening her tone. "Look. We don't have time to talk about this now. But I want you to know one thing, Beth. I loved your son very much. He'll always have a place in my heart."

"But?" she prompted, crossing her arms in front of her chest.

"Yes, you're right. There's a 'but'. I have fallen in love with a wonderful man who loves me in return. And he needs me right now."

Beth narrowed her eyes and glared at her daughter-in-law. "How could you do this to Andrew?"

Emma sighed dejectedly. "I'm not doing anything to Andrew. He's not *here*, and this is what *he* wanted. Please just read what your son had to say about all of this," she added, patting the letter in Beth's hands.

"Is everything all right here? Mom? Emma?" a deep masculine voice boomed, startling both of them.

In the intensity of their conversation, neither had noticed Joe walking up the sidewalk from the curb, where his Jeep was parked.

"Joe! What are you doing here?" Emma gasped. Immediately, she searched his face for signs that he'd overheard their conversation. Particularly the part about her being in love with Justin.

"Aaron called the station and asked me to give you a ride to the hospital. I told him that he was fortunate I hadn't gone home yet. But the truth of the matter is, I owe you."

"You *owe* me?" she repeated. "For what?"

"We all know what I jerk I was at the Fourth of July picnic - and even long before then - about your relationship with Justin. I've been doing a lot of thinking, Em, and I was wrong. As much as I'd prefer to have my best friend back, it's time for me to accept the fact that he's gone. And if I knew Andrew at all, I know that he would've wanted you to find a good man to love you and the kids. So who am I to stand in your way?"

Relief swept through her and she gave him a side-hug. "I have a good brother. And a *good* friend. Thank you for your support, Joe. It means a lot to me," she added, bestowing him with a grateful smile.

"Joseph, you really approve of this?" Beth's tone left little doubt as to how she felt.

He grasped both of her shoulders. "Yes, I do. Andrew was my best friend. But you and I both know he'd be very angry with us if he knew we were giving Emma a hard time about this. Justin's a nice guy, Mom. You just need to spend some time getting to know him. We all do. Besides, if Emma loves him, then he must be okay, right?"

"I don't know, Joe. I just don't know."

Emma took Beth's hand and squeezed it, nodding at the letter clutched tightly in her other fist. "Just read the letter. Please. And thanks for being here, Beth. I appreciate it more than you know. I'll call as soon as I can."

Once they were in the car and on their way to Denver, Emma was struck by an eerie sensation of deja vu. At least Joe hadn't picked her up in a squad car or in uniform. She took several deep breaths, trying to reclaim the peace she'd received earlier.

"Can you tell me anything about the accident? I mean, what happened?"

"After getting off the phone with Aaron, I called a buddy of mine who works in the Denver police department. Apparently, a drunk driver ran a red light and plowed right into the side of the car."

Emma closed her eyes. "Which side of the car, Joe?"

"Passenger's side."

She heaved a giant sigh of relief. "Oh, thank God. I was so afraid you were going to tell me it was the driver's side that was hit."

Joe glanced at her briefly, a worried expression marring his handsome face.

"What?"

"Emma, Justin wasn't the one driving."

Chapter Nineteen

The drive from Cancun to the hospital in Denver normally took about forty minutes. With the aid of his police lights, Joe made it in twenty. But it was the longest twenty minutes of Emma's life. Throughout the short ride, she alternated between boldly trusting in the Lord and succumbing to the crushing anxiety waiting to carry her away. Finally, just when she didn't think she could stand another minute in the car, Joe pulled the Jeep up to the covered drop-off and promised to find her once he'd found a parking space.

She raced through the sliding doors, throwing a glance around the room for a familiar face.

"Emma!" someone yelled above the din.

She halted mid-step and turned in the direction of the voice. It was Aaron. Another eerie sense of deja vu momentarily seized her, reminding her of the last time he'd met her in the entrance way of a hospital, but she forcefully tamped it down. She chose to believe that this situation would turn out differently. Unlike Andrew, Justin would walk out of these doors on his own very soon.

Aaron was jogging down an intersecting hallway toward her, a carrier with four tall styrofoam cups in hand, so she stood off to the side and waited for him. When movement just behind him caught her attention, she was startled to see another person frantically racing to keep up with her brother's long strides and frowned. Red hot jealousy flared. Izobel Sanders--what was *she* doing here?

"Good timing, Emma! I'd popped across the street to Starbucks for some coffee and ran into Izobel on my way back to the waiting room. If I'd known she was coming, I'd have gotten an extra coffee."

Izobel waved a manicured hand at him. "Please don't concern yourself, Aaron. I'm not much of a coffee drinker, anyway. I prefer to feed my caffeine addiction with cold carbonated beverages," she added with a slight grin.

Yeah. A diet *carbonated beverage.* Emma couldn't imagine the svelte Izobel willingly consuming sugar.

Aaron glanced around the room, evidently searching for someone, much as she'd done moments earlier. "Where's Joe?"

"He went to park the car. I'm sure he'll find us in a few minutes," she explained, anxious to be at Justin's bedside. And away from Izobel, if she had anything to say about it.

He grasped her elbow and squeezed gently, understanding her unspoken need. "This way, ladies."

"Have you seen him?" she queried hesitantly.

"Briefly. He's hurt pretty badly, Emma."

"How badly?" she whispered, barely hearing her own voice. She was shocked when a small hand slipped into hers. Glancing to the left, she met Izobel's tentative smile.

"Some fractured ribs and maybe some other broken bones. But those are the least of his problems. He's not regained consciousness since the accident. The doctors are concerned that there might be some swelling on his brain."

A wracking shudder swept through her and she pressed her other fist to her lips to stifle a sob. *Lord, please!*

"So where is he now?" Izobel asked, gently squeezing Emma's fingers.

"They were running tests on him when I got here. As banged up as he looked, it wouldn't surprise me if they haven't brought him up to a room yet."

"How's Mama holding up?"

Jealousy once again reared its ugly head. Izobel was calling Justin's mother *'Mama'*?! First he'd escorted her to the reunion last year, and now this. Just what kind of relationship did they have? Irrational fears began to surface. What if this woman was trying to steal him away from her? Emma began to realize that not once in the last year had he ever mentioned the exotic beauty, or why he was with her that night. But was that a good thing? Or not? She couldn't quite decide.

Aaron turned watery eyes on the women. "Not well. She's lost a son and her husband in the last six years. Justin's all she has left. And now this accident. She's really broken up about it."

Pangs of guilt wracked Emma. How selfish she was being! Justin's poor mother had gone through so much sorrow in the last several years. She certainly didn't need a jealous.... Her thoughts were brought to an abrupt halt. How was she to categorize her relationship? Just what was she to Justin and he to her? She knew what her feelings were for him, but what about his for her? The day of their fight, had she truly lost him for good? With a mental shake, she realized she was doing it again. Selfish. Justin was probably better off without her.

Just outside the doorway to the waiting area, Emma paused, remaining behind after both Aaron and Izobel started to walk through the doorway.

Glancing back at her, Aaron threw her a questioning glance. "What's the matter?"

"I'm not really sure this is a good idea. Justin and I..." she paused, trying to come up with the right words. "Justin and I aren't...well, we aren't really on speaking terms right now. I hurt him pretty badly a month ago. I'm not sure that his mother really wants to see me. I sure wouldn't," she quietly admitted, thoroughly dejected.

To her surprise, Izobel took her hand once more and squeezed it. "Emma," she began, waiting for the woman to meet her gaze. "Just whose idea do you think it was for you to come?"

"She's right, sis," Aaron confirmed, pulling her into a one-armed hug.

Inside the small room, Emma's eyes were drawn to a tall woman sitting with her leg propped up on a stool, a small bandage on the left side of her forehead, her neck in a brace, and her left arm in a sling. She'd only seen Justin's mother once before, but this woman bore little resemblance to the beautiful older woman she'd met.

Izobel raced to the woman's side and carefully sat in the chair next to her, careful not to bump her. "I'm so glad you're okay, Mama. Are you in pain?"

It *was* Justin's mother. What in the world had happened to *her*? In a rush, realization dawned. "You were the driver, weren't you, Mrs. Bennet?"

"Yes, I was. Izobel and Justin made reservations at my favorite restaurant here in the city and we were on our way to meet Iz when that drunk driver ran the light and hit us."

Emma refused to acknowledge the green monster knocking at her door. Not after she'd been treated so kindly just moments ago.

"Lynne, I'm so glad you two were in your car and not Justin's. At least your car has airbags."

"*Had* airbags, Aaron. I'm not sure there's anything salvageable in that mess. And yes. If it had to be one of our cars, I'm glad it wasn't his Daddy's 'Vette." She grimaced and shifted in her seat, trying to find a comfortable position.

"Do you really think you should be up and around, Mrs. Bennet? You look like you're pretty uncomfortable."

"Laying down in a bed or sitting up in a chair isn't gonna make one bit of difference, honey. Pain is pain. As long as I don't move - or breathe -" she added with a tight smile, "I'm all right. Besides, the doc gave me a little something for the pain. Once it kicks in, I ought to be fine."

"Has there been any word?" Aaron asked, taking the chair on the other side of her.

Emma felt awkward just standing around, but she didn't really know where to sit, either. A large part of her just felt out of place in the room with people who knew Justin's mother so much better than she did.

Just as Lynne Bennet was about to answer, the door opened and a doctor entered the room. "Mrs. Bennet, I'd like to talk to you about your son."

The poor woman's trembling pierced Emma's heart. *Lord, please don't take him away.*

"Is he going to be all right, Doctor?"

"That's hard to say, ma'am. He does have some bruised organs and a few fractured ribs, but there's no internal bleeding or damage. We suspected his leg and arm might be fractured as well, but miraculously, neither of them were. He does have some slight swelling on his brain, however, that we are going to closely monitor over the next several hours."

"Will there be any lasting damage, Doctor?"

"It's really too soon to tell. Once he emerges from the coma, we'll know more. I'm sorry I don't have better news for you."

She gave him a tremulous smile. "On the contrary. You've brought me the best news--my son is still with us. God is obviously watching over my boy."

"I think you may be right about that, ma'am. There's no other way to explain it than that. As for tonight, while there's a couch in Dr. Bennet's room, I doubt it would be very comfortable for you in light of your own injuries. I can make other arrangements for you within the hospital if you like."

"That would be wonderful, thank you. As much as I'd prefer to be in my own bed, I can't stand the thought of being so far away from my son."

"The young lady is welcome to use the couch in the room, if she'd care to. She's not technically family, but I think I can make an exception for a fellow doctor's girlfriend," he added, winking at Izobel. "Everyone else will have to wait in here, I'm afraid."

Izobel's face colored and her eyes shot over to Emma's. "No, I'm not..." she stammered.

Lynne Bennet smiled sweetly at both women before nodding toward Emma. "*This* is my son's girlfriend, Doctor."

His face flushed with embarrassment. "I'm sorry, I just assumed. As I said, ma'am," he said, turning to Emma. "You're welcome to stay with Dr. Bennet in his room if you'd like. I'll have one of the nurses escort you to your room, Mrs. Bennet. And if anything changes, I'll let you know right away."

Emma lowered her eyes to the floor and kept them there even after the doctor had left the room. She absent-mindedly reached for one of the coffees and wrapped her hands around it, allowing its warmth to seep through the cup into her cold fingers.

"As much as I'd love getting to know you a bit better, my dear, I'm really too tired and sore to talk much more tonight. Besides, I'm sure you'd rather be with my son."

She glanced up at Justin's mother and shrugged. "Maybe it's better if Izobel stays with him, Mrs. Bennet."

"First of all, I'd like you to call me Lynne," she gently corrected. "And secondly, I think it's only appropriate that the woman my son is in love with have that privilege."

Emma hung her head again. "But our fight... All those things I said to him. He can't really still be in love with me after that."

"If you really believe that, then you don't know him very well after all."

Hope infused her heart at hearing this. Lynne was right. He had loved her through some of the darkest months of her life when she was nothing but a bitter shell of herself. What was she so afraid of?

"Thank you," she whispered, bestowing Justin's mother with a radiant smile.

"You're welcome, honey. Now, go to him."

Emma impulsively pressed a kiss to the right side of Lynne's face before rushing down the hallway to find Justin's room.

The door to his room was slightly open. Cautiously, she peered around it to make sure the room was indeed empty. Taking one look at the man on the bed, her heart sank. He looked horrible! His head was wrapped in a thick bandage that covered every inch of his dark hair. More bandages peeked through over the top of his hospital gown from where his ribs had been wrapped. Despite his injuries, her eyes swept over his beloved countenance hungrily. It was hard to believe she hadn't seen him in a month! Her heart ached at the wasted time. If only she hadn't been such a coward. Wasn't he worth fighting for?

Yes. Most definitely yes.

There was a small couch on one wall of the room, directly beneath a window, with a hard chair adjacent to the bed. She tossed her purse onto the couch and quietly pulled the chair closer to the bed. Before sitting, she leaned over and tenderly kissed him, one hand caressing his whisker-roughened cheek.

"I love you, Justin Bennet. I never should've let you go that day. How can I live without you? You're like the air to me," she tearfully whispered, quoting a line from *A Walk in the Clouds*. Their local movie theater had aired the movie, while not new at the time, for Valentine's Day the year they briefly dated. In fact, Justin had taken her to see the movie for their third date. It was one of her favorite movie lines of all time. Certainly one of the most romantic, at any rate. "We belong together, and it's time for me to stop being such a coward about what people might say.

Besides. You told me a few months ago that you wanted to marry me. I'm still waiting for that proposal, my love."

Emma gently clasped his limp fingers in hers and slowly caressed each one, ending with a kiss upon the back of his hand.

"C'mon, baby. Wake up. I need you."

He was under water in a deep sea, no land or life preserver in sight. Something from the cold depths kept a firm grasp on his ankle, seeking to drag him down to join it. After what felt like hours of trying to break free, he was exhausted. A part of him longed to yield to the firm grip. But there was another part of him, however minuscule it was at the moment, that fought his body's instincts to give in.

Just when he felt the last vestiges of strength leaving his weary limbs, he caught the faint traces of a whispered voice murmuring, *"You're like the air to me."* The gentle voice filled him and strengthened him with a renewed vigor. It somehow gave him the will to keep fighting.

He was almost to the surface. Just a few more strokes and he'd be free of the crushing depths. His hand tingled, as if caressed with the barest of touches.

With one gasp for air, he surfaced.

There was no longer any water, only sweet-smelling air.

Slowly, he began to realize that it wasn't air, but a room with a bed. And he was lying on it. All he wanted was for that voice to fill him with its melodious sound again. The sweet air had cleared his mind somewhat and he realized he knew that voice. That scent.

It was Emma's.

Could it be? Dare he hope she was there with him? No matter their harsh words and hurt feelings. She was there. He knew it...she'd come.

He couldn't move or open his eyes. But that didn't matter. All that mattered was that she had come.

His Emma.

It seemed to her that his breathing changed to a more natural rhythm, as if he were merely sleeping and not in a coma. *Yes, Lord, help him fight his way back to us.*

With the realization that she could be here all night, she called the house to check on her children, hoping Beth would be willing to stay until she could return. If not, she'd have to call her parents. They'd come.

However, surprisingly, Beth reservedly assured her that she'd stay with the kids as long as necessary. She even offered to bring Andrea to the hospital in the morning so that Emma could nurse her if Justin hadn't awoken by then.

Stunned, yet strangely hopeful, Emma rested her chin on the bed railing and settled in for a long night. No matter how long it took, she would be here when he woke up. She had to be. There was so much to say.

And she didn't want to miss one moment.

Chapter Twenty

It was an excruciatingly long night. Emma had slept fitfully in the chair next to his bed, refusing to move even as far as the couch against the wall for fear that she'd miss something. As a result, she was stiff and sore, muscles aching that she hadn't even been aware of having.

She stood and stretched, then wandered around the room loosening sore muscles before using the bathroom and returning to Justin's bedside. Absentmindedly, she rubbed the back of her neck, wincing at the pain.

"Now there's a face," rumbled a familiar voice.

Heart racing, her eyes dropped to the man she loved.

And found him awake--smiling at her.

Legs suddenly weak, she collapsed onto the chair before bursting into tears.

His hand reached for hers on the railing. "What's this? Tears? I thought you'd be happy to see me."

She raised her eyes to his once more, and he sucked in a breath at the love he saw radiating from their depths.

"I was so afraid that I'd lose you, Justin. Just like I lost..." She couldn't bring herself to finish that thought.

He brought her fingers to his lips and kissed them tenderly. "I know, dearest. You don't have to say it. But I'm not planning on going anywhere. We were meant to be together, after all."

Despite his assurances, the tears refused to cease. Weren't tears cathartic at any rate?

"Kiss me," he announced suddenly.

She raised her head in uncertainty. Had she heard him correctly?

"You heard me, Emma. Kiss me."

"Your wish is my command, my love," she replied with a watery smile.

After lowering the bed railing closest to her, she rested her palms on either side of his head and lowered her face to his. Their kiss started out sweetly, tenderly. But when she started to pull away, his hand shot to the back of her head and held her lips to his, his fingers kneading the sore muscles of her neck while he deepened the kiss.

Between the passionate assault on her lips and his fingers kneading away all the tension in her neck, her insides liquefied. Just when she thought she couldn't stand on her own two feet a moment longer, he released her and pulled his face away from hers. She carefully regained her seat, never once removing her gaze from his.

"Was that the kiss of a man planning to leave you anytime soon?"

She shook her head.

"I wasn't sure I'd ever get the chance to do that again," he admitted huskily.

She reached down and caressed his cheek. "Me either."

"So what changed?"

"Andrew."

Confusion marred his handsome features. What did her dead husband have to do with her presence beside him? Maybe he'd hit his head harder than he'd thought; she couldn't have meant that.

"Last night I was cleaning out some of Andrew's things and found a letter he'd written to me before he died. In it, he talked about how he didn't want me to remain single. He wanted me to meet someone and remarry-- sooner, rather than later."

He exhaled softly. "Wow, Emma."

"But it wasn't just the letter, Justin. It only solidified something I'd known for a couple weeks. We belong together. It doesn't matter what anyone else thinks about our relationship."

His lips quirked into a half smile. "There are only four people's opinions that matter. Yours--of course," he added, his lips extending into a full-sized grin, "Emmitt's, Will's, and Andrea's. No one else's." His smile faded. "Dare I hope...has Emmitt changed his mind about us?"

She took his hand and kissed the back of it. "Yes."

A few tears snuck past his closed eyes and slid down his cheeks.

"And Will?"

"They both have been pestering me with questions several times a day: where are you, what are you doing, when are you coming back? But the one that almost killed me was, 'what did we do wrong, Mama?'"

She saw sympathy and pain mixed in his eyes as he raised them to hers. "Oh, Emma. To think the boys believe I haven't been there because of something they did breaks my heart."

Tears rained down her cheeks and she hastily brushed them away. "I know. I tried to explain to them that it was *my* fault you were gone. Not theirs."

"How did they respond to that?"

"Will was very angry with me for about a week. As for Emmitt...well, I think my son is wise beyond his years. He was very sad and thoughtful for several days. And then he actually apologized to *me* for his attitude about us. And for hurting you, as he knows he did."

He squeezed her hand. "Emma, I'm the one that should apologize for the way I handled that whole thing. I shouldn't have forced you to acknowledge our relationship. You clearly weren't ready and all I did was make things worse. I've kicked myself over and over again at my lack of patience. All that time I waited, for what? I'm sorry."

"There's nothing to forgive. I understood why you did it. Not that it made things any easier, but I understood nonetheless. And I think that as hard as it was, it's what needed to happen."

"How can you say that?"

"Because of what happened next. About a week after Emmitt's apology, I ran into Father Miller at the grocery store."

Justin's face again wrinkled in confusion. "Ben Miller? The priest from my hospital? I wasn't aware you even knew him."

She nodded. "The night of Andrew's death, after you took the family into that other room, I came to the waiting room looking for them. He was there reading the paper. We talked for a few minutes and he prayed for me and the family. He's the one who first told me about the reporters."

"And did he remember you when you saw him?"

"Yes. He asked me how things were going, and I broke down in tears right there in the middle of the dairy aisle."

"You didn't."

"Yup, sure did."

"What happened next?" he asked, a mixture of amusement and concern in his voice. He could very well picture that staid gentleman's response to Emma crying in the middle of the grocery store.

"He said that it was clear there were things I needed to sort through and asked if I'd be willing to come to his office the next day to discuss them. I met with him almost every day that first week, and then a couple times a week after that."

To say he was mildly surprised would've been an understatement. "Emma, you're not Catholic."

"I know, and so does he. But somehow, it doesn't matter. For some reason, the idea of talking to my pastor always filled me with dread. Not that he wouldn't have been able to help me. But he knew Andrew. Very well. I just couldn't stand the thought of talking to someone who knew both of us, or would pity me. Father Miller is an unbiased third party. We may not agree on theology, but he's had some really profound things to say nevertheless."

"Can you tell me about them?"

"Losing Andrew was the most painful thing that's ever happened to me. I can't even describe the pain associated with losing a spouse--especially in such a violent manner. Instead of continuously turning to God and pouring out my grief to Him, I ran to you for comfort, Justin. And you were a good friend to offer it to me. But I should've turned to God first. I made you my savior, and no matter how much I love you or how great you are, that is not rightfully your position."

He nodded his agreement and understanding.

"I was also so bitterly angry about the way Andrew died. Angry at the men responsible. Even angry at God for allowing it. So after months of ignoring my rightful Savior and nourishing my anger and hatred toward the men, it's little wonder I was so miserable.

"There's something else that Father Miller helped me recognize and come to terms with."

"What's that, sweetheart?"

She looked down and frowned. "It's very hard to admit to you, Justin, but I feel that it's important there be nothing but openness between us if we're going to make this work."

He squeezed her hand. "You know you can tell me anything, Emma, and I'll never think less of you."

"Father Miller helped me to finally realize what was *really* holding me back. That it wasn't strictly the timing of my feelings for you. It was guilt. You see, when I saw you for the first time the night of the reunion, it was like someone had kicked me in the gut."

"Well, yeah, naturally. You weren't expecting to see me."

She shook her head. "No, you don't understand. I was strongly attracted to you, like I was sixteen all over again. Happy married women should *not* have those types of feelings about other men. It's not like I was in love with you then or had romantic thoughts about us. But the sight of you that night definitely rekindled some of those old feelings. I know nothing would've happened, and I also know that Andrew would've understood and forgiven me. What really got to me, I think, was knowing I had inappropriate thoughts about another man while Andrew was going through all of that and needed me the most."

"Oh, Emma. I had no idea."

"Just like Andrew will always own a piece of my heart, you've always owned your own piece as well."

He nodded. Her revelation, while it greatly surprised him, made complete sense and helped him to gain a better understanding of her actions over the past few months, her reluctance to tell others about their relationship in particular.

But she wasn't finished with the shocking revelations. "There's one more thing Father Miller and I discussed. He said that until I was able to really forgive the men responsible for Andrew's death, I would never be free of the anger and bitterness. His suggestion was for me to actually go to the prison and see and forgive them face to face. Two days ago, I went to the prison and met with the accomplice. I looked him right in the eyes and told him that I forgive him."

Nothing in the world could've prepared Justin for that. He stared at her, stunned completely speechless.

She favored him with a smile. "I know, shocking, huh? But, Justin. Oh, the relief and peace I felt afterward! The anger is gone. The bitterness is gone. I am *free*!" Tears sparkled in her shining eyes.

"Praise Jesus!" he murmured, his own eyes filling with tears. "Emma, you have no idea how long I've prayed for that for you. What was his response?"

"He was shocked, very much like you were. And then he laid his head on the table and cried like a baby. I don't think I've ever seen a grown man sob like that before. Especially one with his criminal background. Then, just before our time ended, he raised his eyes to mine and said 'Thank you.' That was all. But I received a phone call yesterday asking if I'd be willing to go back again. He wants me to go back."

"Do you think you will?"

"Definitely. I have a strong burden for this man, Justin. I can't explain why. Joe thought I was absolutely nuts when I told him I wanted to go the first time. He yelled at me something fierce! But then after he saw how insistent I was about it, he relented and drove me himself. He did, however, insist upon sitting with me in the visiting room. I can't say he was quite as moved as I was by the man's response, but he didn't try to talk me out of going back. I think he realizes God is working in that man's life."

"Would you like me to go with you next time?"

She smiled. "No. This is something I need to do for me. But I'd love for you to pray for him. His name is Zach."

"Then pray I will."

She leaned over him and kissed his lips, shivering with pleasure when he kissed her back.

"I wish I could hold you in my arms, but it hurts to move. What exactly is wrong with me?" he asked with a frown.

"You have a few fractured ribs."

"Ugh. No wonder. And my mom? Is she okay?"

Emma nodded. "She's pretty sore as well, but nothing's broken."

"Thank God."

"I suppose I should let everyone know you're awake."

"Everyone?"

"Oh, the hospital provided your mom with a room she could stay in so she'd be nearby. And last I checked, Aaron and Izobel were camped out in the waiting room."

Hearing the funny way she pronounced Izobel's name, he peered at her sharply. Was she actually *jealous*? A huge grin nearly split his face.

"I know what you're thinking, Justin Bennet, and it's not funny."

"You're *jealous*! Of Izobel!"

She glared at him. "Again, not funny."

"Oh, it most certainly is. Especially if you consider the fact that she is practically a sister to me."

"I doubt you'd take someone who is practically a sister to a reunion or invite her to your mother's birthday dinner, Justin," she replied frostily.

"Honey, what you don't know is that she was engaged to my brother. Even all this time after his death, she's still madly in love with him. She's sworn she'll never find anyone to replace Matt. As far as me taking her to her reunion goes, I was fulfilling a last request of my brother's. He asked me to look out for her and try to help her any way I could. And standing in for him as her date for the reunion was something I know would've made him very happy."

Her face fell. Good grief. Was she really so childish as to give in to jealousy over apparently *nothing*? And even if Izobel's feelings for Justin had been different, didn't she owe it to him to trust that his feelings for her were true and faithful? "I'm sorry, Justin. I should've trusted you."

"Yes. You should have," he replied, then allowed another huge smile to spread across his face. "But it is awfully flattering to know you were jealous."

She favored him with another kiss.

"Did I ever tell you that I made a similar promise to your husband?"

"What? You did? When?"

He took her hand in his once more and repeated the conversation from that fateful night, all the while gently caressing the back of her hand.

"Do you think he knew what would happen by asking you to look out for me and the kids?" she asked, completely surprised.

"I do. And I think that, somehow, he knew it would be a welcome responsibility for me. That I already loved you and would continue to love you. Who knows? Maybe God laid it on his heart to do that."

It was now Emma's turn for speechlessness. To think her husband had been matchmaking with his last breath. And that letter written a few weeks before... God must have indeed prompted all of it. A thrill shot through her at the knowledge that her relationship with Justin was right. Was God's will for all of them.

"Maybe I should get the doctor now."

He nodded. "As much as I'd love to have some more time alone with you, I know my mom will be anxious to see me awake. And I want to hear how long the doctors think I'll be stuck in here. After all, I've got a life to live with the woman I love. And I don't want to lose a minute."

Their gazes met and she smiled again before going in search of the medical staff and their friends and family.

Once she was gone, he whispered prayers of gratitude for all the Lord had done in her heart and life - in both of their hearts and lives - during their month apart. He had brought healing to them both.

One day soon, he would tell her about the healing he had found throughout these last months with Andrea. He still grieved the fact that he'd never had the opportunity to know and raise his child. But loving Emma's children and trusting in Jesus had eased that potent ache in his heart. He knew that his child awaited him in heaven and he looked forward to spending eternity getting to know his son or daughter. In the mean time, he would be the very best father he could be to Emma's children.

And soon, Lord willing, to *their* children.

With that thought, his mind raced with ideas and possibilities for what would come in the next several months.

A proposal.

A wedding.

A long life with the woman and children he loved.

He was a blessed man.

Lynne Bennet stayed with her son long enough to reassure herself that he really and truly was going to be all right, then Izobel drove her back to her house to rest. Before the ladies left, Emma took the younger woman aside and thanked her for being such a great friend to Justin and his mother. And then she apologized for being such a jealous fool.

Izobel merely hugged her. "It's all right. Believe me, I had my moments with Matty the last time he came home on leave. You can imagine how handsome he looked with that close hair cut, tanned features, and thick muscles--all in a sharp uniform. He had ladies swarming all over him!"

Emma was about to remark that surely a woman as gorgeous as Izobel should've had nothing to be jealous of but stopped herself before she could say it. Jealousy was jealousy regardless of looks. Glancing again at Justin, she remembered how strikingly similar he and his brother had been, and she certainly understood that attraction.

They'd not been gone five minutes when Justin received yet another visitor--one that greatly surprised both of them.

Emma was in the bathroom freshening up a bit when she heard Justin's shocked exclamation, "Mrs. Darcy!" For a split second, she thought he was being funny and was actually calling to her.

Until she heard her mother-in-law's voice.

Throwing open the door, she spied Beth standing just inside the door to the room, holding Andrea in her arms. With a tiny squeal, Emma plucked her daughter out of Beth's arms and hugged her to her chest. "Oh, my sweet girl, Mama missed you!"

Andrea cooed back at her mother, gleefully burying her fists in Emma's hair.

Suddenly feeling a wetness on her breasts, Emma realized she was hours past Andrea's usual feeding time. She'd been growing increasingly uncomfortable as the morning went on; Beth had arrived just in time. She sat down on the couch, pulled her nursing cover from the diaper bag, and started to nurse her daughter.

"How are the boys this morning, Beth? Have they been too worried about where I was?"

Beth glanced from Emma to Justin and back. "No," she replied slowly. "No, they haven't been necessarily worried about you, dear. They have, however, been very concerned about *you* Justin," she added, looking back at him without quite meeting his eyes.

"Me? They've been worried about me?" he asked, his voice tinged with hope.

She nodded. "When they heard I was bringing Andrea here for a few minutes, they insisted I bring these as well," she said, opening her bag and pulling out two pieces of construction paper folded in half.

He gingerly reached for them. The first one he opened was Will's. Above a bunch of scribbles, one of the adults had written, "Feel better soon! I love you, Daddy!" Justin's heart turned over with love to see that. He could just hear the adorable little boy calling him Daddy. Next, he opened the second card with greater hesitation. What would this one contain? Emmitt had made his feelings quite clear a month ago.

Instead, a beautifully drawn picture of the three of them playing football together in the back yard greeted him. And at the top a simple, "I love you" written in Emmitt's crooked scrawl. He didn't even attempt to fight the tears that suddenly clogged his vision, but allowed them to pour freely down his cheeks.

Emma watched him from across the room, tears of relief and joy wetting her own cheeks.

"I can imagine what that means to you both," Beth said huskily. "And it brings me to the reason I came." She sat next to Emma on the couch and took one of her hands, clasping it between both of hers. "After you left last night, I was still pretty angry," she admitted with a long sigh. "There's really no excuse for my behavior, but I felt justified somehow. Like I was defending my son's memory.

"Anyway, after awhile, my curiosity got the better of me and I read the letter. After I read it, I didn't really know what to think. So, I called John and asked him to come over so that we could talk about it. You may be surprised to hear this, Justin, but my husband's been your biggest supporter. He was the one who finally made me realize that life hadn't stopped with Andrew's death--as much as it still feels that way at times. All I've been doing, Emma, was pushing you away. I know you loved my son and will *always* love him to some degree. Nothing can really ever take that away, can it?"

"Nor would I want to," Justin interjected gently. "I'd hate to think that I took his place in her heart, or in the kids' hearts for that matter. All I'm asking is that they make a little room for me."

Beth rose, walked over to Justin, and kissed his forehead. "Thank you."

Emma finished feeding her daughter, then held her up and rained kisses on her belly, drawing delighted giggles from the baby. At the sound of a soft sigh, her eyes shot to Justin's face and her heart went out to him. He was gazing wistfully at her daughter, longing evident in every line of his face. Emma rose, holding Andrea to face him.

Very tenderly, he reached out a finger and traced the baby's soft cheek, then ran his hand over her silky hair. "Hello, my little angel. I've missed you."

Andrea smiled at him, reaching with her little hand for his.

When Emma lowered her closer, he brushed her forehead with his lips, inhaling that delightful baby smell. He'd definitely missed this little girl more than he could've imagined. She may not be of his body, but she was his daughter in every way that mattered. "As soon as I get all better, we're gonna have a date. Just you and me."

The baby babbled at him with another smile as if she truly understood what he'd said.

He returned her smile as Emma lifted her back up and turned her in her arms. After pressing a few more kisses to her baby and giving her one last, long hug, she handed her to Beth. Amazingly, Andrea didn't cry, but gave both her mother and Justin one last big smile.

"I left a bag of extra clothes and a few toiletry items on the couch," Beth replied, reaching with her other arm for the diaper bag. "Would you like me to stay with the kids a few more days?"

Emma flashed her a grateful smile. "Yes, if that wouldn't be too much trouble."

"Of course not. John and I will enjoy a little extra time with them. If you'll give me a call later, we can get a schedule figured out. After all, there weren't many bags of prepared breast milk in the freezer, so I suspect you'll need someone to bring this little one again tomorrow morning."

At the mention of the stored breast milk, Justin shot Emma a confused look. Why would she need to pump and store her milk? Sure, keeping a couple feedings' worth on hand was always a good idea, but more than that was really only necessary if she planned to return to work.

He sucked in a breath and cringed, the movement sore on his ribs. She was planning on returning to work. Something they'd talked at length about her *not* doing, as she greatly preferred remaining at home with her children while they were young. He realized, perhaps for the first time, that she'd truly believed their latest breakup to be permanent. He hadn't realized until now just how close he'd come to losing her.

What a miracle it was, then, that she was standing here beside him. *With* the support of her family and friends. He determined anew that he would concentrate fully on a total recovery. The sooner the better. Because once he was recovered, he would not lose one single day before making Emma his. Then she would never again have to worry about providing for her little family, as it would forever be *his* responsibility.

And it was one he greatly looked forward to.

"Do you ever wonder what would've happened if we hadn't broken up? Y'know, the first time," she asked, completely catching him off guard.

Justin looked up to find that she'd returned to her perch in the chair next to his bed.

"Where did that come from?" he asked with a chuckle.

She shrugged. "I dunno. Just something I think about sometimes. A lot more lately, actually."

"I'll admit that it's crossed my mind a time or two."

"We might've been married a long time by now."

He nodded slowly, trying not to move too much. The pain had returned in intensity. "Yes. But if you hadn't married Andrew, there would be no Emmitt, Will, or Andrea."

She sat back in her chair, digesting this new information. She hadn't thought about it quite like that. No matter the agony of losing Andrew, or her feelings for Justin and her desire to be his wife, she would not change a thing. She had deeply loved her husband and best friend. "I am head over heels in love with you, Justin Bennet. As much as I love you, however, I would not trade my time with Andrew for anything. Especially since, as you pointed out, my three wonderful children are a result of our love for each other."

He smiled at her tenderly. "I know, sweetheart. It's only because of a tragedy that you're even here by my side today. I'll never forget that. I meant what I said to Beth. I don't want to take Andrew's place in your hearts--have *never* wanted that. Am I sorry it had to happen? Yes, of course. But I'm also thankful for this chance to spend our lives together. There is not one thing I would change about our history. You were worth waiting for, Emma."

After a brief kiss, she brushed the hair off his forehead, then framed his face between her hands with a half smile. "We're awfully mushy today, aren't we."

"We have to make up for lost time," he whispered with a slight grimace.

"Didn't the nurse give you some more pain medication?" she asked, concern wrinkling her forehead.

"Yes. It just hasn't kicked in yet. I think I've been a bit overzealous in my movements."

"Then, you'll just have to lie quietly. And no kissing," she teased.

He glowered at her. "No kissing? I think I'd rather endure the pain."

"Okay, *less* kissing, then. But no more sudden movements. If you want me to kiss you, then just tell me," she suggested, rubbing his forehead soothingly.

"Like now?"

Emma grinned before lowering her lips to meet his. His light kiss was further evidence of just how much pain he was in. Gone was the passion from earlier this morning.

She continued rubbing his forehead, hoping it would have the same calming effect it often did on her children. It did. In a matter of moments, his eyes slid shut and his body relaxed.

Once she was sure he was asleep, she rose and stretched out on the couch. She planned to sleep when he slept so that she could spend every waking minute with him. They still had much to discuss. But there was plenty of time for that.

All the time in the world.

Chapter Twenty-One

Mid-September

Justin was awake long before his alarm clock sounded. Even then, he took his time rising, savoring the plans made for today. After all, it was a day he'd long anticipated. A day he'd prayed for. Lived for.

Today was the day he'd ask Emma to marry him.

Unable to stay still a moment longer, he carefully eased his bulk out of bed. He'd been home from the hospital about three weeks, but his ribs still pained him after making sudden or jerky movements. And although he'd returned to work last week, his boss insisted that he merely handle surgical consultations for the time being in order to give his body time to fully recover. As a surgeon, he stood in what was often one position for hours at a time. It was a profession that required him to be at his best. Another several weeks or so, and he'd be as good as new.

No matter. He was determined to make this day everything she deserved it to be. After all, it was her birthday as well. Those long days in the hospital, he'd thought of nothing else. He could still remember his joy at finding her there with him. When all had seemed lost, when he'd felt hope abandoning him, he'd sensed her there beside him.

The look in her eyes when he'd first opened his... He'd never forget the love and longing in those eyes. It was then he'd feverishly planned for this day. He wanted it to be as special as she was. He wanted to show her how cherished she was--that she'd have nothing to regret in going against her family to marry him.

But then, a surprise change of heart. Beth and Joe had each given their blessing to the couple. Only God could work such a miracle. God--and Andrew's letter. Although, in actuality, Joe hadn't needed to read the letter to realize he'd been unfair. Bless him. Justin could never thank him enough for all he'd done for Emma in the last couple months.

After a hot shower, he dressed and hastily consumed a banana and a handful of granola. All standing over the kitchen sink, of course, he realized with a chuckle. He was quite sure that once Emma had her way, this bachelor habit of his would quickly come to an end.

But look what he was getting in its place. A family to share all of his meals at home with.

He made a phone call to ensure all of his plans were being carried out, then drove over to Emma's. She believed they were merely truck shopping this morning. He'd convinced her to trade in her minivan for something a little more dependable come winter. Something that would handle the slick roads with ease while being roomy enough to accommodate her little family.

Soon to be *their* little family, he amended with a grin of pleasure.

After spending the morning shopping for a new truck, they'd made plans to enjoy a leisurely birthday lunch in Denver. But he had something else entirely planned for them. Something he knew she'd been waiting for. As had he.

Emma appeared at the door in a knee-length sundress, half-sweater, and cowgirl boots. With her long hair twisted into twin braids, she looked so young and fresh. Very much like the girl he'd first known all those years ago.

"Happy birthday, Emma," he replied with a grin. Then, he wrapped his arms around her waist and pulled her against him for a lingering kiss. "Dressed like that, you make me feel like a teenager."

She favored him with a happy smile. "Thanks. You look pretty good, yourself." He wore dark jeans, a navy plaid button down shirt, the sleeves rolled back to his elbow, and stylish work boots. A straw hat perched on his head at a rakish angle. They were certainly a pair. She grabbed his hand and pulled him inside. "C'mon. The kids want to say hi before we go."

"Just think...next year, you'll be 30."

She rolled her eyes. "Ugh, don't remind me."

"Oh, come on, Em. It's not that bad."

While she gathered her things, he hugged each of the children, pressing a kiss to Andrea's little cheek and receiving a wet kiss on his in return. She was just learning how to give kisses, although they were usually open-mouthed, as she hadn't quite figured out how to pucker her lips. But he didn't mind. Her attempts made his heart turn over with love.

In a matter of months, this little girl's Mama would officially be his. And so, he hoped, would she. He'd love nothing more than to adopt the kids and give them his name. He'd always loved kids, wanted kids of his own. And, if everything went according to plan, once those two little words, "I do", were spoken, he'd instantly become the father of three wonderful children. He was blessed beyond measure.

When Emma reentered the room, followed by Allie, she failed to see the wink Justin passed to her sister-in-law. "Will you boys be good for Aunt Allie?"

"Yes, Mama," they chorused together.

"Be sure to help her take care of Andrea, okay? You know she's been trying to crawl and can be a big handful at times."

Emmitt nodded. Since his sister's birth, the little boy had taken on the role of her protector. After all, he was the man of the family now, wasn't he? He'd once overheard someone saying that and had liked the sound of it. It was one of the reasons he'd had such a hard time accepting Justin as the new man in his mother's life. When he was just "fun Uncle Justin", it was okay. But at first he wasn't eager to relinquish his new role. After awhile, he'd decided he rather liked having Justin around. The way he played with Emmitt and his siblings, coupled with the way he supported their mom...well, he reminded the little boy of his own daddy. And what he missed most about him.

Justin handed the baby to Allie, then knelt before Emmitt and ruffled his hair. "We'll be home later this afternoon, buddy. Then, maybe we can play in the park for awhile. Does that sound good?"

Will threw himself into Justin's embrace, nearly knocking him over. "I tack you!"

"Yes, you tackled me. You really *are* strong, huh?"

Both boys dissolved into gales of laughter.

"Okay, we'll see you guys later. I love you!" Emma called, blowing each of them a kiss.

"Love you too, Mama," Emma replied.

"Too! Wuv too!" Will chirped, not to be left out.

Justin drove Emma's minivan to the car dealership owned by the husband of one of the high school teachers. He knew they would get a good deal from Gary. Even if his wife hadn't worked with Andrew, it was a relatively small town where folks looked out for each other. It was one of his favorite things about their community. And of course, everyone knew Emma. Had known - and loved - Andrew.

All morning, as they looked for the perfect truck for her, the excitement continued to build inside until he thought he would burst. He was dying to drop to one knee and propose to her on the spot, longing to make it official. But proposing marriage - something he'd never done before - in the middle of a used car dealership, was far from romantic. And Emma deserved the most romantic proposal he could give her.

Finally, she found a vehicle she liked. They both had an opportunity to drive the vehicle, and all of the paperwork had been filled out and approved. She handed over the keys to Justin, then climbed into the truck and sat down right next to him on the bench seat.

He wiggled his eyebrows at her, briefly grasping her knee. "I think I like your new truck, Em."

She slipped an arm through his and rested her head on his shoulder. "Me, too. I don't think we can even sit this close in your car."

"Do you have any idea where you'd like to go for lunch?" he asked, knowing full well he had no intention of driving to Denver this afternoon.

"You mean you don't have every minute of my birthday planned out?" she asked with a teasing smirk.

"I didn't say that, did I?"

"Oh, nowhere in particular, I guess. Anywhere you'd like to go is fine with me. Seriously, just being together today is what makes it special."

As they had reached a red light, he leaned over and pressed a quick, but ardent, kiss upon her lips. "I love you. Have I told you that yet today?"

"Not in the last half hour, no."

"Well, then, let me say it again. I love you very much, Emma Darcy."

She squeezed his arm. "And I love you, Justin."

Just as the light turned green, his cell phone rang. He pulled to the side of the road before taking the call. Then, after a short, rather vague conversation, he hung up the phone and pulled back onto the road, this time, headed in the opposite direction.

"What's up?" she asked. "You weren't called in to the hospital, were you?"

"No, that was my friend Ryan."

"The one who remodeled your cabin?"

"Yeah. He and his wife stayed up there for the weekend a few weeks ago for their anniversary. At the time, he mentioned something about a plumbing issue, so I asked him to go back and check it out."

"So what did he say? Did he find something?"

"He just said there was something I needed to see right away."

She pulled a face. "That doesn't sound good, does it?"

"Not really, no. I guess we'll see what's up when we get there."

But when they arrived at the cabin, there were no other vehicles in sight.

Emma looked around, a bit confused. "Where's Ryan's car?"

Justin shrugged. "It's possible he intended to meet us here. Let's go inside and wait."

He unlocked the front door and allowed her to precede him inside, biting his lower lip in an attempt to stifle a smile at what was coming.

She stepped over the threshold and froze. "What in the world is all this?"

Orange, yellow, and white helium balloons filled with confetti were formed into beautiful balloon bouquets all over the main room. Fresh fall floral arrangements were also grouped on each of the end tables, on the window seats, and on the dining table. Lit white candles floated in beautiful vases filled with orange and yellow tinted water. Soft music emanated from the stereo speakers, and platters of finger foods lay at the ready on the kitchen counters.

"Justin, what is this?" she repeated, turning halfway around to face him, while still rooted to her spot in the doorway.

He grinned and wrapped his arms around her, walking her into the room so that he could shut the door behind them. "Oh, nothing really. I just wanted to do something special for your birthday, that's all."

She turned fully in his embrace, leaned up on her toes, and favored him with a kiss. "You didn't need to go to so much trouble to make me feel special, Justin. You do that everyday just by being you."

His arms tightened around her, he spent a few minutes lavishing her face and neck with more tangible proof of his affection.

Once they were both completely breathless, he grasped her hand and led her over to the table, where he seated her at one of the two set places. At the counter, he filled two plates with fruit slices, dainty cucumber sandwiches, assorted sliced vegetables, and several chocolate-dipped strawberries.

While they enjoyed a leisurely lunch, they were serenaded by the beautiful instrumental selections on one of Justin's iPod playlists. It was thoroughly romantic.

After the initial shock wore off, Emma had begun to suspect what his true motives for this romantic surprise were. Anticipation filled her stomach with fluttering butterflies, and each time he took her hand or kissed her, she caught her breath, anxious for him to propose.

But he didn't.

When the meal was over, they walked down to the swing by the stream to enjoy the crisp, fall weather and breathtaking view. The surrounding hills were ablaze with color, from the vivid yellows of the aspens, to the vibrant orange and reds of the other tree varieties. It was, and always had been, Emma's favorite time of year. In her opinion, there was no beating a gorgeous Colorado autumn.

They sat together on the swing, holding hands, with her head against his shoulder. The melodious trickle of the water had almost lulled her to sleep when she felt Justin begin to fidget next to her. Instantly, her heart raced in excitement. *Could this be it?*

"Emma," he began, absently twisting the bottom of one of her braids around his fingers. "If I could bring Andrew back to you, I'd do it in a heartbeat. You know that, right?"

She stilled, completely dumbfounded. Where was he going with this?

"Justin, we've talked about this before. I will always cherish the time I had with my husband, and I'm so grateful for the three wonderful children I have. But neither of us can bring him back, so there is no point in dwelling on the past. Not anymore. You're the only one I want," she added with conviction, turning slightly so that she was facing him on the swing.

He grasped her hands and brought them up to his lips, pressing kisses upon the backs of each. "I just had to make sure you didn't have any regrets or doubts about us."

She reached up and touched his jaw gently. "No, my love. If I have anything to regret, it certainly wouldn't be because of anything you've done. I regret taking so long to let go of my bitterness and anger after Andrew's death. I regret putting you on a pedestal and then blaming you when you couldn't be everything I needed. It was unfair of me to expect you to take the place in my life that should only belong to God. Most of all, I regret hurting you."

He pulled her into his arms for a long embrace, then leaned back until they were face to face once more. "I don't regret that."

She cocked her head in confusion. "Why?"

"Because only by having everything you valued removed from you, could you see the truth and make things right." He let out a deep sigh before continuing. "Just as you placed me on a pedestal, I have to admit that you'd long inhabited one of my own making as well. I just didn't realize it until you walked away. That month apart was as much for me as it was for you. And from it, we've grown closer together."

"And to God," she finished, her quivering voice matching her teary eyes.

"Amen." *Thank You, Lord, for blessing me with this woman. She is a rare jewel that I will never take for granted.*

They didn't linger long after that, as Justin had promised the boys they would be back in time to play ball. Emma was a little disappointed when he didn't propose, but only momentarily. One day very soon, he would ask her the question that would change their lives forever. It just wasn't today.

There wasn't much cleanup to be done in the cabin, as most of the platters of food had been disposable. The flowers and balloons he promised to bring to the house in a day or two so that everyone could enjoy them.

Once more, she handed him the keys and then sat close beside him in the truck as he drove back to her house. At home, the boys were excited to see Mama's new wheels and begged for Justin to take them on a ride before their promised trip to the park. While he installed the boys' booster seats and Andrea's car seat in the back of the extended cab, she fed the baby and gathered a few supplies for the diaper bag.

They spent a couple hours at the park, the ladies ensconced on a stone bench overlooking the football field, where Justin and the boys played football. Emma thoroughly enjoyed watching the three of them play together. The tenderness and gentleness Justin showed her children melted her heart like nothing else could.

As the sky was beginning to darken, they picked up fried chicken and took it home for supper. Once the boys had eaten their fill, she bathed them and readied them for bed while Justin snuggled with a sleepy Andrea.

Finally, all three kids in bed, Emma wandered back into the living room and stopped in surprise. He'd turned all of the lights off; the only light coming from the many lit candles around the room. She sat down on the couch next to the man she loved and leaned into his chest, her feet pulled beneath her. "How lovely! What a great way to end a perfect day."

"What makes you think it's over?" he asked, his voice husky.

When she looked up at him in confusion, he pressed a lingering kiss to her lips. "I love you, Emma. I've loved you for as long as I can remember. You are beautiful, inside and out. I know this has been a difficult road to walk. But it has been my privilege to walk it with you."

He stood up and her heart raced into double time, expecting him to kneel down.

But he didn't.

Instead, he grasped her hands and pulled her to her feet, leading her over to the sliding door that opened onto the deck.

"Close your eyes. No peeking, now!"

She squeezed them shut, completely confused and clueless as to what was occurring. She heard him open the screen door, then felt him gently, carefully guide her to the railing. The night breeze teased her long tresses, freed earlier from their braids.

"Open your eyes."

Her sharp intake of breath was immediately followed by eyes that filled with tears.

In the yard, in brightly colored lights, were the words, "Marry me?" She glanced from the display to his beloved face and back, over and over, the tears spilling down her cheeks.

He reached into his pocket and took out a small jewelry box, then opened it to reveal a heart-shaped diamond surrounded by tiny sapphires, her favorite jewel. It was the most beautiful ring she'd ever seen. "Oh, Justin."

He dropped to one knee and took her left hand in his. "I want to share each of life's moments with you, both the good and the bad. I want to raise our children - both the ones we already have, and any more the Lord blesses us with - to know and serve Him as Savior. Most of all, I just want *you*, Emma. I lost you once and I don't want to make that mistake a second time. You are the missing part of me, my better half. Emma Joy Darcy, will you please do me the honor of becoming my wife?"

"Oh, yes, Justin! *Yes!*"

His face lit up with the biggest grin she'd ever seen. He slid the ring onto her finger and stood in one fluid motion, pulling her tightly to him once he'd regained his feet. "You have made me the happiest man in the world," he whispered, capturing her lips in a sweetly passionate kiss.

Later, as they snuggled together on the couch, she managed to get the whole story from him.

Ryan, Aaron, and Julia had been the ones to prepare the cabin for their romantic lunch. Originally, he'd planned to propose next to the stream, knowing how much she enjoyed it there. It had been Allie's suggestion, however, to use the colored lights. Just to fool Emma into thinking it wasn't all part of the proposal, so she wouldn't be suspicious.

Emma was shocked by how many of her family members had been in on the surprise. She was even more surprised to hear that not only did the family members know about the proposal, Justin had actually gone to both Emma's *and* Andrew's parents and asked them for permission to marry her!

All because he wanted to reassure the Darcys that he wasn't taking Emma and the kids from them. Not for the last time, she marveled at the wonderful man God had blessed her with.

They sat together for a long time, talking about the wedding and about their dreams for the future. Finally, when they both realized how late it was, Justin stood, pulled her to her feet, and kissed his fiancé goodnight.

"I can't wait until we don't have to do this anymore," she replied.

"What?"

"Say goodbye for the night."

He kissed her one last time. "Me, too."

She watched him practically strut down the sidewalk to his car, then blow her a kiss before driving away. After shutting the door, she leaned on it and let out a contented sigh.

Engaged to be married! In just a few short months, on the first Saturday in January, she would officially become Mrs. Justin Bennet.

The mere thought filled her with unspeakable joy. She was happier than she'd been in a very long time. Was it only a year ago she was stranded in a pit of sorrow, depressed after Andrew's death, and struggling to accept a new pregnancy?

So much had changed in the last year. Would *continue* to change over the next several months.

The kids would receive a new Daddy.

And she would become someone's wife again.

Chapter Twenty-Two

January 3

As always, Emma awoke to the aroma of percolating coffee. She opened her eyes reluctantly...and smiled. Today was her wedding day. Only seven months ago she'd marked the first anniversary of Andrew's death. And only seven months ago she and Justin had first voiced their true feelings for each other. It didn't seem possible that only seven months had passed. But it had. Regardless of what had occurred before, today she was marrying a man she'd grown to love dearly. A man she couldn't wait to spend the rest of her life with.

She flew out of bed and hastily donned her robe, excitement racing through her. In just a few hours she would officially become Mrs. Justin Bennet. Glancing back at the bed, she smiled. Never again would she have to sleep alone. She'd have someone to share *all* of life's moments with. Joy filled her anew at the thought.

Picking her way through the maze of boxes, she slipped quietly into the kitchen for her morning cup of coffee, careful not to awaken anyone. Her parents were staying with them and would remain with the kids while she and Justin spent the week at the cabin for their honeymoon.

All of the family members had been so wonderful, helping her box up the family's belongings in preparation for their move to Justin's home--the home he'd grown up in as a boy, purchased from his mother over a year ago. They planned to sell this house and put the money away for the kids' futures. She'd used some of the life insurance money she'd received when Andrew died to pay off the mortgage, so they were in no rush to sell. In the current economy, that was a huge blessing.

Emma sat at the breakfast bar, sipping her coffee, merely savoring the unhurried, peaceful moment before the day's excitement began. They really did need this fresh start as a family. That was primarily why they'd chosen this first Saturday in January as their wedding day. They wanted to mark the new year with a new beginning. A new house. As a new member joined their family and they became a *new* family.

She couldn't imagine sharing the same bed with Justin that she'd shared with Andrew. The memories of their marriage and their time together as husband and wife deserved to be set apart. Private. She didn't want to constantly be reminded of Andrew when she was with Justin. Not that she'd ever forget him. Indeed, looking at her children would be a stark reminder of him. But her heart belonged to Justin now. He deserved to have it fully, undivided. Then, the same worry that had been plaguing her for the last few days gripped her. She caught her lower lip between her teeth and frowned. What if she *couldn't* forget Andrew? What if she constantly thought of him...and especially at the most intimate times? Comparing the two men? She didn't want to forget Andrew, no. But nor did she want to think of him when she was with Justin. Immediately, she lifted up a prayer to God. *Lord, please bless this marriage. Help me to be a good wife. To focus wholly on Justin, because my heart and life belong to him, now.*

Feeling a bit better, she finished her coffee, rinsed her mug and set it in the sink, then went to take a bath. Her parents were giving her the luxury of having the next few hours before the wedding to herself. They would make sure the kids were fed and cleaned up in time to leave for the church. This time was hers alone.

She enjoyed a long, luxurious bubble bath, using Justin's favorite scented shampoo. Her makeup carefully applied, she twisted her long hair into a chic chignon, leaving several tendrils loose to frame her face. These she curled with a curling iron, wishing for the millionth time that her hair was curly like her son's. At least it was thick enough to hold a curl fairly decently, she thought with chagrin.

Once she was finished, she slipped into the silky white dress she'd purchased. The top of the gown was form-fitting, with a modest scoop neck bodice. At the waist it flared just a bit, falling to mid-calf. The trim on the peasant-style sleeves, along the bodice, and at the hem of the dress was made of lace. The entire ensemble was so soft, so silky, that she felt like she was wearing a cloud dipped in the purest of sugars.

Gingerly she perched on the edge of the bed and pulled on silvery-white leather boots. Then, she spritzed a bit of perfume at a few of her pulse points, smiling to herself at the memories the scent evoked. When she'd spotted it in the drug store last week, she'd immediately known she had to have it. For him. Finally, she pulled the furry white cape around her slim shoulders and fastened it at her neck.

She placed a few last minute items into her suitcase, then zipped it and left it for her father to carry to the truck. A quick glance at the clock on the nightstand let her know that it was time. The car would be here any moment.

In the kitchen, her mother took one look at her and began to cry. "You look beautiful, honey."

Emma embraced her tightly. "If you keep that up, I'll start crying, and then we'll *both* be a mess," she teased. "The kids ready?"

Grace nodded. "Don't worry about a thing, sweetie. They're back in the boys' room watching a VeggieTale on my laptop."

Her dad emerged from her bedroom, suitcases in hand. "Is this it?"

She nodded.

He eyed her up and down, grinning. "Justin is a lucky man, m'dear."

"Thank you, Daddy."

"You're welcome, sweet pea," he replied, tenderly pressing a kiss to her forehead. As long as he lived, and regardless of how old *she* was, she would *always* be "sweet pea" to her father. "You want these in the back of your truck?"

"Please."

He stopped at the doorway and peered at her, concern etched on his face. "I know it's got four-wheel drive, and I'm thankful that Justin convinced you to trade your van in for something that handles the winter weather a bit better. But his cabin is up in the foothills. I'm not sure even having the four-wheel drive is adequate to get up and down those roads if they get icy."

She smiled. This was such a dad thing to worry about. "Justin came by yesterday and put the chains on. We'll be careful. I promise, Dad."

He smiled with relief. "I'm glad to hear it, sweet pea." Glancing out the window, he turned to her with a grin. "Looks like your ride is here for you. You go on to the church. We'll load up both vehicles and be about fifteen minutes behind you."

When the front door rang, claiming her attention, she opened it to find Aaron standing on the step.

Much like their father had, he eyed her up and down, the corners of his mouth lifting appreciatively. "You look beautiful, Em," he whispered, kissing her cheek.

"Thanks, Aaron. So are we going in your car?"

He grinned. "Nope."

Curious, she peeked around his shoulder...and her heart melted. Justin's Corvette was parked at the curb, washed, waxed, and seemingly spit-shined. It appeared that both of them were feeling a bit nostalgic today.

"Shall we?" Aaron offered his arm to her and helped her down the snowy sidewalk and into the car.

They were quiet during the ride to the church, each content with their own thoughts. At the church, he shut off the car and then turned to her. Took her hand in his. "I know what today means to you, sis. I know what it took to get here. And I believe that Andrew is smiling down on you from Heaven."

She carefully brushed errant tears from her eyes, not wanting to mess up her eye makeup. At least, not before the pictures were taken. "I know he is." In some weird way, she couldn't have gone through with this if she hadn't felt a sense of blessing from him. Permission to move on, even though he was no longer here.

Aaron helped her out of the car and into the church where the minister was waiting for them. "Justin would like a few minutes alone with you before the pictures."

Anticipation filled her. In just a few moments, she'd get to see the man she loved. The man she would shortly pledge her life to. Her children's lives to.

"He's waiting for you in the sanctuary."

Justin glanced at his watch for the umpteenth time in the last five minutes. Where was she, already? Surely she'd arrived by now. Concern knifed through him as a million possibilities raced across his mind. Just as he'd begun to imagine her injured on the side of the road, he heard the door open, turned to face the back of the church, and froze.

She was here. Standing there, with an impossibly long church aisle separating them. He'd never before realized just how *long* that aisle was! He was so overjoyed at seeing her that he all but ran down the aisle to her side. And then, finally, she was standing there before him. Within arm's reach. Never in all his life had he seen a more radiant woman. She was more beautiful than he'd ever seen her. Ever. He reached out and tenderly caressed her cheek. Wanting to save their kiss for the wedding, he instead brought her hand to his lips and kissed the back of it. "I've been dreaming about this day for a very long time, Emma. But even in my wildest dreams, you never looked this beautiful."

Her eyes glistened with unshed tears. "I can't wait to become your wife, Justin."

He leaned closer and pressed his forehead to hers. "We don't have much longer to wait, my love."

They stood there for several minutes, foreheads touching, clinging to each other for support. Finally, he took a tiny step back and gave her a tremulous smile. Reaching into his coat pocket, he extracted a long, slender case.

She raised curious eyes to his before opening it. Inside was a lovely string of pearls. With a gasp of pleasure, she turned to allow him to fasten them around her neck.

"I keep my promises."

Confusion filled her eyes before the memory surfaced. "I can't believe you remembered," she whispered. Back when they were teenagers - back even before she'd developed feelings for him - while one day daydreaming of what her wedding would look like, she'd mentioned that all brides should wear pearls on their special day. He'd teased her about it, jokingly promising to give her a string of pearls on her wedding day. She'd forgotten all about it until just now.

"Of course," he replied with a grin, pressing a kiss to the back of her neck. A familiar scent tickled his nose *and* his memory. Memories of a pretty young girl who'd adored him--one who'd teased and delighted his senses with this same perfume. "Vanilla Fields? I didn't know they made this stuff anymore." He wrapped his arms around her from behind and drew her firmly against him, nuzzling the back of her neck. "You have no idea how badly I want to kiss you right now."

Emma's eyes slid shut. Chills of pleasure raced up and down her spine. She swallowed. "Justin Lee Bennet," she warned, resolutely stepping out of his embrace.

"Uh-oh. The full name."

She ignored him. "You're just gonna have to wait until later."

He chuckled. "Fine. But once we're alone at the cabin, you are *mine*."

The promise thrilled her. She eyed him up and down. Man, he looked good. Oh, how she liked a well-dressed man. Specifically, the well-dressed man in front of her. She raised her eyes to his smoldering gaze and smirked. Two could play this little game.

With a playful laugh, she raised up on tiptoes and kissed his smooth cheek.

"You're killing me, woman!" he groaned.

Thankfully for the two of them, Lynne Bennet poked her head in the door, gaining their attention with a loud, "Ahem!"

Once two pairs of eyes were on her, she stepped fully into the sanctuary and hugged them both. "I just wanted to let you know that everyone's here. We can do the pictures any time."

"Give me five minutes to talk to the kids, first, Mom. I haven't seen them all day," Emma requested.

"I'll come with you. I'm just dying to see them in their little outfits. You coming, son?" she asked, turning expectantly toward him.

"In a minute."

Watching them leave the room, talking companionably, warmed his heart. What a blessed man he was. Not only was he marrying the woman of his dreams, but he was also becoming a father to three wonderful children he loved more than anything.

He'd long dreamt of making Emma his wife. But never in his dreams did he imagine that on the same day he married her, he'd also become a father. It was a big responsibility. One he knew he was unprepared for.

With that thought in mind, he took a few moments to kneel at the altar before joining the rest of the family, asking God to help him be the best father he could be.

The three children waiting for him deserved nothing less.

Hours later, the newlyweds kissed the children goodbye and left for their week-long honeymoon at the cabin. Neither had bothered changing out of their wedding clothes, although Justin had long since abandoned his tie. He was definitely a man accustomed to the loose-fitting scrubs he wore at the hospital.

At the cabin, he picked his way gingerly across the snow to his bride's side of the extended-cab truck. It was a lot more slippery than he'd anticipated. With the four-wheel drive and the chains on the tires, he'd barely noticed the snow and ice on the road coming up the mountain. His dress shoes certainly weren't making things any easier. Too bad they didn't make chains for shoes...

Emma must've read his mind, because without waiting for him, she opened her door and stepped carefully out. "Honey, don't worry about carrying me over the threshold. There's no need for either of us to break any bones to honor a silly tradition."

He pulled her arm tightly through his. "It's not a silly tradition, Em. But I am thankful that my new wife has a practical side."

She slapped at him with her other arm. "Thanks a lot! That makes me sound totally unromantic, Justin."

He rewarded her with his most devastating smile.

After only sliding once, they made it to the deck without any major mishaps. He unlocked the door and swung it open, barring her from entering when she attempted to step past him.

He lowered his hands to her trim waist, pulling her closer. Ever so slowly, he leaned down and placed a tender kiss on her lips. She moaned and closed her eyes, leaning her body against his for support. Gently he lifted her, holding her tightly in his arms. "Welcome home, Mrs. Bennet," he whispered, carrying her over the threshold of the cabin. She reached behind them and pushed the door closed.

He strolled over to the sectional and sat down, settling her comfortably across his lap. "Now, my dear. Where were we?"

Justin spent several minutes lavishing his bride's face and neck with kisses before reluctantly letting her go. He had something special planned for her. That is, if he didn't forget himself and continue his tender assault on her lovely features.

"I have a surprise for you, but I need a few minutes to get it ready. Can you please wait here?"

She nodded, overheated from his passionate kisses.

Once he was gone, she unfastened her cape and draped it over the sofa. Then, she removed her boots and settled back against the cushions, drawing her legs up underneath her. From where she sat, she had a lovely view of the distant mountains. What had been tiny, intermittent flurries when they'd left the church nearly an hour ago were now big, puffy snowflakes. She was thankful he'd insisted upon leaving their reception early. Not for anything did she want to attempt the trip up *or* down the mountain in heavy snow. She gazed idly out the window, daydreaming about their special day. Without realizing it, her eyelids sank and she drifted to sleep.

This is how Justin discovered her after preparing his surprise and bringing in their suitcases from the truck. He bent and woke her with a kiss. "Wake up, sleeping beauty," he teased.

Emma noticed he'd removed his coat and shirt and was clad only in his suit pants and an undershirt. A rather snug-fitting undershirt which emphasized his torso and muscular arms. Her heart raced. This gorgeous hunk of a man was her *husband*.

He led her down the hall to the master bedroom and stopped, allowing her to precede him. Her soft gasp of delight brought a smile.

He'd drawn the curtains and placed lit candles throughout the room. Red rose petals were strewn all over the bed. Next to it was a chilling bottle of sparkling grape juice and two champagne flutes. Soft classical music drifted from a stereo in the corner near the bathroom, where he'd also been at work. More lit candles and rose petals decorated the edges of the Jacuzzi tub. It was sexy and romantic. And thoroughly Justin.

"It's beautiful," she breathed, then stepped into his embrace and wrapped her arms tightly around his waist.

He reached behind her head and pulled out the pins holding her chignon in place. Her luxuriant hair cascaded around her shoulders, half-way down her back. He slid his fingers through the silky mass and gently kneaded the back of her neck, eliciting a tiny moan from her. With her face held between both hands, he lowered his mouth and captured hers in a passionate kiss. A kiss of promise for what was to come.

Breaking the kiss, he leaned his forehead against hers briefly before meeting her heated gaze. "I've looked forward to this for a long time, Emma. I've loved you for what feels like forever. And now I get to *show* you just how much."

He swept her up into his arms and laid her gently onto the bed. Looking down upon his beautiful bride, he smiled. "I love you, Mrs. Bennet."

Mrs. Bennet. She loved the sound of that. The name she used to dream of having was finally hers. As she gazed up at her handsome husband, she silently thanked God for all He had brought her through in the last nineteen months.

She may have lost Andrew. But she'd found something infinitely more precious in the long run---a renewed relationship with Jesus, her Savior. And from that relationship had come a renewed relationship with the wonderful man before her. Emma could not wait to see what blessings awaited their marriage.

"And I love you, Dr. Bennet," she answered, making room for him next to her.

For days she'd been afraid that she'd be torn between both men she had loved. But as Justin took her in his arms and kissed her, her thoughts were of him alone.

And soon, she ceased to think at all.

Epilogue

5 months later

Emma Bennet eased her husband's Corvette along the cemetery road past rows and rows of tombstones, coming to a stop in front of one underneath an ancient weeping willow tree. She emerged from the vehicle and reached back inside for a bag and the bouquet of lilacs sitting on the passenger seat. She shut the door with her leg and carefully made her way over to the tombstone.

She lovingly placed the bouquet on Andrew's grave, thrilled to see that the small marble box she'd left last year was still there after all these months. There would be time to reveal her treasures later. Right now, she just wanted to take a moment and think back over all that had happened to her in the last two years. Two years! It was strange to think Andrew had been gone for two years already. While that first year had drug slowly by, this last year had passed in a blur. Wasn't it only yesterday she was marking the first anniversary of her husband's death?

She drew her knees up against her chest, leaning against the bench for support. What a year it had been! There was much to tell him--God had brought her through so much.

"Where do I start?" she pondered aloud. She'd long ago developed the habit of talking to Andrew when she visited his grave, even though she knew he could not respond. But did he even hear her? Perhaps God gave those who had gone before a window into their loved one's lives on earth. It comforted her to believe so.

She told him about meeting Zach for the first time and how God had changed her heart for him. She also told him about their subsequent bi-weekly meetings. While she was sad to think that the other was still hardened to her extended olive branch and wanted nothing to do with the message of forgiveness she brought, she was overjoyed and amazed at how the Lord had gotten a hold of the other. About two months after she'd first begun meeting with him, he'd accepted Christ as his Savior. The transformation in the man's soul was utterly remarkable. Transformed by the saving grace of Jesus and afire with the Holy Spirit, he was preaching the Gospel message within the walls of the prison. Several of the prisoners and even a couple of the guards had also accepted Christ as their Savior as well! It was nothing less than a miracle. A miracle that had begun in her. She still wondered anew at the work God had done in her heart not that many months ago.

Swatting at an errant bee, her eye caught the sparkle of the diamond ring on her finger and her lips spread in a huge grin. If it hadn't been for Andrew's letter to her... "The kids and I miss you very much, Andrew. It is still hard to comprehend that you've been gone from us for two years. After your death, I didn't think I'd ever survive. I doubted it possible that I'd ever learn to love again.

"But you knew otherwise, didn't you? I still can't believe you wrote me that letter, encouraging me to find love again. To remarry if possible. Well, I did. You made it all possible, my darling. Without your encouragement, I'm not sure I ever would have married Justin."

She closed her eyes, wistfully remembering the wedding ceremony that had taken place almost five months ago. Five months ago tomorrow, to be exact. They'd chosen the first Saturday of the new year, desiring the new year to begin with a fresh start for the whole family.

"Tomorrow will be our five month anniversary. Oh, Andrew, it really was a beautiful wedding, although it wasn't as big or as fancy as ours. I wore a simple white dress, and he wore a black suit. Only our family members and closest friends were there. It was absolutely beautiful."

"He told me about he day you died, Andrew. About how you asked him to look after as. Well, he has. He's taken very good care of us and I know he'll continue to do so. I want you to know that I'm very happy. And the kids are happy, too. Justin loves them very much.

"He also told me that a couple weeks before he proposed, he had a dream about you. He was at the lake, sitting on the rock you and I often used to sit on to watch the water. In his dream, you appeared out of the trees and sat next to him. The two of you had a long talk about me. About the kids. You told him not to be afraid to marry me. You also told him that it was all right for him to adopt the kids as his own. For them to formally take his name. He told me that after he woke up, he had the greatest sense of peace about our future together. He believes that dream was from God...and from you. After our wedding, we did a lot of talking about what we should do. Last week, we unexpectedly received your family's full blessing and approval for us to move forward with the adoption. They have completely accepted Justin's new role in the kids' lives, and in mine as well. It's been nothing short of a miracle.

"At the same time, Andrew, I promise you here and now that I will not keep the kids from your family. They will always be our children's family, even though you are no longer here with us."

She pulled a plastic bag of pictures from her bag and spent a few moments describing each one. Pictures from their little daughter's first year of life, and her first birthday. Pictures from Emmitt's preschool class. Pictures from Will's active toddler days. Then, she added these to the ones already nestled in the marble box. Instead of replacing it in front of the tombstone however, she tucked it into the bag, then rose to her feet, hooking the bag's straps over her shoulder.

"I'm taking this box home for our children to have. You have no need of it, of course. I think that in some way, *I* needed you to have this. To know that you were still a part of our family circle, because I just couldn't imagine letting you go. You told me to move on with my life, to find happiness and love. Thanks be to God, I have. But to move ahead, I think it's finally time for me to let go of the past, Andrew. Of you. You will always have a place in my heart, and I will always be grateful for our time together as husband and wife--for the beautiful children you gave me. But my heart and my life belong first to Jesus, and now to Justin as my husband.

"It's time for me to say goodbye until we meet again in heaven. I'll love you forever. Goodbye, my darling."

She blew a kiss into the bright sky, then made her way back over to the car.

As she left the cemetery and drove home, Emma realized that throughout the last two years she'd experienced many different reunions. The reunion with an old friend that had in some ways marked the beginning of her journey. Then, during those dark months after Andrew's death, she'd experienced a reunion with her Savior. If there was anything she'd learned during that time, it was that God was enough--He was all she'd ever need. And then, just when she doubted she could ever really love again, He'd blessed her with yet another reunion.

A reunion with love.

The End

Author's Dedication and Expressions of Gratitude

This book is dedicated to the One who first gave me the idea, my Lord and Savior, Jesus Christ. Without Him, I wouldn't be where I am today.

To my husband, Troy - You've always encouraged me to go for my dream, no matter what it took. I'm overjoyed that you get to share this with me, babe. I love you.

To my four babies, Tayler, Clayton, Tori, and Cody - Y'all have been my biggest cheerleaders throughout this process. I am so privileged that God blessed me with the opportunity to be your Mama.

To my "Fence Friends" (you know who you are) - Thank you for the opportunity to learn from you all. Y'all truly are gifted writers who use your gifts to the glory of God alone. What an encouragement y'all are to me.

To my amazing editor, Nat Davis - Thank you for all your assistance and encouragement; especially at a time when things were upside down in your personal life.

And finally, to all my family and friends (who are too numerous to name individually) - Thank you for the encouragement over the years (especially those who had to read my earlier stories from elementary school). It truly is a blessing to have such wonderful people in my corner, continually pushing me to realize my dream with this novel.

About the Author

Jennifer Gentry has been writing stories since the third grade, one of which was published in her high school periodical. She is also a voracious reader whose favorite book, like that of her heroine, is "Pride and Prejudice", by Jane Austen. As to which "Darcy" camp she belongs to, Jennifer is a staunch Matthew Macfadyen fan.

Generally preferring Christian fiction, Jennifer's favorite novels are those in which the authors are able to pull a large range of emotions from their readers throughout the telling of the stories. She also enjoys novels where she walks away encouraged -- or even challenged -- in her faith.

Jennifer Gentry is a missionary, serving with an anti-human trafficking ministry whose primary goal is to prevent human trafficking. This is accomplished by educating churches how to identify those most at risk of being trafficked, then working together to provide ways to decrease these individuals' risk levels. She and her husband and four children live and work in Mexico City.

When not living in Mexico, Jennifer and her family make their home primarily in the South. Her favorite place to visit is the Great Smoky Mountain National Park, especially in the autumn when the mountains are ablaze with color. Jennifer's ideal spot to sit and drink in the beauty of God's creation is a mossy rock next to a gurgling mountain stream.

Visit Jennifer Gentry's blog at http://www.jottingsbyjenny.blogspot.com.

Made in the USA
Charleston, SC
03 August 2014